Acclaim for Dai Sijie's

ONCE ON A MOONLESS NIGHT

"An ex⋯⋯⋯⋯⋯le of strange and
noble⋯⋯⋯⋯⋯roams across cen-
turies⋯⋯⋯⋯⋯na, Mali and Paris."
—⋯⋯0 Books of the Year

"Haunting and complex. . . . Told with a spare elegance of
prose. . . . Abounds in inventive mythology darkly threaded
by a tragic love story." —*The Washington Times*

"A freewheeling meditation on language as the divine current that buoys human experience. . . . As a piece of art,
encrusted with meaning and mystery, it is rich and strange."
—*Los Angeles Times*

"Much of this wonderfully written book is set against the col-
orful backdrop of Old Peking and the crisply written narrative is as exciting and powerful as a typhoon."
—*Tucson Citizen*

"At its heart the novel crafts an ode to the power of language." —*National Geographic Traveler*

"[This] complex and well-written historical novel . . . grips
the audience thoroughly with its poetic look back in time."
—*Mainstream Fiction*

"Mesmerizing." —*Audrey* magazine

"Elegant and thoughtful. . . . Worthwhile and captivating with a beautiful ending sure to resonate with its audience. . . . A celebration of the joy of a good story. [Dai] Sijie delights in storytelling."   —Bookreporter.com

"Filled with twists and turns of fate, backstories, symbolism and intersections of politics and religion worthy of a Dan Brown novel. . . . Dai adds layer upon layer of meaning. . . . [*Once on a Moonless Night*] pulls the reader along, as does the language, which is pungent and immediate. And as for the scroll itself: this is one mystery, one message, that really makes it worth reading until the last lines of a novel to discover."   —*UPI Asia*

"*Once on a Moonless Night* is full of tales within tales and worlds within worlds, ranging from ancient Chinese empires through communist China to modern Beijing."

—A. S. Byatt, *The Guardian* (London)

"[Dai] Sijie's ambitious work spans a thousand years of Chinese history . . . [with] a rich repository of tales, traditions and sensibilities [the book's] theme of indeterminacy of meaning is braided into the clash between East and West. . . . [Dai] Sijie has a gift for the spectacular."

—*The Times Literary Supplement* (London)

"*Once on a Moonless Night* evokes the past with all the eerie clarity of a dream, its outlines blurred, but every tiny, telling detail extraordinarily alive. Anyone in search of a brief history of China would do well to begin right here."

—*Financial Times*

DAI   SIJIE

ONCE   ON   A   MOONLESS   NIGHT

Born in China in 1954, Dai Sijie is a filmmaker and nov-
elist. He left China in 1984 for France, where he now
lives and works. He is the author of the international
bestseller *Balzac and the Little Chinese Seamstress* (short-
listed for the Independent Foreign Fiction Prize in the
United Kingdom and made into a film) and of *Mr. Muo's
Travelling Couch* (winner of the Prix Femina).

ONCE ON A MOONLESS NIGHT

DAI SIJIE

ONCE ON A MOONLESS NIGHT

TRANSLATED FROM THE FRENCH BY ADRIANA HUNTER

ANCHOR BOOKS

A DIVISION OF RANDOM HOUSE, INC.

NEW YORK

FIRST ANCHOR BOOKS EDITION, AUGUST 2010

The Library of Congress has cataloged the Knopf edition as follows:
Dai, Sijie.
[Par une nuit où la lune ne s'est pas levée. English]
Once on a moonless night / by Dai Sijie, translated from the French by Adriana Hunter.
p. cm.
I. Hunter, Adriana. II. Title.
PQ2664.A437P3713 2008
843'.92—dc22   2008041089

Anchor ISBN: 978-0-307-45673-1

Book design by Iris Weinstein

www.anchorbooks.com

Printed in the United States of America
10 9 8 7 6 5 4 3 2 1

ONCE ON A MOONLESS NIGHT

PART ONE

CHINA

1 9 7 8 — 1 9 7 9

I

LET'S CALL IT THE MUTILATED RELIC, this scrap of sacred text, written in a long-dead language, on a roll of silk which fell victim to a violent fit of anger and was torn in two, not by a pair of hands or a knife or scissors but quite genuinely by the teeth of an enraged emperor.

My chance meeting with Professor Tang Li sometime in mid-July 1978 in a conference room of the Peking Hotel, and what he revealed to me about that treasure, both shine out to this day like a little square of light in the hazy and confused labyrinth that my memories of China have become.

For the first time in my life I was being paid in my capacity as interpreter in a meeting set up by a Hollywood production company to discuss the screenplay of *The Last Emperor*, which went on to be the major film that everyone knows, garlanded with nine or ten Oscars and generating astronomical box office takings. With permission from the University of Peking, where I was enrolled in the Chinese literature department as a foreign student, and armed with a notebook bought the day before specially for the occasion, I made my way to the Peking Hotel in the middle of a summer afternoon

so hot it vaporised everything, turning the city into a caul-
dron steadily stewing its population. Creaking their last, my
bicycle wheels sank into the cloying asphalt, softened by the
heat and giving off little spirals of blue smoke. The foyer of
the eight-storey hotel (the city's only skyscraper at the time)
was overflowing with excited activity, the revolving glass
door besieged by a noisy succession of fifty, a hundred, two
hundred people, I couldn't tell. Judging by their accents they
had come from every corner of China. Parents laden with
provisions and children carrying violin cases on their backs
and, despite the heat, wearing Western-style blazers with
white shirts buttoned up to the neck and ties or bow ties,
even though some of them were barely six or seven years
old. As soon as each child appeared in the foyer, a riot broke
out; the others would swarm over and huddle round, peer-
ing anxiously and bombarding the newcomer with impatient
questions. It looked just like a crowd of worried refugees
jostling at the doors of an embassy. After a while I gathered
that they were each waiting for a private audience with
Yehudi Menuhin, who came to China once a year on a mis-
sion that was as charitable as it was artistic (and in which
there was a certain element of personal publicity): to find
one or two child prodigies, a new Chinese Mozart. This was
a golden opportunity for these young violinists, an unhoped-
for chance to set off for the United States and attend a music
school directed by the master himself.

The lift wasn't working and the climb to the eighth floor,
where my meeting was being held, required considerable
effort, especially as there were violinists everywhere in the
stairwell too, milling about like ants, sitting or even lying on
the stairs, along corridors and in the corners of window

ledges. Eventually, almost rigid with exhaustion, I reached the meeting room and found that it was, quite by coincidence, right next to the budding violinists' audition room, which had its door closed.

I was invited to join a group comprising a representative for the Italian-American director, a production assistant, another translator and a dozen eminent Chinese historians. We were seated around a rectangular table covered in a white cloth dotted with tins of Coca-Cola, cups of tea, ashtrays and vases of plastic and paper roses, and in the middle, in pride of place, stood an imposing and majestic professional tape recorder. On the wall hung an enlargement of a black-and-white photograph of Puyi, the last emperor, taken in the Forbidden City on a particularly raw winter day in 1920. He was wearing a Western-style jacket and glasses with rimless round lenses, his features tense, his expression dark.

The introductions and handshakes were accompanied by my halting translation from Chinese into English laced with a strong French accent, while the other translator, who was barely more at ease than I was, translated from English into Chinese; protocol was strictly respected. I noticed a Chinese man of about sixty, not like the others who all wore short-sleeved shirts; he was draped in traditional Chinese dress (a tunic in dark blue satin, buttoned at the side and falling to the floor) which, bearing in mind the season, made him look slightly absurd if also touching. He alone bowed to greet the organisers of the meeting, but with no hint of sycophancy, and occasionally he raised an elegant hand, in a gesture so slow it seemed to date from a different age, to stroke his long white beard, which wafted gently in the draught from the fan hanging from the ceiling. It seemed time had stopped over him, he alone was the incarnation of an entire era, a separate universe. When he spoke his name, in just two characters, I was struck by their simplicity and familiarity, which I mentally associated with . . . I searched and searched as I looked at his face, but in vain. The memory stayed buried in some recess of my mind, paralysed by the nerves of this first professional experience.

When I translated the nickname that his Chinese colleagues gave him—the Living Dictionary of the Forbidden City—the director's representative burst out laughing and promised, rather condescendingly, to hire this "gentleman" for a walk-on part or even a minor role. The other Chinese people present fell about laughing, but not the old man. I heard the hum of mosquitoes dancing in the artificial draft from the fan, flitting across beams of light that striped the room. The sound of a violin through the wall acted as background music to the meeting, a Mendelssohn sonata or concerto, gentle, slightly mawkish.

Two or three hours elapsed before I turned to look at the man in traditional dress again. The meeting, during which he had remained silent, was drawing to a close and the participants were glancing impatiently at their watches when he suddenly began to speak in a cracked, reedy, almost strangled voice.

"If we have a few more minutes I would like, very humbly, as humbly as my background dictates, to plead the case for re-establishing the truth."

In a fraction of a second, as I translated what he had said, I thought I knew what his name reminded me of. It was . . . Just then a large mosquito which was stuck to the forehead of the director's representative caught my eye; I saw it take off, hover, veer back and land very precisely on the end of his nose, probably a less oily site. A verse from a Russian poet whom I had just read in translation came to mind: "the mosquito beatifically raised its ruby belly." That was exactly it. As for knowing who the old Chinese man was, my vague recollections were extinguished almost before they were lit.

"I would beg the director and his writers," went on the old man, "either by your intermediary or through the tape recorder on which my eminent colleagues cannot help focusing, to throw this screenplay—or at least this version—in one of the hotel's bins, where, despite the establishment's reputation, there's quite a substantial population of hidden little scrabbling creatures who, I can only hope, will nibble it page by page, word by word. So very far is it from the true character of Puyi, who, contrary to the untruthful biography on which your screenplay is based, was a pathologically complex person, and I'm not referring here to his homosexuality, for many an emperor before him had similar tendencies. That is not the question, but his sadistic cruelty and frequent fits of delirium—as unpredictable as they were uncontrollable—were due to schizophrenia, in the purely medical sense of the term."

In our collective silence we could make out through the wall the individual notes in the opening melody of the allegro from a Beethoven concerto, then a slap rang out, one the director's representative administered to himself. The mosquito, which I could no longer see, must have avoided the blow and escaped.

"Piece of shit!"

With this vengeful cry, the man leapt from his chair,

crushed the insect between his hands and threw its oozing, bleeding corpse into an ashtray, where he burned it with the tip of his cigarette.

"What the hell was that mosquito doing here?" he said. "Did he want to get into movies too?"

He roared with laughter and declared that, on that note, the meeting was closed. Before leaving he turned to me.

"Tell the old man I'm sure he knows the truth, but it's too dark, too negative, it won't work with a Western audience, it has nothing to offer a movie, no one's interested in that, least of all a world-famous director whose ambitions can be summed up in one word: Oscar."

He left. While I translated, struggling to find attenuating words and turns of phrase, the Living Dictionary of the Forbidden City stared at me with eyes bulging from their sockets, his smooth beard and white hair stiff with rage.

It was only after his blue-robed figure had vanished, still reeling, through the doorway and I had closed my scribbled notebook in relief that—without even searching my memory—the thing I could not remember earlier came to me. Tang Li, well, of course! The author of *The Secret Biography of Cixi*. I stood up, reached the door, launched myself into the corridor, bumped into someone and thundered down the stairs, which were still heaving with future Mozarts so I had to zig-zag my way through them on every floor. As if finally seeing the Bearer of Good News, the highly strung crowd, tortured by their long anxious wait, sprang to life again. The fact that I was obviously in a hurry, my little translator's notebook, my Western appearance . . . all insignificant details, granted, but enough to whip up their emotions and create ripples of excitement that escorted me all the way

down to street level, along with waves of questions, suppli-
cations and fears concerning the choices made by the king of
violins. They clearly took me for his powerful assistant who
worked behind the scenes scheduling the on-camera audi-
tions. Despite my explanations (and my futile swearing in
the name of film and of another king—this time of cine-
matography), the young performers' parents continued to
hound me, God knows why. One mother of about thirty, a
hunchback with permed hair and a sweaty face, picked up
the hem of her cheap skirt, dragged her offspring by the arm,
followed by her bald husband, and bore down on me like a
determined predator, descending the stairs with the fervent
energy of a good soldier, close on my heels all the way. But
she must have tripped on a step, because her bag fell, scat-
tering tins of food, sandwiches, bottles of water and a red
apple, which bounced from stair to stair right to the bottom
of the flight.

It was almost dark outside. I had to leave my bicycle
where it was parked and, by dint of various acrobatic
manoeuvres, cross the tightly packed streams not of cars
(which were rare commodities at the time) but of bicycles
advancing inexorably, in order to catch up with the old man
in the long blue robe at the tram stop on the other side of the
widest boulevard in China, built in the passion for all things
huge that was the 1950s, in imitation of Moscow's Red
Square. Another couple of seconds and I would have missed
the tram. The driver set off, but my relief evaporated when I
saw—still running and now out of breath—the father, the
boy and the violin case, but not the mother, at least. I rushed
to the door, which shuddered under the father's blows and
eventually opened. Once more they interrogated me furi-

ously; I explained who I was, helped by the testimony of the old historian who had come to my aid and whose hostility seemed to have vanished on that imposing grey boulevard, known the world over for its military parades, its huge mass demonstrations and, years later, the student massacre. The father, floundering between the names Menuhin, Bertolucci and Puyi, eventually gave up and a group of schoolchildren surging towards the door pushed him and his son aside, helpless.

Rather than the old historian's steady, motionless, almost bulging eyes, it is his voice that comes to mind and still rings in my ears, a quivering thread of a voice, cracked and very gentle, drowned out most of the time by the racket of the tram. His voice and the way he cleared his throat when he succumbed to a wave of sadness or indignation. Standing among the other passengers, holding on to a leather strap, with no comment on the lurching corners which threatened to throw him over, without looking at me, he took up the subject of Puyi exactly where he had been interrupted that afternoon, as if nothing had happened in between and the meeting were carrying on quite naturally in that dusty tramcar.

"History tells us that the two child emperors, Guangxu and Puyi, appointed successively and thirty years apart by their aunt, the empress Cixi, were struck by the same mysterious disorder: impotence, to give it its name, and this brought an end to any hopes of perpetuating their lineage. Puyi's case seems all the more fateful as, bearing in mind his status as last emperor, the phenomenon takes on an almost metaphysical dimension far beyond his personal destiny. He was, anyway, a sickly child and his fragile state was aggravated over the years by countless Chinese and Western remedies, high-dose injections, prayers, rituals and all sorts of cures, aromatic fumigations and aphrodisiacs extracted from the testicles of various species of mammal, bird and fish, the most famous of which is incontrovertibly the Tibetan 'grass worm,' a small flatworm, a plathelminth of the peziza order, about two or three centimetres long, it looks like the grey silkworm and is called *Bombyx mori*. This worm owes its name to the fact that after it dies in winter its body, buried beneath the Himalayan snow, turns into grass, which eventually pokes through the snow and grows all through the spring, now enjoying an entirely vegetal existence. Even so, massive doses of this powerful aphrodisiac famous for its success were unable to stir the imperial organ from its lethargy. Worse than that, they plunged the emperor into states of extreme panic, bringing on outbursts when he believed he was prey to tiny creatures writhing inside his stomach, invading his liver and making their way up to his heart and brain, sometimes claiming it was caterpillars with pearly grey fur that were inside him, breaking him down, eating him up and coupling in his insides to the death, sometimes pointed bamboo shoots that he felt he could see gleaming green, springing up from every part of his body as it cooled, cooled, cooled like a field the day after a lost battle, like a drifting iceberg. Then he would throw himself body and soul into calligraphy, a true art at the time as it still is now. From morning till night he applied himself to copying out the works of another emperor, Huizong (1082–1135) of the Song dynasty, an artistic genius but a very mediocre administrator who also experienced a long period of sterility and undertook an arduous military campaign until the late arrival of his first child, not before he had had an artificial mountain erected to the north of the capital on the advice of a soothsayer. At the end of his reign the country was in ruins and he lost the war. When the 'Northern Barbarians,' the Jins, headed for the capital he gave the order, on the advice of another soothsayer, to open the gates of the city, believing a celestial army would come to his aid. He lived his last years—as Puyi would later—in captivity in the absolute silence of the far north, eight thousand kilometres from the palace he could now visit only in his dreams. So few of his works were left in this world that each of them, even down to fragments of letters, assumed an immeasurable value; they were of primordial importance in the imperial family's collection, and Puyi, who was its sole heir, could enjoy not only admiring them but also copying them. He would spread out on the table a masterpiece, often written on hemp paper coloured yellow by a concoction of vegetable pulp used to protect it from worms and insects, a type of paper used only for transcribing sutras and which acquired an attractive warm grey patina with age. Then he would lay over it a thin sheet of translucent paper covered with a light coating of wax, which meant he could trace with perfect accuracy. He had brushes made just like those used by his predecessor, with bristles of polecat hairs, reputed for their stiffness, arranged around a central point; mastering them takes years of assiduous practice but produces an elastic resistance that lends each stroke a keen powerful edge and transposes every nuance of the calligrapher's personality. In the Forbidden City there is still a graveyard for the polecat-hair brushes once used by Puyi; each has its own tomb, a headstone and an epitaph written by the emperor himself with the maker's name, the date it was first used, the day it was scrapped, etc. During these long daily tracing sessions, Puyi felt the giant of Chinese calligraphy guiding his hand, entrusting to him the secret held within each stroke and every character; if we are to believe the diagnosis made by the Court doctors years later, this activity created a hypnotic, emotional, besotted relationship between the tracer and the man whose work he traced, and gave rise to the particular brand of self-sublimation referred to by the strange term 'transference.' So the young emperor felt he was slipping into the persona of another captive monarch; when he dipped his brush in ink, when the bristles swelled, filling with the exact measure of ink Huizong would have used, Puyi found himself in a prison camp eight hundred years earlier, looking at a snow-covered landscape, at the tents for guards and prisoners, at vast plains and the summits of distant hills. He held his breath, his hand exerted its gentle pressure, a concentration of all Huizong's stylistic precision and elegance. Under this pressure, the point of long polecat hairs released the correct amount of ink onto the paper, or rather it was Puyi's person-ality which was released onto it, or, as he often claimed, Huizong's. Over time he confused the traces of ink with trails of urine that left furrows in the thick carpet of snow inside Huizong's tent one stormy night. The unfortunate prisoner, tormented by a prostate problem, had woken in the middle of the night but not had time to reach the latrines outside. Sometimes, while he was copying, Puyi shed tears which ran over the waxed tracing paper, and the traces of those tears can be seen to this day on the yellow hemp paper of one of Huizong's works conserved at the Tokyo Museum. He would fly into a tantrum when he failed to master a vital technique—one that was not particular to Huizong but also adopted by other great calligraphers—which consisted in always working with a raised hand, without leaning either hand or elbow on the table so that, by suspending the entire arm, the pressure exerted by the point of the brush on the paper could be regulated, allowing each movement to take wing with complete freedom, and creating a rhythmic sequence of downstrokes and upstrokes. The moment Puyi lifted his wrist in the air it stopped obeying him and quivered like a leaf, which put him into a paroxysm of rage and, perverse as he was, the only way he could calm himself was to take pleasure in the suffering of others: with a gloved hand he would whip or cave in the skull of one or several eunuchs who had witnessed his failure, his sadistic inspiration conceiving hideous tortures for the sole pleasure of hearing his victims weep and beg and shriek in pain.

"Early in April 1925, thirteen years after the fall of the empire, Puyi was released from his gilded prison, the Forbidden City, guarded by the newly formed Republican Army, following a sort of epileptic fit which plunged him into a profound state of lethargy and left him more dead than alive. He was moved to the Japanese concession of Tianjin, south of Peking, where he stayed in bed for weeks on end, and only smiled again when a procession of porters some two kilometres long arrived, their shoulders chafing under great swaying trunks. There were three thousand of them, all filled with precious objects collected by his ancestors, but in his eyes the most beautiful of these trunks full of national treasures, of streaming pearls, rivers of diamonds, cascades of jade, gold, porcelain, copper, sculptures, paintings, calligraphy, etc., was the one set aside for the works of Emperor Huizong. As soon as his convalescence was under way, he threw himself back into his master's works in order, this time, to copy the paintings, a field in which Huizong excelled perhaps even more than in calligraphy, occupying a position comparable to that of Modigliani or Degas in Western painting.

"No one could be absolutely sure what his recovery could be attributed to: Was it Huizong's painting or the Japanese sumo wrestler by the name of Yamata whose body was so huge his tiny head seemed to be tucked inside his sloping shoulders, and who played an indispensable part in the emperor's day-to-day life? Towards noon Puyi would indicate he was awake by ringing a bell and the sumo wrestler, naked as the day he was born, would approach him, moving like a silent mountain, and carry him to the bathroom in his warm arms that were as soft as any woman's. He would lay him in a marble bath where the temperature of the water had been regulated and was scrupulously monitored—using a German thermometer—by the sumo himself, who knew that the least discrepancy in heat would provoke a fresh outburst from his obsessive master. And so, still half asleep, as Puyi once described to his cousin with whom, as with everyone, he referred to himself as the emperor and in the third person," the professor explained, "the emperor listened to the creaking and groaning of his frame as it swelled in the warm water, lulled by the voice of a young virgin who sat beside the bath reading a novel he had chosen the day before. It was usually an extract from *Jin Ping Mei,* read by a succession of Chinese girls each more beautiful than the last. Sometimes, on the advice of his sumo, the emperor might also ask for erotic Japanese works; then the reading would be done by a Japanese girl and, although the emperor didn't understand a single word of the language, the girl's voice mingling with the misty steam bewitched him so that, when he found the strength to open his eyes for a fraction of a second, he thought he saw a mermaid, for the young girl's pearly grey skirt shimmered in the steam room like a fish tail, whose scales (according to legend) would come away in handfuls if a man so much as looked at them, scales that the emperor thought he could see floating on the surface of the water like slivers of silver all around his body beached in the bath. He rang again to signal the conclusion of his bath, the sumo came in, lifted him from the tub, carried him at arm's length into his bedroom, laid him on his bed and wrapped him in large, soft, thick towels impregnated with a heady perfume. The emperor lay in complete darkness for a long time, hearing and seeing nothing, inhaling the exquisite scent of flowers, plants and musk, until he dissolved into it. Time, which flashes past elsewhere, drew itself out so slowly for him that every minute seemed an eternity.

"Late in the afternoon, if we are to believe what his cousin remembers," the professor went on, "the emperor would shut himself in his study where the windows were permanently covered with wine-coloured blinds that let in no sunlight, and sit at a desk lit by a lamp with a green shade. There, like a studious pupil, he copied a bird perched on a bare branch painted on silk by Huizong, who initiated this sort of Court painting, the height of Chinese refinement and studied elegance, dominated by a singular kind of purity, unadorned, ghostly, always light but laden with meaning. No one could say whether the bird was in a heavenly sky, an underwater world or a dark aquarium, so utterly devoid was the work of coarse earthly realities. Needless to say, the emperor displayed a particular predilection for this kind of painting. The sumo prepared his ink, spread out a length of silk specially manufactured for him by a workshop in Suzhou to replicate exactly the silk used by Huizong eight hundred years earlier: with thick, closely woven threads on a double weft, not like these modern silks, vulgar satins with fine threads doubled up in the warp. His craftsmen used a technique dating back to the era of the Song dynasty, steeping the raw silk in a mixture of glue and alum, firstly with a brush, then by pressing, beating and rubbing it to ensure it was better adapted to take the successive applications of colour washes, a technique invented by Huizong and of which he was master. The emperor sat motionless for hours on end, contemplating the bird he intended to copy, trying to penetrate the secret of its ashen plumage made up of juxtaposed lines that, on closer inspection, disguised infinite precision beneath a continuous quivering; the secret of those clouds of red, sort of shapeless unidentifiable leaves that metamorphosed into petals, stamens, pistils . . . around the bird's crimson tail; and that black beak with a single very fine line describing its contour, crystallising it in a fluid shape shot through with invisible vibration; and above all the miracle of its eye, which, even more disturbingly, constituted an enigma that neither the emperor nor anyone else would ever be able to resolve: how had the painter succeeded in giving it such brilliance and power that you felt—although this was manifestly impossible—that the creature was watching you, crossing over an invisible boundary? The emperor sometimes imagined Huizong had not used a brush, but just his fingernail, applying a drop of ink to it and projecting the droplet a metre's distance so that—either by chance or thanks to a minutely planned gesture—it landed on the painting just where it needed to. The bird's head was painted in transparent colours with delicately deepening shadows, a detailed and natural anatomical depiction, a fragile, vibrant head infused with profound solitude, portraying for the emperor the image of himself as a small boy of three, perched on a throne of filigreed gold, borne by four intertwined dragons, raised to a height that a child's eye could barely reach, the throne on which he had felt his weightless body transformed into that of a little bird huddled in its nest way up high in the audience hall, which was filled with both an icy cold and, paradoxical though this may seem, deathly silence, where the deafening cries of the tens of thousands of courtiers prostrating themselves before him rang round as they would in a vast abyss, merging into a series of long, dark and terrifying echoes.

"What Puyi did not reveal to his cousin," the professor pointed out, "was that, despite the endless time he spent in contemplation, he never succeeded in putting down a single brushstroke, the least spot of ink, the tiniest scribble on the silk. In the end all that Huizong's works inspired in him was profound self-loathing. At the end of each session, the sumo put away the paintbrushes—brushes that had never been dipped into the ink, which slowly thickened, gradually coagulating and clouding irremediably—then he would gather the scraps of virgin silk torn up and thrown away by Puyi, and bury them in the courtyard beneath a layer of earth and rotting leaves. This period of 'meditation on painting,' as Puyi called it, ended in a spectacular episode, not devoid of an element of comedy: late in November 1926, towards the end of a snowy night, some courtiers were horrified to spot Puyi, who was twenty at the time, in the feeble morning light, his frail naked body wrapped in a long boa of black and white feathers as he perched, shivering, on the branch of an elm tree just like the bird painted by Huizong eight hundred years earlier. Not one of his servants dared approach him, except for the sumo, the only person allowed to enter his study (strictly out of bounds to anyone else) so that he could put more wood on the fire in winter and stand behind him mutely waving a fan in summer. No one will ever know what degree of intimacy there was between the young fallen emperor and his Japanese sumo but, if the recollections of one of the last eunuchs in Tianjin are to be believed, every time Puyi descended into unshakeable lethargy after a hysterical outburst, the sumo would lie down beside him in his bed and hold him in his arms, day and night. But on the morning in question when the sumo reached out to his master to take him in his arms, the elm branch—which had already bowed considerably under Puyi's weight—snapped with a deafening crack and both men fell, in each other's arms, though neither was injured thanks to the snow on the ground in the courtyard.

"Another singular detail is that Huizong, himself a painter and calligrapher, was also a great collector or even the greatest ever, an area that no doubt requires vast wealth but also a knowledge of art, in a word: taste. Even I, who am no artist," the professor confided, "have read and reread once a year the catalogues of Huizong's collection, which list six thousand and three hundred works with their titles, descriptions, painters' biographies and, most importantly, the emperor's own comments, piecing together the genesis of each creation. Almost all of these works have now disappeared, but reading the catalogues affords the same pleasure as looking at an old map of a town or neighbourhood, where the observer can wander through imaginary remains, recognising crossroads, losing his way in a market, following the course of a moat, looking out for its ripples along the sinuous outline of city walls, although it will vanish the moment he feels he has grasped it. Can you understand why a great wave of happiness washed over me when, looking at an enlarged photograph, I spotted the titles of two works from this mythical catalogue on the label of a chest that was handed down to Huizong and later belonged to our last emperor?

"The first was a piece of calligraphy by Li Bo, the great poet of the Tang dynasty, an autograph transcription of his poem 'The Terrace of the Sun' on hemp paper. Three centuries lie between Li Bo and Huizong, but in his day, as in ours, men of letters were divided into two camps, those who loved Li Bo and those who admired Du Fu, another great poet of the Tang dynasty and an intimate friend of Li Bo. Huizong clearly belonged to the first camp, since, according to the catalogue of his collection, he owned six autograph works of calligraphy by Li Bo (six poems he had written), two in semi-cursive script and executed at the palace before his emperor, who had commissioned them, the other four in full-blown cursive script, and all of them, judging by their titles, eulogies to alcohol improvised in a drunken state and which Huizong—with a flourish that went beyond his role as an expert—annotated with these words: 'Li Bo and alcohol, ever running to meet each other, became so interchangeable that eventually, like a vanishing apparition, they formed just one creature, compact yet ill-defined, and quite unique.'

"I couldn't help doing some research on the poem called 'The Terrace of the Sun,'" said the professor. "What a journey it must have had, through all the political upheavals, the founding and floundering of dynasties! After Huizong was exiled, the work disappeared, then re-emerged in the Yuan dynasty, at first in the hands of Yan Qin, then Ou Yangxuan (1274–1358), the famous master of the Imperial Archives, then it disappeared again, only to reappear three centuries later in the Ming dynasty in the catalogue of Xiang Zijing, the famous collector, before becoming the property, some time in the late sixteenth century, of the Qing emperors, Puyi's ancestors. Calligraphy may well be simply an artistic version of another form, that is the ideograms which make up the poem, but then not only does it reflect the character and temperament of the artist but (you can believe me on this) it also betrays his heart rate, his breathing and the alcohol on his breath, and all this affords the enthusiast a feeling of euphoria comparable to that of a music lover discovering or, better still, acquiring a two-hundred-year-old recording of a Beethoven piano concerto played by Beethoven himself.

"The hypnotic psychological effect of a piece of calligraphy or a painting (which, according to doctors, was in itself nothing short of miraculous in Puyi's case) is, like all other artistic responses, only ever short-lived and was not enough to affect his pathological condition or to maintain a mental equilibrium, however fragile. And yet, unless I am mistaken, that is exactly what he did experience with the second treasure from Huizong's collection—a manuscript on a roll of silk in a language that was not known at the time—an object that meant more to him than anything else in the world. The hypnotic power it exerted over him was such that, while

Puyi had had the calligraphy by Li Bo hung beside his bed, he hardly ever looked at it, for he was quite incapable of tearing his eyes away from this scroll of manuscript.

"I can see from your expression," the professor remarked, "how interested you are in this roll and I feel I must put you on your guard before this interest becomes more passionate, as it has for anyone who has come close to the manuscript. I myself, I have to admit, developed a keen enthusiasm for it when I looked into its history, exhausting all available sources, some of which must be viewed with caution, for they are too closely tied up with legend; but I felt that by reconstituting its peregrinations, however tortuous a course they may have taken, I would be better equipped to talk about the late emperors on whom it had left its mark and to put together lost fragments from the lives of fallen nobility, such as Seventy-one, whom I mention in the book you have read. Time and again I regret the fact that, when it was published, your compatriot Paul d'Ampère had not yet come to China, that the paths of that noble madman and this manuscript had not yet crossed, depriving my book of a chapter that would have been more disturbing than all the others.

"This precious roll is made up of two strips of silk sewn together with tiny stitching; the first of them contains the text in an unknown language and the silk is stained an orangey yellow. There is no indication of a date, but, from a scientific study of the weaving, it has been established that the stain was made using a concoction extracted from the bark of the Huangbo tree, characteristic of the Han dynasty, and analysis of the ink, which is of exceptional quality and has retained all the intensity of its strong dark black, seems to prove that this mysterious work probably dates from the second or third century of our era, which makes it the oldest roll preserved to date.

"On the second strip, which is in more luxurious silk stained light blue, there is a long colophon of thirty columns of ivory-coloured Chinese ideograms, with calligraphy details by Huizong in gold dust—which still gleams in places—mixed with glue, a technique used in Buddhist temples for copying sacred texts. (Did Huizong have some premonition about the nature of this text written in an unknown language?)

"The colophon begins with a short biography of An Shih-Kao, the first Chinese translator of Buddhist sutras, a hereditary prince of Parthia in the Middle East, who converted to Buddhism, became a monk and, when his father died, gave up his inheritance in favour of his uncle. Leaving the confines of Indo-Iran, he followed a route through the oases of Central Asia, Khotan, Kucha, Turfan . . . all the way to Gansu, having travelled through the cosmopolitan cities of Dunhuang, Zangye and Wuwei. He reached the valley of the Yellow River in northern China and his presence there is recorded in the middle of the second century, in the year 148 to be precise, in the capital, Luoyang. Alongside his reputation as a linguistic genius—he spoke some twenty languages—was his vast historic erudition, and not a day passed when he did not devote several hours to his works of translation. He spent ten years in his room translating into Chinese the many sutras brought home from his travels. His translations were usually in verse, honed and restrained, betraying no trace of his previous existence as a Parthian prince or indeed of any personal pretension; they stir the reader's very soul, whereas his spoken Chinese was hesitant and tainted by a strong accent and grammatical errors. Once in the middle of the night—as he later told his emperor—during a visit to Xi'an, the former capital of China, where he had come to preach in the outskirts around Fufeng, he saw beams of light springing up from the ground on a stretch of wasteland, lighting up certain areas as in mystic visions depicted in religious paintings. According to the report he made to the Court in the year 480 before our era, once the Buddha Shakyamuni achieved the unfathomable peace of Parinirvana, his disciples shared his relics among themselves and set off in several groups, heading in different directions to spread his word all over the world. Those who reached China met with insurmountable problems, for the country was ravaged by war, and they died one after the other. The last of them, a very elderly man, died when he reached the Wei valley along the course of the Yellow River, where he had had to bury the Buddha's relics, which then revealed themselves to An Shih-Kao with those beams of divine light piercing through the earth. It was the first time the Court had heard the name Buddha, which amused everyone; even so, on the emperor's orders, the army carried out excavations and found crystal structures in the shape of teeth and finger bones, but larger than normal size, golden in colour and translucent, gleaming in the bottom of a ditch. That was how An Shih-Kao succeeded in converting the emperor of China, who, in memory of this miracle symbolising the triumph of Buddhism, erected a ravishing stupa on the site (a stupa being a tall edifice made of wood and brick and painted white), in whose crypt the Buddha's relics were kept. He had a house built beside it for An Shih-Kao to spend the rest of his days praying, meditating, translating and teaching. After

An Shih-Kao's terrible death (he was assassinated during one of his frequent religious pilgrimages), his house became the first Chinese Buddhist temple, the Temple of the Gates of the Law.

"Almost a thousand years passed, the colophon written by Huizong goes on, and in mid-August of the year 1128, deep into a stormy night racked with thunderclaps and squalls of hail and torrential rain, the superior at the Temple of the Gates of the Law had the extraordinary sensation of the sky being torn in two by lightning and a hallucinatory vision of the stupa floating several feet above the ground, defying the laws of gravity and eventually vanishing in a puff of smoke. He woke the two hundred monks in the temple, announced his vision to them and asked them to pray with him all night for the stupa to be removed to the eternal peace of Parinirvana. As dawn broke the rain slackened, the dark mists stopped swirling and there was a huge thunderclap, creating so much electric discharge that the sky seemed to explode and the ground to disintegrate. The framework of the temple cracked and shuddered; then, in a fraction of a second, the left side of the stupa, which had been struck by lightning, collapsed. The right side remained standing in the rain, its damaged silhouette—bearing the clear tear line, which ran from the highest point right down to the ground—outlined against the sky like a fragment ripped from an architectural drawing. The following morning, in among the lightning-blackened bricks and planks at the foot of the building, soaking wet pages of the Avatamsaka Sutra were found lying in concentric circles on the ground. This was Buddha's 'Flower Garland' Sutra, which the monks were not surprised to see here, as, for many centuries, faithful wealthy donors had had the right to lay down offerings (rolls of silk or sheets of paper on which scribes had been paid to copy out sacred texts) inside the thick walls of the temple. But when the superior of the monastery climbed to the top of the broken stupa to take down a pitifully damaged bronze statue of Buddha, a manuscript rolled on valuable shafts made of white sandalwood, jade and ivory fell from the belly of the statue. Unsettled by the unfamiliar language on the roll as much as by the circumstances in which it was found, he presented himself to Emperor Huizong in person to offer him the manuscript, convinced that it bore a message concerning a higher authority. What came next proves that deciphering this text would have tremendous repercussions on the country's fate as much as on that of the emperor himself.

"Huizong, a weakened sovereign, an artist shipwrecked on a throne, ended his colophon in a hand that admittedly proved he still had a dazzling mastery of the skill but increasingly lacked discipline: 'My imperial person, in his concern to decipher the manuscript, devoted all his erudition and hours of research, reading and reflection to every last sign. In vain.' As this item seemed to date back to the period of An Shih-Kao, the emperor asked the then king of Parthia, where this genius originated, to send him a delegation of intellectuals and experts, but they too were unable to identify the language. They pointed out that, according to the annals of history, An Shih-Kao was familiar with some twenty languages, most of them dead. The mystery remains impenetrable but the emperor is convinced that, despite its brevity, the text is a sutra, since it was positioned at the very top of the reliquary, inside the most sacred statue. This hypothesis is joined by another, from Su Shi, the emperor's favoured poet with very pronounced inclinations towards Buddhism: remembering that An Shih-Kao was assassinated, Su wondered whether there was any secret link between this crime and the roll of silk in which An Shih-Kao might reveal something about the authenticity of the relics.'

"As for Puyi," the professor went on, after gazing for a while at the silent streets flitting by through the tram window, "his fascination with the manuscript took an unexpected turn. Towards the end of the 1920s, before the beginning of the Sino-Japanese War, Puyi, who was then twenty-five, was confronted with the dilemma of behaving patriotically at the risk of never regaining his throne or collaborating with the Japanese who might one day restore him to his imperial role, albeit at the expense of his honour. It was at this point, as if trying to find a message to resolve his dilemma, that he threw himself into deciphering the unknown language, firstly on a whim but later with a nervous intensity that gradually consumed him. Books translated by An Shih-Kao began to overrun his study, dining room, bedroom, bed and soon his whole existence. For the most part these works, devoted to various techniques of dhyana meditation or to numerical categories, made him feel faint and dizzy, bringing on migraines that clouded his little round eyes and made imaginary motes of dust dance across his field of vision, but he forced himself to apply a system conceived by one of his former tutors with the aim, after considerable circumnavigations, of identifying one word or phrase that might have sprung from the great translator's hand in an unguarded moment, betraying the secret to the labyrinthine construction of this unknown language. One day, when he was reading the nineteenth volume of one of the seven versions (the number of pages and contents of each version vary and even contradict each other depending on when they were written, constituting several areas of controversy) of the *Buddhanusmri Tisamadhi-Sutra* (a meditative sutra that evokes different manifestations of Buddha), he had a sudden conviction that all An Shih-Kao's translations belonged to the classic tradition of Hinayana, a school of thought known for its strict discipline and which had fallen out of usage long since in China but was, and still is to this day, very widespread in Burma, Sikkim, Nepal, Sri Lanka, Cambodia, etc. Convinced he was on the right track, Puyi then noted these countries down in red ink and sent their heads of state or their British guardians official letters essentially asking for their help in deciphering the signs. At first these letters went unanswered without upsetting Puyi at all, because he had now turned his research to another field of investigation: the origins of Chinese writing. His aim was to find the oldest glyptic signs which might have a link to those in the manuscript and that a linguistic genius like An Shih-Kao would have been able to write. Puyi would certainly never have thrown himself into such an enterprise had he had any idea of the complexity this work entailed or the erudition it required. To some historians, this long march towards the origins of the Chinese language represents a final flurry of patriotism from the last emperor, but they also hold that he ended up losing himself along the way, which, in my humble opinion, is by no means a certainty, because a man in a state of mental torture is sometimes better equipped to approach the truth than scholars. Puyi had three thousand chests of national treasures and he started by asking to see a collection of small, thin-walled bronze alcohol flasks made during the Zhou era (late eleventh century–256 B.C.). Using a magnifying glass, he studied their minute inscriptions, where he found no trace of the unknown language, but—examining the signs that soothsayers had had carved onto these small yet solemn and imposing receptacles—he felt for the first time that they constituted a separate ritual language with little connection to Chinese writing. This idea was reinforced when he scrutinised another, still older glyptic language used by soothsayers about two thousand years before our era. He found it in his collection of rare antiquities that had never belonged to previous emperors, but had been given to him by a private collector at the beginning of the twentieth century: inscriptions on sections of tortoiseshell, which had been used for divination by reading the patterns of cracks on them, kinds of diagrams that soothsayers created by burning the shells; the interpretation (in some cases propitious, in others not) of these diagrams, the date, name of the interested party and reason for the sacrifice were later engraved on the shells, themselves so thin and fragile that most would barely want to touch them with their fingertips for fear they would crumble to dust. During this period Puyi's doctors, concerned to see him laugh a great deal of the time for no apparent reason, worried about his mental health. I myself am convinced he was at last savouring a brief moment of happiness when he could forget the outside world, his political dilemma, his impotence, etc., as he laid out those tortoiseshells and wandered along pathways through an ornamental garden of signs as far removed from Chinese writing as the unfamiliar language on the manuscript. To Puyi those signs did not belong to a language at all, but to a system of purely graphic symbols with no grammatical rules or syntactical relationships. It was the language he had always been looking for, one he had found only in dreams or as a child, a language without verbs, just nouns, nouns and nouns—a language, I like to think, with which he could have written his own motto, painted in large characters on the walls of his residence: *No verbs, therefore no concerns*.

"After the inscriptions on tortoiseshell, Puyi was inspired by patterns suggesting a primitive sort of writing, painted or engraved on two ceramic articles in his possession: a pot with openwork sides to display its contents and a jar with a narrow neck. He then widened his field of research, obtaining photographs and copies of prehistoric engravings found deep inside legendary caves in far-flung provinces. In 1980 a distant cousin of his published a two-volume work entitled *Glyphs and Rock Carvings Acquired by Puyi*.

> Little by little, [the cousin states in his preface,] as he copied and recopied them, Puyi managed to hear a dialogue between these patterns, the suns, human bones, birds, frogs, fish, plants and insects, not unlike Egyptian hieroglyphs. As several weeks could pass without his speaking to anyone but his Japanese sumo, this verbless exchange thrumming round inside his head constituted his only conversations. In a wine-coloured leather diary for 1930 (probably a gift from his English tutor and now conserved at the Museum of Contemporary History), there are some brief notes sufficiently explicit to demonstrate that, in his mind, these glyphs and rock carvings were associated with images of paradise, which ended up haunting his dreams. On the page for the 8th of November, for example, he writes: "dreamed of Banpo, a giraffe" . . . Banpo was known from pictograms dating back to the second half of the second millennium before our era.

"One day," the professor went on, "he received a letter from Borneo, an Indonesian island whose Dutch governor had had copies made of the alphabets of several languages once used by native peoples. Among them was one letter of the Phoenician alphabet, which attracted Puyi's attention because it resembled a sign on the manuscript. Peculiarly, instead of leaping for joy, he simply glanced at a map of the world, placed his finger on this land lost in the middle of an ocean which—in An Shih-Kao's day—had not yet been crossed and cried: 'Oh, for goodness' sake, no!' With which he removed his finger and had the letter filed in archives still known as the Court Archives, the better to forget it.

"Another letter, a surprisingly thick one, its envelope smothered in strange stamps and postmarks, arrived in Puyi's residence in Tianjin in mid-August 1931. The place was shrouded in gloomy silence, this was a month before the Japanese invasion of Manchuria. The sumo came into his room and put the letter on the emperor's bedside table while he lay huddled in his freezing bed, tortured by worry and migraines, haunted by the thought of becoming a puppet for the Japanese who would name him emperor of Manchuria, casting infamy over the entire Chinese people. That same day the only Chinese scholar familiar with Sanskrit, the sacred language of India, was summoned before Puyi to read the letter. All that emerged from this consultation was that the author of the letter was a ruler from a region which once belonged to ancient India but was now part of Nepal, and its Kapilavastu district had been Buddha's birthplace two thousand five hundred years earlier. On orders from his superior, a British governor who had fought the Boxers in Peking in his youth, he was sending Puyi a copy of *The Hitopadeśa*, a collection of fables written in a local language called Newari, a combination of Sanskrit and a north Himalayan dialect used by nomads. This letter fostered an infatuation with Sanskrit in Puyi, who was quite won over by its grammar, as it was explained to him by the scholar, or rather by one essential grammatical point, the only one that held his attention: in this very rich, very precise language, verbs existed only in the passive form. You could never say, for example: 'The cook is preparing rice,' but rather: 'Rice is being prepared by the cook.' Tormented by a feeling of failure and the thought that he would soon leave his residence and be no more than a puppet emperor in captivity, Puyi felt every sentence pronounced by the scholar resonating in his ears like some gentle incantatory formula, his every word opening a new doorway through which he alone could reach the skies with his magician by his side. In the space of an afternoon an idyllic world was born in his mind, a world where verbs—actions—were reduced to their passive form, thus making every kind of threat disappear. No gesture or movement had any meaning now other than submitting, like a virgin sheet of paper that accepts having print over its entire surface, sometimes even being deeply dented in the process.

"That evening the Sanskrit scholar, exhausted by his new pupil's ardour, took his leave immediately after dinner to sleep in one of the many empty bedrooms. Puyi, on the other hand, as he later recounted, spent a sleepless night learning the alphabet and a dozen or so Sanskrit words by heart, floundering in the contrast between long and short vowels, their solemn weight, the way they alternated, and in the framework of consonants, the voiced and unvoiced, the aspirates and the unvoiced aspirates. He even tried to compose a sentence—his first in Sanskrit—to taste the pleasures of passive experience and passive desire; he succeeded and it was beautiful. Then he discovered, and this too was beautiful, how to decline the concept of despair in the passive form and, better still, in passive past participles. Oh, the power of passivity!

"He did not close his eyes until daybreak, sinking into a half sleep, and, in a fleeting fraction of a second, he saw two strangers leaning over him, one tall in a monk's habit with a beard that completely covered his cheeks, the other small and slight, still young but with a greying goatee on the tip of his pointed chin. They disappeared just as they had appeared, before a single word had been exchanged. Only afterwards did Puyi recognise them as An Shih-Kao and Huizong, even though the latter had not been wearing an imperial headdress. He had two votive altars erected to them in a large hall in recognition of his gratitude for this first visit, which he saw as a very good omen, a mute baptism of the sacred language.

"In the last fine days of autumn—which were also, although he did not know this yet, the last fine days of his apolitical life as emperor—to be sure that he could immerse himself in this language to which he was recently converted, whatever the time of day and wherever he might be (in his study, the dining room, the bathroom, the toilet, along a dark corridor, in the disused ballroom or the deserted court-yard), he gave his guest, the professor, sheets of white paper and asked him to write out the names of almost everything in Sanskrit, as in the village struck down with amnesia in *One Hundred Years of Solitude*. His servants copied out the labels in whitewash letters a hundred times the size on the

.ground, the walls, doors, windows, armchairs, beds . . . even the sumo, who pinned the words *raja purusa*, 'the emperor's servant,' on his capacious tunic. For the first time in a long while Puyi could be heard roaring with laughter again, yes, real laughter, in his falsetto voice, granted, but glorious laughter which filled the gloomy house with joy. One morning he met his scholarly visitor in a corridor and greeted him in Sanskrit but, instead of saying 'Good morning,' he employed a polite formula with all its attendant protocol, meant for the emperor alone, without realising he was making a mistake. His guest bowed to thank him but, moments later, was packing his bags, and it was only when he came into Puyi's study with his suitcase and said a simple 'Goodbye' in Sanskrit that light dawned in the emperor's mind and, understanding the absurdity of his mistake, he was filled with elation and laughed till he wept. He experienced similar sensual ecstasy when his wife—a general's daughter he had married six years earlier and to whom he vowed platonic love, although he did not truly know her sweet face or her tender body—came into his study disguised as a young Indian prince, sat on his lap, covered his face in kisses and whispered in his ear: '*sā bhāryā yā pativratā*,' a Sanskrit sentence which he had made her learn by heart in the tomb-like chill of her bedroom, impregnated by a strong smell of opium, and which could be translated as: 'me wife devoted to my husband.'

"But time had run out for Puyi to use the words of this sacred language, which he had learned so quickly and with such appetite as an effective means of defence. Events took an ironic turn when two Japanese officers, in civilian dress, came to fetch him and take him out to a car parked by the front door of his residence (for the rest of his life he would remember the squeak of that car's brakes and the furtive sound of footsteps—or rather the absence of any sound of footsteps—made by those two ghosts). He struggled to keep his composure and, with all the dignity of a head of state, responded to the officers' military salute by uttering, syllable by syllable, the longest Sanskrit sentence he knew by heart: *Brāhmanah Kalaham asahamāno bhāryāvatsalyāt svakutumbam parityajya brāhmanyā saya desāntaram gatah* ('After his house was abandoned, unable to bear the disagreement any longer, out of love for his wife, the Brahman fled with her to a foreign country'). After such an exploit and having surprised even himself, Puyi was overcome with joy and experienced patriotic pride for the last time in his life, particularly as, although they understood absolutely nothing, the two ghosts from the land of the Rising Sun had bowed before him on three separate occasions during this interminable sentence.

"But when it came to saying goodbye to his scholarly guest he again used an inappropriate Sanskrit formula without realising it. For reasons of intellectual integrity, his embarrassed guest reminded him that he should have used the term meaning 'goodbye,' and not the one for 'hello' in the present tense. Puyi, who had managed to keep his madness in check up until this point thanks to Sanskrit, succumbed to a violent fit of hysteria and, shaking like a leaf, called the man every abusive name he could think of so that their farewell scene descended into nightmare. An hour later, at the airfield, his anger subsided when the sumo, the only person permitted to travel with him, appeared with two padlocked, chrome-plated metal chests, which bounced glints of sunlight round the stark, tattered and uncomfortable cabin. He put them down opposite the emperor on an iron seat with cracking dark green paint. These two chests—one filled with works of art counted among the most precious treasures in China if not the world, the other quite priceless, once the property of Emperor Huizong and now Puyi—were cited as exhibits years later by an international tribunal, proving Puyi was not innocent: he had prepared his departure and had, therefore, been guilty of treason when he stepped into that Japanese aircraft. A crime that was all the more shameful for being premeditated.

"The six other people on board—a pilot, two co-pilots, the two officers and the sumo—died during the war without leaving any testimony about the incident which happened inside the plane when Puyi, gripped with sudden madness, opened the cabin door in mid-air and threw out torn shreds of various works of art.

"Puyi had never flown before, notes Li Ping, a specialist of the Sino-Japanese War, in an article published in the twenty-third edition of the magazine *History,* and was taken to a dirty, cramped aircraft intended for transporting freight. It was chosen deliberately by Japanese generals for its sorry appearance and, more particularly, its poor state of repair, as a way of thoroughly duping the Chinese administration, a fact revealed by the few documents concerning the future emperor of Manchuria's camouflaged departure. In *Memoirs of a Japanese Colonel,* which I was lucky enough to buy for a handful of coins from a second-hand bookseller in Kyoto, the author relates, among other things and with supporting photographs, how his own nerves were sorely tested the day he had to take one of these planes that were kept for secret missions, in order to get out of Mongolia. Take-off was delayed and the pilot had to get down from the cockpit, find a long bamboo ladder, lean it against the plane, climb up it and wipe the cabin windscreen by hand, because it was too dirty to begin such a long journey. No one knows whether Puyi was subjected to similar inconveniences, but the state of the plane, I'm quite sure, heightened his fear and exerted such pressure on his already disturbed mind that it brought on a fit of hysteria. According to Li Ping, the violent jolting like a constant earthquake under his seat, and the whining motor like a siren announcing the end of the world, along with his loneliness and the feeling of being held captive by brutal creatures exhaling their steaming breath over his face, shouting and playing childish games, laughing at obscene jokes, one cruel jibe leading to another, not that he could understand a single word—all of these elements combined to induce another mental breakdown.

"The causes of the incident have raised little if any controversy. Some of his contemporaries attributed it to a rush of arrogance on Puyi's part, humiliated to be travelling in that ugly little freight plane, or even a final patriotic reflex, an indication of his self-loathing for failing to reject the idea of resuming the imperial throne, even if only as a puppet for the Japanese. At various symposia I discussed it with other, more sceptical specialists who felt Puyi's gesture was a tad too spectacular, as if he were trying to leave an image of himself as an emperor who, even after his downfall, would not collaborate without rebelling, and this very attitude meant he was actually more than a collaborator, he doubly collaborated."

As the professor explained his colleagues' opinions to me, we arrived at his house and went into a small dark room, which served as dining room, sitting room, kitchen and study all at once. He lit the gas hob with a plastic gun and started making tea next to a sink filled with a teetering iceberg of filthy washing-up.

"One of my former students works at the Party Central Committee Archives where, as you know, they keep all documents classed as 'state secrets.' One time, in this very room, when we were talking about drug use in China, she mentioned a file relating to Puyi, which she came across by chance when she was filing archive material. This came as a surprise to me, because I thought she catalogued only documents about the Party. She recited from memory a few pages from an interrogation which took place in a Manchurian prison in 1954. It was the first time I had heard this version of the facts and, while I made notes, I prayed silently that there would be no gaps in her recollections. But she accomplished quite a feat and earned my respect. How precious they are, people with the prodigious gift of memory, who can record things in their heads, like the three-hundred-page book by Dmitri Shostakovich, which was banned but later published by one of his pupils, who made it through to the West and found all those quantities of words written by his master still anchored inside his head. I shall read you an extract of the notes I made:

INTERROGATOR B: Prisoner, can you describe for us the plane that took you to the site of your betrayal? And don't try and make the same mistake you made in the last interrogation: when talking about yourself, you won't say "the fallen emperor" or put all your verbs in the third person, you'll just say "I" like everyone else.

PRISONER: I don't remember it clearly any more, either the shape of it or the interior. I felt as if I were in a different world, not on this earth, less still in heaven, but in a world I didn't know and which I don't really remember. I do recall certain sounds and sensations, smells, images, but very few of the thoughts that came into my head that day, and even less of what they might have meant. I think we stayed in the plane on the ground for quite a long time, until it started to rain. But I couldn't hear any sound, as if I were deaf. Through the open cabin door I could see the rain falling on the dusty runway, on the wings of the plane, harder and harder. Suddenly a colossal silhouette appeared at the end of the runway, looming out of nowhere and slicing through the rain carrying a chest wrapped in wet cloth in each hand. He ran over to the plane, and his feet—I'll never forget this, he was wearing white flat-heeled thonged sandals—his feet now looked tiny in the middle of a huge raindrop, which fell slowly and made a great puddle on the ground all by it-self, silently splashing his white skin and the ivory gleam of his sandals. First one then the other, his feet stepped into another raindrop, just as big as the first one, and it made me laugh, but when I got up to go to the door the vision van-ished. Sound came back to my ears. The sumo was at the foot of the plane, bowing and smiling at me as he held out the two chests as though in some ridiculous theatrical per-formance or to celebrate a victory, but I couldn't remember what he was bringing me or why. I think I had lost my mem-ory. The sumo handed the two chests to the officers inside the plane. But he didn't get in straight away. He stayed where he was, speechless, possibly humiliated because I hadn't recognised him. A temporary lapse, but its intensity terrified him because he knew from experience that memory loss often heralded death. To avoid dirtying the gangway, even though it was well rusted, he took off his sandals and climbed up the steps, which rocked beneath his weight. Once again I couldn't resist the urge to laugh as I saw his bare feet coming towards me, shrunken like two expertly sculpted miniatures, held in a single drop of rain as it fell on the steps, and that wading sound, *psh psh psh,* echoing round . . . I suddenly realised the significance of the situation: those raindrops were tears shed by Heaven for the last seconds of the last emperor of China, a farewell; so I reached my arms outside, and the drops splashed thrillingly over my hands, laden with a sadness that chilled me to the bone.

INTERROGATOR B:　Superstitious nonsense! Listen to me, prisoner, make an effort to confess your crimes without any of your propaganda for reactionary superstitions! All that's been wiped out by the great Chinese people.

PRISONER:　I acknowledge my crime, comrade interrogator, and I swear I will not re-offend.

INTERROGATOR A:　In your opinion, was this hallucination you've described the symptom of an illness such as schizophrenia, or the effect of a drug, opium, for example?

PRISONER:　I'm not an opium addict, sir.

INTERROGATOR A:　Perhaps the Japanese drugged you? Gave you an injection claiming it would calm you down? Or some pill for travel sickness? Tell the truth. This detail could mitigate your guilt.

PRISONER:　No injections . . . or pills . . . Wait, I do remember something. I can see an officer handing me a bottle. It was in the car on the way to the airfield.

INTERROGATOR A:　What sort of bottle?

PRISONER: The glass was matt, very opaque, with a white vapour inside, which I breathed through a straw as if drinking it.

INTERROGATOR A: Probably "ice" as the Americans call it, "crystal." The more fanatical doctors in the Japanese army gave astronomical amounts of it to kamikaze pilots at the end of the war before they crashed themselves into American ships. Go on.

PRISONER: The rain stopped shortly before we took off. We reached a certain altitude, but the pilot couldn't get the plane to go any higher; it was shaking so much I thought it would explode, and I held on to the sumo's arm as I looked down through the window at the town of Tianjin, which I was probably seeing for the last time in my life. I told myself all those tiny black dots milling about in every direction, smaller than ants, that they were Chinese people who were my enemies now. Then we flew parallel to the coast of the Eastern Sea before cutting northwards. Ships, fishing boats, a couple of little islands appeared, framed by the window, then vanished. Then we were wrapped in thick fog, which looked as if it had come from the depths of the sea. Despite our low altitude I could hardly see anything now, except the dark silhouettes of a funeral procession. I couldn't make out the musicians, but the music drifted up to me in snatches and tears of nostalgia clouded my eyes. When the fog dispersed, I saw the faint outline of a river mouth beneath us and the riverbed flooded by the high tide, with the funeral procession winding its way along it, crossing a bridge so insubstantial it almost wasn't there, ephemeral, ready to vanish into thin air at any minute. The sight of it revived memories of my thwarted experiences as an artist, because painting would have meant that, with a few swift brushstrokes, I could have captured this devastating image of death, this burial of my Chinese identity, which was apparently being celebrated before my eyes. Long after it disappeared, the funeral tune—a strident, almost vulgar air—stayed with me like a melancholy obsession, so insistent that, when the sumo opened the chests and I looked through the purest masterpieces in the imperial collection—I'm sorry, in my collection—which were going to travel all the way to Manchuria with me, all I could see was the funeral procession with its black and white banners rippling in the wind, shrouded in autumn mists. Most of the rolls were not very large and I personally opened a work by Huizong chosen at random, unrolling it a section at a time. One by one birds spread their wings before my eyes, but, all of a sudden, the roll slipped from my hand and fell. Not that the jolting of the plane was too violent, or that the roll was weighed down by the tears I couldn't help shedding. No. But a long, long snake had sprung from the depths of the clouds and smacked against the misted window in mid-air. I wanted to get a closer look at it, but it melted away and it was only when the sun broke through the low cloud that I saw it again, stretched out beneath us, dead, or nearly, its black dragon's jaws opened to the shimmering sea, paralysed in its final agony, swept away by the tide. I watched that snake in terror; its heart had stopped beating but the body still displayed all its arching beauty in the sinuous trajectory winding through the mountains, or rather in a thousand and one trajectories, in arcs and spirals, sometimes in loops, until together they formed the biggest and most mysterious question mark in the world: The Great Wall of China. The contours of the wall quivered slightly, making it look as if it were squirming, suffering, a reptile smeared with saliva, unable to sleep until it was sated. That was when I picked up a roll of manuscript, written in an unknown language; I went over to the sliding door and opened it. A gust of wind snatched my glasses. My hands were so weak I had to tear the roll with my teeth, into two pieces initially, but before I could tear it further I saw the reptile, its rings paler than before, springing once more from the depths of a cloud, and I threw the two halves of the manuscript at it. Just as it raised its hideous head to take this sacred food in its gaping jaws, I noticed its uneven grey teeth, some long and pointed, others as small as the teeth of a saw. The monster hurled itself at me, wrapped itself round me from head to foot, squeezing me so tightly that its icy scales punctured my skin. When I regained consciousness, I don't know how much later, I was lying on my seat, still shaking from the experience. Under the implacable watchful eyes of the two officers, the sumo was picking up what was left of the mutilated roll, in other words the strip of silk bearing the colophon written by Huizong, and the valuable shafts it was rolled on, made of white sandalwood, jade and ivory."

2

THE PERIPATETIC EXISTENCE OF THIS mutilated scroll, although captivating, would have remained insurmountably removed from me, like the earth from the sky, had I not met Tumchooq a few months earlier in a certain Little India Street. This street, which had nothing Indian about it, partly justified its name: it really was very little, barely six metres wide. Every time two lorries crossed they toyed with catastrophe: there were horn-blowing duels, exchanges of cursing and insults, but mostly a test of each driver's determination with neither prepared to yield a whisker. Little India Street was to the west of my university, running alongside the grey bricks of the campus, sketching a gentle slope and lined with small shops: a grocer, a baker, the Zhang sisters' haberdashery, a tailor, a traditional pharmacy, which wafted aniseedy smells of bark, dried herbs, cinnamon and musk and which had big glass jars on the counter with snakes coiled inside them bathed in greenish alcohol, ophidians imprisoned in the land-locked sea of those jars, the geometric patterns of their faded skins almost completely lost. At the top of the slope, in once white stone blackened by smoke and dust, was a statue of Mao in a raincoat that flapped in the east wind to symbolise political storms, while, perched limply on his head, was a Lenin hat with a visor in proportion to the size of his head, so large that one day a nest of straw and twigs caked in saliva and gastric juices appeared on it, complete with a swallow on a clutch of eggs. From the full height of its twelve metres the statue overlooked a clump of ugly single-storey administrative buildings: a police station from which the occasional isolated cry of despair could be heard as if from a psychiatric asylum; a post office where my grant arrived at the end of each month, a postal order for a pitiful sum; a small hospital; the Revolutionary Council where public records were registered, a haunting, sinister place I sometimes visited in my dreams, where I was married, registered the birth of my child, and where my death certificate was presented; the People's Bank; the People's Militia; the Community Arts Centre; a former library converted into a hall for political studies; and the premises of the Party Committee and the Communist Youth. The profane swallow that appeared on Mao's cap was shot and her nest destroyed. The anti-revolutionary trails of saliva and white droppings that had covered one of his ears, carving a diagonal torrent across his face and streaming untactfully all the way to the leader's astonishingly prominent chin, were meticulously cleaned, but, if the rumours are to be believed, the swallow's ghost, slightly smaller than the live bird, as if shrunken in death, zig-zagged across the sky at night, even in winter, making piercing, mournful sounds like the shriek of a rusted saw, tormenting the ears of insomniacs.

After this political high point, Little India Street started on a downward slope as gentle as its rise. Two modest restaurants stood facing each other: The Peking Kitchen to the right with a menu that horrified me (grilled scorpions, pan-fried pig intestines . . .) and The Capital's Kitchen on the left with grilled scorpions, steamed pig intestines . . . ; next came a shop selling salt, soy sauce and vinegar; a butcher; a cleaner's; a bookshop; a little bicycle-repair stall; and at the end of the street, where it met the main road into the centre of Peking, between two shops which owed their prosperity to ration tickets sold on the black market, was a greengrocer's.

At nightfall this shop was the site of a strange ritual, which I would surely never have noticed if a spring shower had not interrupted my evening stroll one day in 1978, forcing me to shelter under the bicycle-repair man's awning. At seven o'clock the shop selling alcohol was the first to close, then the tobacconist and the bookshop. I watched the lights dancing through the rain and going out one by one, like a fluorescent millipede gradually being swallowed up by the darkness before disappearing altogether. The bicycle-repair man, with his pipe in the corner of his mouth, was spinning a wheel in the air, listening for any resistance.

On the other side of the street the greengrocer's, which was usually so ordinary, attracted my attention with its inexplicable goings-on. At first sight, the small, hunched salesmen looked like a group of schoolboys sitting in a classroom, but, on closer inspection, they made you shudder. They were unusually short, sitting in the harsh light of the bare bulb hanging from the ceiling, and had faces that seemed a hundred years old, their features hollow and furrowed like masks sculpted in rock. I'd be frightened of going into that place, I thought, among all those men with their wild eyes, the salesmen wearing butchers' white aprons and the deliverymen dirty blue ones, looking like something straight out of an annual meeting for some crime syndicate. They sat holding their breath, all eyes on a man in glasses, the youngest of them (perhaps the only one who could count and write?). Standing under the bare light bulb, he opened a drawer and took out handfuls of banknotes and coins, piled them on a table and started counting them. He behaved as if it were some unimaginable booty amassed by pirates disguised as greengrocers, when in fact it was simply that day's pitiful takings, earned entirely for the benefit of their employer: the State. A pile of cash collapsed under its own weight, and like something in a silent film the coins rolled to the ground without a sound. They picked them up quickly and, using the tip of a knife taken from a hook on the wall, eased out those caught in cracks or swallowed up by holes hollowed out over time in the beaten earth of the floor.

One of them stood up, his back stooped, and headed haltingly for the door. He stopped in the doorway, emitted a stream of spittle, which described a long curve before melting into the rain, then lowered the metal shutter. Motionless as a statue, leaning slightly onto his good leg and with a majestic air of contempt, he disappeared centimetre by centimetre, along with his colleagues, behind the metal shutter, which creaked as it came down, soon leaving just a narrow strip at ground level, a crack of light. All at once the light went out inside. (Who switched it off? The man with the glasses?) The golden line between the doorstep and the metal shutter had evaporated. As I wondered what they could possibly be doing in the dark the light suddenly came on again and the metal shutter was immediately raised with the same oriental nonchalance and by the same limping salesman leaning on his good leg. How long did the power

cut last? Ten seconds? Twenty? Thirty at the most. No hope
of guessing what had gone on inside the shop plunged in
darkness for those thirty seconds. There they all were again,
some on a bench, one on a cardboard box or a crate of cabbages, carrots or turnips, like actors back on stage after a
short interval, sometimes clearly visible and then less so,
depending on the oscillations of the light bulb. As if unaware
of the interlude, they picked up the scene in the same place:
the money was piled carefully on the table again and the
young man with glasses started counting it. Impossible to
tell the colour of his eyes, because of the distance. (Although
I did see him closer to in different circumstances, the colour
of his eyes, which altered according to the light, was always a
mystery to me. Most of the time it hovered between deep
black and a bright, intelligent brown, but sometimes the
thick coating of grease accumulated on his glasses had a
capricious and even rather fanciful way of altering his eyes,
giving them different nuances: the green of a jealous lover,
the grey of gentle fog, the list could go on and on, but never
blue.)

From the far side of the street I could hear him murmuring numbers and, even at that distance, his voice seemed
spellbinding, somewhere between a teacher's and a sor-
cerer's, but with a hint of self-mockery. I was amazed by his
prominent chin, the strange shape of his head, which was
not as wide as his companions', but most of all by his name,
which one of them used, a name with a gently exotic ring to
it, like birdsong, like a grain of sand in the far-off Gobi
Desert or the northern steppes, whipped up by the wind,
carried by storms, swirling through the sky, travelling, crossing whole countries without knowing quite how, and ending

up in the crook of my ear. Incredible though this may seem, jealousy was my instant reaction, jealousy for the beauty of that bespectacled young man's name: Tumchooq.

My instinct was not wrong.

Tumchooq: Toomsuk in Pali, the language in which Buddha preached; Toomsuk in Sanskrit; Doomchook in Mongol—all meaning "bird beak." This was the name given to an ancient kingdom because of its very small size and the shape of its territory. In 817, when it had been in existence for some ten centuries, Tumchooq, which had resisted wars, invasions, coups and droughts, was completely buried by a sandstorm.

Paul d'Ampère, *Notes on Marco Polo's Book of the Wonders of the World*
(Paris, Éditions de la Sorbonne, p. 518)

"Not one centimetre of our vast territory evades the State," ran a slogan at the time, and the modest vegetable shop huddled at the end of Little India Street demonstrated to everyone that these were not empty words. No gain was too small to feed the greed of our all-powerful State, and it never recognised the limits of its own power, even when confronted with vegetables, disobedient, anarchic, often mad vegetables . . . occasionally even vengeful. Take cabbages, for example, they simply could not be sold on some days, but, depending on plans made in an anonymous office, industrial quantities of the things might descend on the unfortunate little shop, even though it had nowhere to store or preserve them; at times like this, mountains of cabbages piled up everywhere, swamping the pavement and encroaching into the road, rotting, oozing, mingling with filth, metamorphosing into trails of mould on which passers-by slipped and fell. At other times Little India Street was viciously struck by long shortages of cabbages, not a leaf was seen for weeks, whole seasons even, until people forgot what they tasted like. Sometimes a decision-maker would suddenly come up with the idea that that year, instead of cabbages, the population should be eating turnips, and waves of turnips would instantly stream into the shop, flooding it for weeks even though they could not sell half of them.

I often find myself thinking of that shop; I can still see it now: a basic, single-storey building with just one long narrow room, its brick walls painted with greying, flaking whitewash and lined with shelves made from cardboard or plywood which, under the weight of unsaleable goods, had lost their original colour and horizontal form; curving, undulating shelves that shook and looked ready to snap with the very next crate but had not actually collapsed for years, even though they were far beyond any acceptable level of deterioration. There was no ceiling. Chinks of sky filtered through gaps between the roof tiles along with dead insects, raindrops . . .

When I think of that shop, more than its smell, it is rather the state of the floor that comes to mind: the rest of the room was so drab I could barely take my eyes off it, they were glued to it. It was made of beaten earth. I just have to close my eyes to picture those arabesques worthy of a Rubens or a Matisse formed by thousands of fine, sinuous grooves creating images that were bold in places, more delicate in others, like a lip or ridged like vertebrae. A floor worn down with use, its bumps encrusted with filth and scraps of vegetable; I felt I could read in it the sophisticated, labyrinthine fingerprints of time, furrowed by countless forking and intersecting paths, and the footprints the salesman had made in it day after day, month after month, year after year with their daily comings and goings, especially as six of them (a good majority of the staff) were lame, including a former general and two ex-colonels of Guomindang's army, men who had once been enemies of communism and were now prisoners of their physical infirmity as well as their shameful past. What heavy footsteps they had, those political cripples living a form of penitence in that greengrocer's shop.

In theory, every sale, which often represented only a few pennies, had to be recorded in minute detail (name of the vegetables, quantity, time of the transaction, price per kilo, price paid, etc.) in the beautiful upstrokes and downstrokes of the ex-officers' handwriting in a booklet which was meant to hang on the wall but often drifted about on the floor, evidence of the Government's impotence. One feature of vegetables, in comparison to other State merchandise, is how they vary in weight depending on the time of day: a hundred kilos of celery in the morning becomes eighty at noon and seventy by evening, with no external intervention; like a piece of cloth washed for the first time, vegetables shrink, they dry out of their own free will, refusing to collaborate, showing utter contempt for figures and evading any system of control. On top of that, it was always possible to claim they had rotted, victims of some blight or other, and a large proportion of them had had to be thrown away to avoid contaminating the rest of the stock. The relativity of their turnover was, therefore, a source of delight to the salesmen. Still, only those closest to them would ever know the truth about the ritual they performed every evening when the light went out between the lowering and the raising of the metal shutter.

"I was nineteen when I had that fantastic, intoxicating experience for the first time," Tumchooq once told me. "The exhilaration! I shook with fear and excitement. My glasses slipped off and I don't know where they landed. Before I even knew what I was doing, my hands were in there with all the others, blindly raiding what was on the desk: the State's money, the day's takings. We were so violent I thought the desk would tip over and I heard the drawer sliding open. The masks were off, we'd thrown off any simulation of obedience or admission of guilt; the good socialist workforce had disappeared; in the dark we were stripped bare like worms, like animals hungering, thirsting, greedy for money. The little shop had turned into a sort of lair: we couldn't see the others, but we could feel their breath, our hot animal breathing.

"When the light came on and I put my glasses back on I felt a bit dizzy; the bulb hanging from the ceiling seemed higher up than usual, not so bright, not so harsh, wobbling slightly, in slow motion. I thought I could see specks of dust suspended above our heads. I looked, one by one, at the faces of the colleagues I thought I knew so well; I knew exactly who hated whom, who had borrowed money from whom and never paid him back, who had denounced whom, who suspected he had been denounced by whom, etc., and there they were now, pretending to count the coins left on the desk, as calm, impassive and serious as real accountants. I was touched by the trust they showed in initiating me into their game. We were accomplices now, old friends, fellow soldiers who had fought the same battles. In fact, the thought did cross my mind: Were they all from the same regiment, had they known each other since the war? I was so happy it wouldn't have taken much for me to start imitating the lame ones and join the halting ranks of that shadowy army of one-legged veterans as if a communist bullet had struck me in the leg long ago, happy to be part of the collective alibi and of this perfect crime where no one could give anyone else away, because no one could see a thing in that hellish moment of darkness."

I do not know how much money Tumchooq took from the State that first evening, and I am not sure he would have known himself. Something as concrete and down-to-earth as a figure would only have belittled this act of grand larceny; he knew that no sum could truly represent the scale of what they did. Nothing about this adventure, as he described it, really surprised me except for his strange identification with his invalid colleagues two or three times his age. It was not entirely a joke. Later he gave me a fairly convincing demon-stration of his talents as a mimic. He could fake a limp per-fectly: he came to a stop, put his good leg forward, twisted his other foot on the floor so that all his weight came down on his ankle, and bent over to pick up a coin. (I suspected he practised after work when he was alone in the shop, given that he lived there for a long time, because he was not only a salesman but also nightwatchman. In the evenings that desk on which everything inexorably converged became his bed; he covered it with a bamboo mat for a mattress, then a blan-ket and his apron, which he folded in four to act as a pillow for his big head, but it was always on the floor by morning, crumpled like a dirty rag.)

I only remembered Tumchooq's fake limp recently after reading the memoirs of a Russian film director who died about ten years ago, yet whose films—which have sound but no dialogue—have such a pure beauty they bowl me over every time I see them. In his book he talks about the "stammering period" of his childhood, which had started as a game, imitating a friend with this handicap. He got into the habit of stuttering, struggling to find words and uttering snatches of unfinished sentences until he ended up stammering more than his friend and having to resort to singing at the top of his voice, like something from a comic film. "I'm grateful to my stammering friend because, thanks to him, I discovered not the misery of being unable to communicate but an even more significant trait: the vanity of the spoken word."

"One day," Tumchooq told me as he sat on the desk in the greengrocer's with the lights out so that his eyes lit up to the red glow of his cigarette every time he took a drag on it, "I was looking for something to read on my mother's bookshelves. She's the vice curator of the museum in the Forbidden City now, so you can imagine the sort of books she has. Anyway, I came across *The History of Theatrical Presentation in the Court of the Qing Dynasty,* written by Goo Ying and published by the Museum of History. On page 156 there's a paragraph I know by heart:

At the beginning of October in the Year of the Cockerel (1862), on the occasion of the one hundredth day since the birth of Zia Lan, better known as Seventy-one, the long-awaited first son of Prince Yi Lin, a celebration which coincided with victory for the Chinese army in a battle waged with the French on the Chinese-Vietnamese border, the Dowager Empress Cixi showed her gratitude to the Heavens for this double happiness by inviting every prince, minister, general and high dignitary in Peking to attend a huge performance laid on by troupes of singing eunuchs in the Pavilion of Pure Sound within the Forbidden City and lasting from morning till night for three whole days. Two pretexts [the book's author comments] to demonstrate her power. Manifestly, she wanted it—this power—to be noticed, and for people to know that she was Her Majesty the New Master of China, Her Majesty the War Leader, a patriot and a nationalist—a very popular image two years after the fire in the Yuanmingyuan Palace. (This event was collectively perceived as bringing shame on a China defeated by eighteen thousand English and French troops who had marched into Peking and burnt the palace: "The smoke spread through the whole city," wrote one English officer in his diary, "and the Yuanmingyuan Palace was so vast that flakes of black soot fell from the sky onto the city's inhabitants for three whole weeks.") That is how Seventy-one, so favoured by his greataunt, the supreme regent, embarked on a fatal involvement with the anti-Western struggle from as early as his hundredth day. Unfortunately for him, this was the only time in his life his name was associated with a victory."

The following day Tumchooq and I went to the Pavilion of Pure Sound. The sky was overcast, with low clouds drifting over the frozen sea of the Forbidden City's golden roofs in the middle of which four buildings surrounded by red columns form an enormous square around the famous Pavilion of Pure Sound, its three stages set one above the other, rising several dozen metres into the air and thus, according to the museum brochure sold on site, allowing performances to take place in three different spaces simultaneously: Hell, the earthly world and Paradise. This same brochure indicates that the imperial palace actually has two theatres, a small one kept for romantic dramas and more intimate plays, and a large one, the Pavilion of Pure Sound, which, during Cixi's fifty-year reign, was almost exclusively devoted to performances of her favourite production: *Mulian Saves His Mother*.

For the first performance, the scene was set and the audience watched the protagonist's plural lives simultaneously on the triple stage: past, present and future, each occupying one level of the building and establishing its independence by ignoring the existence of the other two. The viewer was offered three different theatrical styles: tragic, comic and poetic. (On the first day, Tumchooq told me, the audience displayed general indifference to these tales they had known by heart since childhood; only visual pleasure triumphed, a pleasure due not to the magnificent sets or sumptuous costumes, but to the physical beauty of the performers, young eunuchs aged between fifteen and eighteen, dressed as men or women and some of whom had that gift beyond human perfection, beyond categories of male and female: the ravishing voice of a castrato.)

The next day the performance still took place on three separate stages: on the top level, seen from far below, the protagonist Mulian stood at the gates of Paradise, but his thoughts, both conscious and unconscious, were expressed by the sublime voice which guided the viewer's gaze towards the earthly world where one could see his mother abandoning him as a child, then towards the infernal world where the mother was quite unrecognisable, transformed into a demon consumed by perpetual hunger and condemned to suffering cruel torture for all eternity. The mother's and son's voices seemed to answer each other, letting fly mutual accusations of sometimes extraordinary violence, from Heaven to Hell. Then came the reconciliation and their two voices crossed the earthly world to find each other, embrace and be united.

It was not until the third day that a vertical staging was laid on, celebrating the triumph of filial love, which lies at the heart of the Chinese moral code. The protagonist progressed from top to bottom using ladders and ropes camouflaged behind elements of the set, or taking perilous leaps to propel himself from one space to the next to save his famished mother. When the son succeeded in controlling his mother, who was trying to devour him, the performance reached its climax: to stop them from escaping, the Lord of the Underworld transformed the lowest space into a gigantic inferno. The hero had to carry his mother on his back and climb up to the intermediary space, the earthly world, but floodwater from the Yellow River, drowning everything in its path, kept driving them back down to the Underworld, where they were swallowed up by flames. As they vanished, a light suddenly sprang up on the highest stage, ripping through the floorboards of the triple set so the hero could rise up with his mother, ascending vertically, climbing ever upwards, unhindered, to Heaven.

Following the map in the brochure, we entered Cixi's private box: a low-slung building with a large opening facing the Pavilion of Pure Sound. There, from behind a wide, finely sculpted screen, she had enjoyed a panoramic view of the triple stage, sheltered from the gaze of her male guests, who were seated in two other buildings on either side of hers. The large room she used as a box was empty, there was nothing left—not her seat, the lacquered screen, any furniture or the great fan wafted by four indefatigable eunuchs silently re-creating the gentle breath of a soft summer breeze for her. In that Year of the Cockerel 1862 she would have been in mourning; her husband, the emperor Xianfeng, having died the previous year. Did her son, the child emperor Tongzhi, who was then four, ever come to this box? If so, where would he have sat? The brochure had nothing to say on the subject.

"I imagine," Tumchooq said, "that in one of the many intervals Cixi would have had her great-nephew brought to her box, given that the celebrations for his first hundred days were theoretically the main reason for the festivities. As an amateur soothsayer, Her Majesty the Master of China had probably felt the baby's still-soft skull, fingering its topography centimetre by centimetre, trying to find a sign of the nation's destiny, some irregular protuberance announcing military talent or anti-Western feelings. In a thirteen-hundred-page book called *An Anthology of Archives from the Intendant to the Court of the Qing Dynasty*," he went on, "I found a few lines indicating the sort of favours Cixi bestowed on her great-nephew: throughout his childhood the intendant's department sent him birthday gifts on the orders of the dowager empress; never the silk cloth or ink made in the Court workshops that other children in the imperial family received, but silver stirrups, a Mongolian saddle, a miniature suit of armour, a soldier's helmet, a compass . . . always things imbued with virile, if not martial, aggressiveness, as if to proclaim: 'Be a hero who will win the wars I wage.' In 1874, for his twelfth birthday, the book records simply: twelve arrows.

"I remember seeing one of those arrows," Tumchooq adds, "at the bottom of a metal box that my mother always kept padlocked; in among her jewellery, some old stamps, official family documents and ration tickets for rice and oil, wrapped in blue brocade decorated with little pearls and tied with a thin yellow silk ribbon was a sheath made of rhinoceros horn, also tied round with yellow silk ribbon. It housed a wooden arrow thirty centimetres long, which, unusually, was painted white; one end was tapered and black, fitted with a rusted iron head, the other still had the vestiges of fletching with balding feathers, and it had a small whistle attached to it: an ancient Chinese invention which dates back several centuries, a sort of flute shaped like a tiny gourd, as thin and light as an empty eggshell; and, if you looked with a magnifying glass, you could see Chinese characters engraved on it: Cixi's name and title in stylised form. Long ago these were known as coded whistle-arrows. When a general received one of these, falling from the sky, sent by Her Majesty, he had to act immediately on the instructions secretly implied by the arrow, its secret so closely guarded that the sender would not allow herself to write it down or have it transmitted by word of mouth."

Tumchooq and I were now heading towards the communal living quarters for the employees of the Forbidden City, where his mother lived; although, he claimed, she had gone to work, even though it was Sunday.

"Eighteen seventy-four saw a key event in Cixi's life," he went on. "After thirteen years as regent she had to restore imperial authority to her son, Tongzhi, the child emperor who had now grown up and reached the age of maturity: eighteen. The law of the Empire requiring Cixi to renounce all power would deprive her of the only pleasure she had known in widowhood. Like a pre-programmed death. Soon she would be the subject of monstrous slander, accused of causing the downfall of the Empire, bringing disaster on the entire country and having blood on her hands. Her victims' families would testify to her cruelty and perversity, making a tally of the dead and clamouring for her head. I think those twelve arrows asked her favourite great-nephew to avenge her or save her from Hell."

When Tumchooq lifted the lid on the box that belonged to his mother I stood for a long time looking at that fascinating arrow, its slender, pointed end made of lead pocked with greenish rust, which I feel I can still see gleaming before my eyes to this day. I couldn't help bringing it up to my mouth and was tempted to dab it with the tip of my tongue to see whether it was poisoned, when I had an idea: Had Cixi ordered her great-nephew to carry out an assassination? Did she simply want to hear this arrow whistling through the air or did she, in fact, want to see it piercing the chest— the very heart—of the son who had driven her from the throne?

Neither *Mulian Saves His Mother* nor *The White Arrow* was played out on the stage of history, but the pages written then were worthy of the darkest noir fiction: Emperor Tongzhi had barely assumed power and started presiding single-handed over Court audiences in the Palace of Eternal Peace, when he was struck down by a violent illness— smallpox, according to the diagnosis of Court doctors— and died the following year, 1875, at the age of nineteen. Shortly afterwards an official announcement stated that his wife, who was pregnant, had brought an end to two lives, hers and that of the future hereditary prince she carried in her belly, a suicide called into question by most historians, some of whom even suspect Cixi was so incapable of renouncing power that she assassinated her son, daughter-in-law and unborn grandson. In any event, Cixi, Her Majesty the Master of China, still bearing the title of dowager empress, installed her nephew Guangxu on the throne, another child emperor who was just four, descended from the same lineage and of the same generation as his predecessor, Tongzhi.

It was the most contested succession in China's history. Cixi was trampling a sacred protocol which had seen the Empire perpetuated for two thousand years: when an emperor died without an heir, his succession had to be secured by a child from the imperial family, but from a different lineage and of the previous generation. Any breach of this Confucian law risked the collapse of the Empire. Cixi's method for silencing protests proved simple, efficient and irrevocable: any ministers or courtiers who confronted her were condemned to decapitation, with the exception of just one or two who were each granted the favour of being sent a long, sturdy silk belt embroidered with celestial landscapes and graciously offered by the merciful dowager empress for them to hang themselves and, therefore, have the privilege of arriving in the afterlife with their bodies intact.

No one will ever know the true causes of the Empire's collapse. Was it pure coincidence? The combination of several negative events? Or simply the inevitable consequence, foretold by Confucian law, of Tongzhi's illegal succession by Guangxu? The latter grew up in turn, took power, initiated political and economic reforms and was eventually brought down by his aunt Cixi and imprisoned on an islet in the middle of the lake within the Forbidden City. He died aged thirty-seven, in 1908, also childless. The ultimate mystery was that Cixi, unable to resist her own impulses, installed another child emperor on the throne, only to die the following day. Two years later the dynasty was overthrown and replaced by the Republic. A new era dawned.

"In 1975," Tumchooq told me, "a hundred years after Guangxu was appointed as heir, I read a book which was banned at the time, called *The Secret Biography of Cixi*. It was given to me by Ma, an old friend from primary school, who'd moved away to Sichuan just before the Cultural Revolution to join his parents, who were both doctors. We hadn't seen each other for about ten years and I didn't actually recognise him straight away. He was sitting on the ground outside my house. I thought he was a beggar at first, because he was so thin and dirty and raggedy. The State had sent him off to some mountain in Sichuan for seven years to be re-educated by so-called revolutionary peasants. Poor as he was, he'd come to give me that book. I could have cried. He'd travelled by train—but like a vagrant, without a ticket—for three days and three nights. No one else in the world would have done that for me. I'm sure they wouldn't. He'd found the book on the black market and swapped it for another banned book, the second volume of *Jean-Christophe*, a French novel translated by Fu Lei. His favourite novel. I remember asking him what he'd done with the first volume. 'I gave it to a doctor who did some important stuff for a girlfriend'—'What sort of stuff?'—'An abortion.' Silence. 'Your girlfriend?'—'No, Luo's, a friend who was sent to be re-educated in the same village as me.' Ma had other friends besides me. Lots of friends. He always did, wherever he went. People being re-educated, locals, prisoners, thieves, tramps, girls, boys, young, old. I didn't. I'm lonely as a red-haired horse. My life, no, let's say the chapter on friendship, began with Ma and he's still the only protagonist.

"*The Secret Biography of Cixi* was published in 1948, six years before I was born. It's a minor historical masterpiece written by Tang Li, a professor at Peking University. I think of him as a geographer devoting the best years of his life, if not his whole life, to studying a river, following it all the way up to its source, in a boat or on foot, stopping every now and then and pursuing a tributary, however small and remote and insignificant it may be, so that eventually he knows the river by heart the way a lover knows his partner's body. It's the only decent book with a few well-documented pages about the life of Seventy-one."

Tumchooq lent me that book, which took me on a journey through the vast labyrinth that is an imperial family, a dynasty. Limited until then to school history books, I felt with every page I turned that I was finally getting somewhere in my understanding of China.

I was impressed, among other things, by the family tree drawn up by the author in the chapter about the illegitimacy of Tongzhi's succession by Guangxu. A representation as clear and precise as an anatomical illustration with all the ramifications of blood vessels, veins and prolific, converging arteries. By following one of these branches I found the name Zai Lan, followed by the word "Seventy-one" in brackets, born to one of the great lineages of direct imperial descent which ended two generations after him.

There is no doubt Cixi knew every detail of this genealogy

by heart, the author pointed out. She knew, her clan knew, the Court knew that when Tongzhi died the only legitimate heir by his relationship and degree of descent was Zai Lan, the dowager empress's favourite great-nephew. But in Cixi's eyes he had a fatal flaw: he was thirteen years old, nine years older than Guangxu.

Nine years! She must have counted those nine years again and again. As the author of the biography related, during the first weeks of mourning for her son, she spent days on end calculating, weighing up the pros and cons, wandering like a ghost through the huge gardens of her palace in the middle of the night. Sometimes she was so exhausted that she asked to be carried by her great eunuch, Li Lianying, so that she could continue her nocturnal walk all the way to the Pavilion of Silk Worms, a luxurious place she adored, lit by flickering lantern flames. She would sit between the racks waiting for inspiration as she watched one of the countless caterpillars metamorphose into a beautiful moth. She eventually made up her mind, choosing the other child to reign, because, although illegal, he would guarantee her nine more years' enjoyment of the absolute pleasure of being Her Majesty the Master of China. More's the pity!

No one would have believed [wrote the historian] that the thirteen-year-old adolescent, Cixi's great-nephew, would be able to recover from such frustration: on the threshold of an earthly paradise, within reach of the throne borne by dragons, he was thrown out. All the politicians, of aristocratic descent or otherwise, thought he was lost. His family was disgraced. No one ever stopped outside their residence to the west of the Pavilion of Peace, not any more, no prestigious visitors in palanquins, no nobles in carriages, once so numerous they created bottlenecks and their drivers argued for space with local porters. The cacophony of noise and shouts fell silent. The Court intendant stopped sending generous or at least symbolic gifts to mark special occasions. When, at the age of sixteen, he married the daughter of a low-ranking administrator, the ceremony was held in his quarters in a low-ceilinged, all but deserted room. At about this time he started visiting instructors in the art of the *pipa* (a sort of Chinese lute). They gradually put him back on his feet and one of them—a blind man who was both a musician and a soothsayer and whose word was respected as an oracle by the population of Peking as well as in the realm of martial arts—predicted his future, a prediction that remained confidential with the exception of one sentence: "The flame of your life will be extinguished at the age of seventy-one." From that day Zai Lan adopted this number as a nickname, as if trying to master his own destiny. A neutral nickname with no social or political complexion, but sufficiently mysterious for some to perceive it as a code name for a clandestine anti-Western organisation which would go on to be a driving force in the Boxer Rising years later.

As well as for the *pipa*, Seventy-one earned a tremendous reputation in the art of falconry; each of his eagles, bred from pure royal strains, wore a bell attached to one foot, and this would ring even when the bird was invisible, flying one or two hundred metres above Peking. He used his own money to publish a work called *The Art of Falconry,* written in delicious rhyming verse in the same style as nomadic songs. Always respecting the rules of alliteration (according to which the two or four lines constituting each rhyme have to begin with the same sound), he guides us one step at a time through a vast field: he examines the vitreous body of the eagle's eye with a magnifying glass, analyses their sight and the colour changes in their feathers, studies the best places to train and fly them, the influence of meteorological conditions and warm and cold airstreams, gives details of their diet, which must not include pork, and explains how to prepare meat for them, including how it must be stewed in spring and autumn; he establishes medical diagnoses based on the colour of their droppings, indicates relevant remedies copied from old books . . . A fascinating work, even in the censored version amputated of the chapter on the art of divination based on interpreting eagles' flight, probably learned from his blind *pipa* instructor. During the Boxer Rising, which erupted in 1900, various collaborators of Western powers thought they detected a coded language in his book, claiming the rebels used a sort of mnemonic process taking the rhymes at the beginning of each phrase to memorise orders from their superiors and transmit them by word of mouth so that no written message could ever fall into enemy hands. When it comes to finding a scapegoat, human imagination knows no limits.

Seventy-one's personality [the historian goes on in such a professorial tone that I felt I could almost hear his voice ringing round a lecture theatre] is a perfect illustration of what is known in psychoanalysis as the frustration complex. Like every frustration, the one he experienced at the age of thirteen engendered aggression. Granted, he never attacked his great-aunt Cixi, remaining loyal to her to the end, as required by the Confucian moral code, but he demonstrated violent tendencies when he met Cixi's new allies, the Westerners, and this coincided with the hostility the whole country displayed towards enemy powers at the end of the nineteenth century. Seventy-one used to send his sovereign reports about crimes committed by European missionaries, and some of these were circulated at Court and spread widely through the streets of the city. On the strength of the injustice he had suffered and his legendary marginal status, Seventy-one became so popular that, when the Boxer crisis struck, Cixi asked for his help and appointed him as a senior member of the State Council to act as an intermediary between herself and the rebels. At the end of this blood-soaked episode, the eight Western powers—including Great Britain, France, Germany and Russia—invaded Peking again; history was repeating itself: acts of revenge, palaces ransacked, pillage, arson, rape and the signature of a peace treaty. In the text of the treaty, between the first article (in which China was to concede a significant portion of territory to each of the eight allied countries) and the third (stating there would be astronomical payments), the second focused exclusively on the personal fate of Seventy-one: Chinese government authorities undertook to condemn Prince Zai Lan, senior member of the State Council, to decapitation. In their great leniency and out of respect for the empress, the allied countries agreed the criminal should be granted mercy, his punishment taking the form of permanent exile beyond the Great Wall, in Manchuria, but he could not be granted imperial amnesty.

His farewells were the most dramatic I have ever known. He was exiled to a minor district of Manchuria where countless anti-Western rebels had perished before him. Acting on Seventy-one's orders, his wife had had an aviary built so that, with special permission from the law courts, he could take his eagles with him. Day after day the dimensions of the aviary grew, adding new levels until there were four storeys of small compartments, because his friends, his admirers and even complete strangers came in droves to offer him birds, the poorest of them bringing humble chickens. It was a Noah's Ark: eagles, nightjars, turtledoves, cranes, mandarin ducks, parrots, cockatoos, nightingales, canaries, red-beaked crows, tawny owls, barn owls, pigeons, flamingos, swallows, pheasants, skylarks, magpies, kingfishers, pelicans, storks, grebes, woodpeckers, sparrows, chaffinches, hoopoes, cockerels, hens, ducks, geese . . . As dawn broke one morning in late autumn, escorted like a criminal by a dozen Chinese soldiers and wearing a wooden yoke round his neck, he left the city in which he had spent all thirty-eight years of his life. He had barely stepped through the West Gate of Peking before the soldiers took off the yoke so he could breakfast with them in a small inn, but a group of horsemen from the army of the foreign powers caught up with them. Speaking through a translator, the captain announced the order given by the commander in chief, General Valleri, to kill all the birds on the spot to ensure they did not become messengers between the exiled prince and Peking's last remaining rebels. The horsemen dismounted, guns in hand, loaded their weapons, arranged themselves in a firing line and opened fire at point-blank range on the aviary. Strangled squawking and frantic flapping of wings in the blood-splattered Noah's Ark. According to some witnesses, Seventy-one completely lost his head at the sight of this massacre and punctured his own eyeballs with a knife he found in the inn's kitchen. After a month-long journey he arrived in Manchuria blind and mad, with his gigantic empty aviary, which, for many years to come, he took with him on weekly authorised trips deep into the Manchurian desert. His children would steer the little cart over to a dune and he would approach the empty aviary, his hands easily identifying the spaces originally reserved for eagles. He stroked the bamboo bars, inhaled the smell left by his birds of prey, lifted his face to the sky and admired their invisible flight, revelling in the long, mournful ringing of their bells. He called them by name, giving them a succession of incomprehensible instructions and orders to attack. His cries rang out in the infinite desert, fierce as a shepherd gathering his flock, filled with hatred and bitterness. Eventually he would put on the thick leather gauntlet that covered his arm up to the elbow, and raise his arm so they could come to rest on it while he stood like a pillar of salt on the sand dune.

During one such outing, one of his children felt a tingle down his spine because he heard a bird cry out, answering his father's calls. "And I saw an eagle" [he later related to the author of the book] "hovering several dozen metres above the ground, dark against the sunlight like the shadow of a dead leaf on the wind, then it flew up until we could no longer see it. A black dot. But it came slowly back down towards us, as if checking the calls were real; the tips of its wings reflecting the sunlight, projecting a display of glittering flashes onto the dune, dazzling my eyes. Calling. More calling. A blind man and an eagle, their voices mingling in a duet which, even years later, still rings in my ears."

The book's author, to whom Seventy-one granted an interview, asked him about a legend which claimed that, during one excursion with the empty aviary, his children changed their route to go to a "singing dune" where Seventy-one's calls to his imaginary eagles combined with the children's ascent of the steep slope to produce a rumbling from the dune, a natural acoustic phenomenon, which the locals had known for a long time and which was of considerable interest to many scientists. On that particular day the "Song of the Sands," as it was known, started as a muffled murmur and grew in volume until it merged with the engine noise of a plane passing over the dune at the same time. The plane flew on and disappeared, but not before dropping an ancient Chinese silk painting which floated through the air, twirled in the wind and landed, nonchalantly, close to the prince's aviary, like a gift fallen from the skies. The son denied, not the episode in its entirety, but the nature of the object in question:

"It wasn't a painting" [he corrected] "but half of a text, calligraphic signs on a torn piece of silk. I don't know the origins of the signs and I can only find one way of describing them: tadpole signs with a huge head joined to a soft body, elongated with frail, squiggling limbs. A friend of my father's, the exiled poet Zhang Zigang, examined the mutilated artefact and announced that it was a language he didn't recognise written in horizontal form from right to left, unlike the Chinese language, and this was almost certainly a piece of immense value if not a priceless treasure, as was suggested not only by the great age of the cloth and the colour of the ink but, more significantly, by the seals of its successive owners above the text: two emperors of the Song dynasty, a prime minister of the Ming dynasty, a sovereign of the Qing dynasty, and Qianlong, whose Seal of the Five Joys of the Sons of Heaven (a very rare seal recognised only by his close entourage) proved the pleasure he had taken in owning the work."

"Do you remember the aeroplane?"

"It was a Japanese plane."

"Why do you say that?"

"It wasn't a combat plane with an open cockpit, but the Japanese emblem painted in red became clearly visible as it glided lower and lower, going very slowly, just skimming the stunted trees."

"Planes at the time looked like geometrid moths."

"This one, with its earth-shaking, drumming engines, was like a winged monster suspended in the air, growling, furious. When this horrible monster darkened the sky over us, a young man in glasses opened the door while still in full flight. It seems far-fetched now but at the time you could open the doors of aeroplanes. His glasses were snatched by the wind straight away, the craft was thrown off balance and one wing dipped dangerously. The man didn't seem to want to commit suicide, he was just brandishing something in his hand, as if to throw it out. The plane seemed to go into a sort of spasm, shuddering frighteningly, as if paralysed. All through the struggle that was going on inside the door stayed gaping open, then I saw the wheels of the landing gear peeling from the monster's body like talons. That was when a shredded piece of silk flew out of the door and was swept away by the wind. Several other pieces of paper or silk flew down, and were carried off by another gust of wind. The pilot managed to right the plane but, as he attempted to regain height, he was heading straight for the side of a dune with the door now closed and the landing gear retracted; the whole incident or spell of madness hadn't lasted more than a minute. The plane disappeared into the depths of the sky, not leaving a sound. And in that silence a ghost of transparent silk sketched a trail of white across the dusk, drifting on the wind with a nonchalant fluttering, and eventually landing on our cart with its empty aviary."

The historian pointed out that when he wrote his book Seventy-one was still living in exile in Manchuria and was over eighty, a much greater age than his blind instructor had predicted for his demise. What had altered his fate? He had stopped his expeditions in his cart at the age of sixty-nine, that is, two years before the anticipated date of his death, on the day that he came into possession of the mutilated silk artefact, which he considered to be a gift from Heaven. "At last," the oldest political prisoner in the world confided in his son, "I have received my rightful inheritance. I've been given back my legitimacy as a prince. Justice has been done to me."

3

I COULDN'T HAVE IMAGINED THAT THE greengrocer's on Little India Street, where I spent more and more of my time after my university lectures, would mark such a turning point in my fate. Seen through the prism of my growing affection, those ordinary cheap vegetables on the brink of decay took on a rainbow of iridescent colours, deploying every nuance of the spectrum: the emerald green of peas, the scarlet of chillies, the sulphurous pink of pumpkins, the purple-blue of aubergines . . . even the swarms of cockroaches as fat as Manchurian soya beans crawling in every corner were decked in jet-coloured velvet in my eyes. Late one afternoon in March 1978 I was at the top of the hill which looked down over the Forbidden City ("Wait for me here," Tumchooq had said, before running off to his mother's home in the quarters for employees of that prestigious establishment, old houses of grey brick next to the grey moat beneath the grey walls) when I was bewitched by the spectacle of the sun sinking into the waves formed by the palace roofs—the marriage between Heaven and Earth, as Tumchooq called it—and the first thought that came into my head couldn't avoid the tyranny-by-vegetables that now irrevocably dominated my entire mind: I saw countless grains of corn coming towards me, endlessly reflected in the matt gold mirrors of those magnificent roofs, and, when the huge red disc was half-masked by heavy clouds, the grains of corn metamorphosed into the gently curved shape of an aubergine, the lower half distorting into serpentine contortions before shrinking, shrinking until it turned into long, gleaming bean sprouts. At the climax of this copulation between yin and yang, the sun broke up into a diffuse force bathing the roofs with its shimmering fluid, flowing dark red over the golden background that still shone through.

In his only novel, *Fortress Besieged,* the great Chinese writer (and probably the most famous scholar of the twentieth century) Qian Zhongshu tells us, with an irony all his own, that in Chinese love stories the one who loves always starts by borrowing a book from the beloved, be it simply a manual of Japanese grammar, a knitting pattern or a bicycle-repair leaflet. In fact, when I decided a few years ago to make enquiries on the subject, I couldn't find a literate person in the whole country who had made their first advances in any other way, even in the disadvantaged circles of restaurant waitresses, little urchins hanging about in station waiting rooms, young apprentices . . . except for me. My love story began with a wilted yellow-green cabbage eaten away by a worm that I thought I could see lurking in the folds of a leaf, a cabbage that Tumchooq—the salesman at the shop on Little India Street—offered me out of generosity, or perhaps contempt, when he still thought of me as just a foreign student with a little rabbit to feed.

White-Tuft was the name I had given the animal bought at a Sunday market, and I had cobbled together a hutch for him out of wooden bars secured with huge nails flattened with a hammer, covered with a piece of rusting zinc and positioned in my backyard against a scaly, whitewashed wall. Apart from a few mosquitoes and a spider scuttling on flimsy legs around my room and my bed, White-Tuft was the only creature I could talk to on those long, icy cold nights. His favourite food was leafy vegetables, which I would go and pick up from the shop on Little India Street every day. This daily task soon brought me closer to Tumchooq, I even got friendly with his mostly lame colleagues and was almost allowed to witness their evening ritual around the oily cash register, which sat crookedly in its casing and made a grating noise. When money was very short, Tumchooq sometimes took me out to the country on his bicycle to pick wild herbs to replace the "socialist vegetables," as he called them, and sometimes after work he would walk me home to the foreign students' halls, watched by invisible eyes. It was an old bicycle from the 1950s, an East German make, and its brakes, unlike current models', were connected to the pedals so you had to back-pedal to operate them, making a long mechanical graunching sound and going into a protracted slide fraught with danger as you exposed yourself to all sorts of accidents before the two wheels, firstly the rear wheel, then the front one, stopped turning altogether.

"It's my only inheritance," Tumchooq told me, flirta- tiously; "every bit of it is extremely precious, because you can't get hold of the parts any more."

The grips on the handlebars, the forks at the back and front and various other parts of it were wrapped in red fab- ric, blackened with age; this made it look from a distance like a swaying horse covered in wounds, its deep gashes bound in heavy, blood-soaked bandages. When he pedalled and I sat on the rusted luggage rack, which creaked at the slightest bump in the road, I thought it miraculous that the thing kept moving and didn't leave us both stranded.

Despondency isn't the precise word to describe my state of mind during my time in Peking. When I went out walking I felt I was swimming through the cabbage soup in the canteen, and when I drank the cabbage soup in the canteen, I felt I could see Peking reflected in it, their similarities seemed so obvious to me: same blackish grey texture in the bowl of soup and the moat of the Forbidden City and, once the frost lifted, the bland, sickening smell of sludge drifting up from it. My university, which was almost deserted, was worse still. It had the best reputation in all China, but you never saw real Chinese students there, just revolutionary farmhands, workers and soldiers—the people the university was open to. In my isolation, the only thing I learnt in class by way of literature were the words of Mao; I could recite whole sentences, some as long and convoluted as a labyrinth. There were also the revolutionary songs I had to sing with the others so many times each day that I sometimes found myself inadvertently humming them to the little rabbit I had bought in the market. Lying in bed in the mornings I would often picture myself at death's door, struck down by some fatal illness, and I would start composing my own obituary under the title *A Revolutionary Parrot Beneath the Peking Sun*. At night, locked in my room, I would sleep for ten hours, sometimes more, as there were no nightclubs anywhere, or concert halls or cinemas screening anything other than propaganda films . . . and there wasn't a single restaurant in the whole city that stayed open beyond seven o'clock in the evening. There was a great wall covered in weeds and moss between China and me. If I needed to use the bathroom in the middle of the night, whatever the season but particularly in winter, I had to get dressed from head to foot, trousers, coat, etc., and cut across a dark, deserted, freezing courtyard with a torch in my hand, because the bulbs had been broken in all the lamps. Eventually, after my long journey, I would reach the far side and the door to the latrines, also plunged in shadow. I had won the first round of the game; now for the second: rotting wooden planks wobbled beneath my feet, spanning a slurry ditch, which gave off the oldest stench in the world. With a feeling of terror but no surprise, I heard my shit fall through the air and then, after half a second that seemed to last an eternity, an echo reverberated through those unfathomable depths, a disproportionate, eerie echo laden with menace, which made my blood freeze. ("When two Chinese words have the same pronunciation," Tumchooq, my instructor in swear words and Peking slang, once told me, "there must be a mysterious connection between them. Take *shit,* for example; it's pronounced *shi,* exactly like the word for the start of something, a beginning.") I only ever felt like the proud winner of this dismal nocturnal game once I was back in my room. Occasionally, I would stop halfway and make a detour round the back of the house, where my rabbit lived in its little lean-to next to a telegraph pole. By torchlight I took a handful of grass and vegetables from a basket and slipped them through the bars of the cage under the rabbit's nose. For a long time my only source of happiness in Peking was watching my friend chewing fresh grass in the darkness, hearing his gentle, rhythmic mastication against the sound of the wind humming through telegraph wires.

One evening Tumchooq parked his bike and actually stepped inside my hall of residence and came into my room in order, if memory serves, to help me with some work, and afterwards I made him a cup of Western coffee and played cassettes of French songs for him. When we went back out we found his bicycle knocked over, sprawled on the ground; the caps from the valves on his tyres had disappeared; stolen, we felt, as a warning. Condemned to pushing his bicycle, Tumchooq walked off into the night, laughing and whistling out of tune. On another of his visits the bell disappeared, then it was the grips on the handlebars and their red bandaging, and finally the saddle, which meant from then on he had to pedal standing up, proud of his calf muscles and his love. With me on the luggage rack, the pair of us must have made the most spectacular sight on a bicycle in Little India Street, because we couldn't find the spare parts anywhere, as East Germany had broken off all trade with China.

Only White-Tuft's death brought an end to his visits: we came in one evening and found my little rabbit assassinated in his hutch, blood still trickling over his flattened ears and dripping to the ground, testifying to the cruelty of the attack, his body still warm as it lay there on his vegetable leaves. His heart stopped beating in my hands.

In the days immediately after that sordid event, Tumchooq continued his visits to demonstrate our determination to whoever had taken out the contract on the assassination but, once in my room, nothing was the same; there was a strange atmosphere because White-Tuft's presence was still so tangible, not to say all-pervasive. My cassettes of French songs sounded like funeral marches and, anyway, they kept getting stuck in the tape player, introducing long silences in which we felt we could still hear the soft regular noises of our late friend chewing his cabbage leaves. The coffee didn't taste the same either, and we had lost the knack for concentrating with childish innocence on my Chinese grammar. To avoid descending into a prolonged period of mourning, Tumchooq suggested I go home with him to do my homework in the shop, where he slept on a bamboo mat that he laid out on the desk in the evening, then rolled back up in the morning and hid behind crates of vegetables, leaving all sorts of rubbish, peelings and dust behind on the table that served as his bed.

"I love money so much," he joked, "I sleep on the desk so I can hear coins rolling around in the till when I move."

That was how the greengrocer's shop definitively took possession of me. Every day after lectures, at closing time (my favourite time), I would run over there like a little girl, carrying our supper, which I had bought at the university canteen, in two bowls covered with lids. Tumchooq often told me stories—they were my addiction, but his too—after we'd eaten. Occasionally, he gave me a brief glimpse of his childhood as he drained a glass of sixty-degree-proof maize spirit, but sometimes he would get carried away, drunk on his storytelling, and expand on a myriad different details until late into the night. As I listened, trying to picture him as a toddler or a schoolboy, another image came to mind, Marlow in *Heart of Darkness,* lying on the bridge of an old boat under a sky littered with stars, and I could no longer tell whether the words I was listening to came from Marlow or Tumchooq as he, too, related events of crushing, inhuman enormity in a slow, slightly cracked voice, which wrapped itself round you, lulled your senses, paralysed your limbs, made your head spin and swallowed you up.

"They were nothing earthly now . . . ," says Marlow. "I began to distinguish the gleam of the eyes under the trees."

White-Tuft's death was never far from my thoughts, and the slightest noise outside—a stray dog barking, a screech of car brakes, a pigeon cooing feebly—made me sit up sharply, terrified, as if it had been a policeman's boot kicking at the metal shutter.

"Mr. Liu," Tumchooq began, "was my class teacher, but was also in charge of drawing lessons for the whole school. He was thirty-five, a very happy, enthusiastic man with a slight weakness for alcohol, not that he was ever drunk in lessons. His life's work, and he'd clearly given himself to it heart and soul, was a portrait of each of the world's five Great Revolutionaries, using models in Tiananmen Square, where Karl Marx had pride of place surrounded by the other four: Friedrich Engels, his close collaborator and faithful financier with a beard just as exuberant and tightly curled as his own (he's not so famous in the West, but very popular in communist countries, where he's seen as a co-founder of the proletarian revolutionary movement), Lenin, Stalin and Mao, the only one without a beard. (It was the late 1950s and China, still passionately in love with the USSR and only just flirting with Maoist idolatry, still respected chronological precedence, so Mao was positioned behind his bearded precursors, two Europeans and two Russian 'big brothers.' Mao never lost his infallible respect for the first two. Towards the end of his life, whenever he mentioned his imminent death, he talked as if it were an appointment with Marx and Engels.)

"Those five portraits painted by our teacher—with real paint which gave off exquisite wafts of turpentine for a whole academic year—were a source of great pride to our class for a long time. If you looked at them closely, which is what pupils from other classes who came to admire them did, all you could see was a swampy delta of colours you would never have guessed were there, throbbing, swirling, mingling and clotting into countless tiny mounds, uniting together with one aim—complying with the artist. Everyone agreed on one thing: these five 'saviours of humanity' looked more real than on the printed posters hanging on the walls of other classrooms. The nuances of his work (products of his tipsy state, who knows?) translated as clearer lines, more natural colouring and particularly as more real, personal expressions on their faces, transforming those serious, feverish 'helmsmen' into smiling, sympathetic individuals, and this was a lesson we would never forget (his only failure was Engels, the great German theorist, who seemed sullen, with a less confident and determined look in his eye, betraying the sort of anxiety rarely attributed to political figures).

"The author of these portraits, our teacher, never failed to remind us how lucky we were to be in that classroom, so envied by pupils in other classes. He even went so far as to imply we had privileged status as protégés chosen by the five great men who watched our every move from above the blackboard. When he came down from his raised desk to walk among us you'd have thought he was an archangel stepping down from the altar. He saw himself as guardian to the pantheon of those five revolutionary gods, and whenever he mentioned enemies of the proletariat who attacked them, his face twisted with loathing and his eyes burned with anger, such anger that he literally ground his teeth. In that silent classroom, if you held your breath, you could hear the extraordinarily brutal sound of his teeth grinding the bones of the imaginary Enemy.

"Every now and then, particularly early in the morning, at daybreak, he would go over all the mistakes we had made the day before, turning towards the portraits, looking up, waving his arms, telling them what an onerous task it was being a teacher, and begging them to help him . . . until the day when plain-clothed policemen turned up at school to arrest him only an hour after he'd chaired a meeting with pupils' parents. According to rumours circulating the next day, someone's father had denounced him. Uniformed policemen swarmed into our classroom, interrupting our lesson, and took photos of the five portraits from various distances and different angles. One of them stood on the desk and, with his gloved hands, took down the picture of the sullen, bearded Engels. He carefully slipped it into a cellophane bag, which he sealed with black tape as you would a piece of evidence in a criminal enquiry. They left without a single word to help us unravel the mystery.

"A few days later, Mr. Liu was released. He came into the classroom behind the headmaster, completely transformed, stripped of his pride; in a barely audible voice he read a long, self-critical tract, accusing himself of the unforgivable crime of painting—under the influence of alcohol—an inaccurate portrait of Engels, having taken as his model a photograph of another bearded man, Professor Ivan P. Pavlov, the famous Russian physiologist, who had been on the front cover of a scientific review at the time. (As far as I could see, Mr. Liu's mistake was a very interesting Freudian slip: Professor Pavlov's name is associated with his discovery of conditioned reflexes, a theory which greatly inspired the concept of brainwashing and was, therefore, just as important to tyrants and the populations they bullied as Engels's theories, if not more so.)

"That was the last time Mr. Liu set foot in our classroom. Even though we were young and didn't understand the facts, his long, self-accusatory speech rang in our ears like a farewell lament. He was demoted to the rank of workman, sweeping the floor and carrying hot water for the teaching staff to which he no longer belonged, working in the outhouses that housed the coal boiler, behind the main building. Some mornings when I arrived at school before dawn for athletics training, I heard him sweeping the cement surface of the playground outside the classrooms. I couldn't see him, but listened to his invisible, rasping brushstrokes reverberating as he gathered dead leaves from the plane trees and cleaned the ground with such stubborn insistence you'd have thought he was scratching out a stain. Along with the white smoke coming from the chimney of the outhouses, those rather slow sounds punctuated my early-morning arrivals in the dark, sometimes in the rain and often in temperatures so cold not a single moth fluttered around the lampposts.

"Mr. Liu's disgrace marked the end of a clandestine collaboration, a secret exchange set up by two boys on the same bench—Ma and me—which had worked a treat until then.

"Do you remember Ma? Yes, the one who gave me *The Secret Biography of Cixi*. His parents were both doctors in Chengdu and in 1964 they were sent to a very remote region of Sichuan on the border with Tibet. Ma was nine at the time and he came to live in Peking with an uncle who worked at the Forbidden City with my mother, first as a night watchman, then as Assistant Security Manager. When Ma joined us, the dunce of the class—that was me—was put next to him because he was the arithmetic champion in his province and brilliant at writing; full of naïve hope, Mr. Liu gave him the weighty task of helping me improve.

"I was immediately struck by the size of his head. He was a weedy little boy with such narrow shoulders that, as one of our Pekinese sayings goes, they were in a straight line with his feet. But his head was more than big: enormous. When he bent over to write, it covered almost half his desk, hiding it from the prying eye of his dunce of a neighbour, cruelly dashing attempts at the espionage and cribbing that would have been his salvation. Nothing. Especially as this genius suffered from myopia, which grew worse at an astonishing rate all through our schooling, forcing him to lean closer and closer to the desk.

"Witnessing the rapid decline in his eyesight, I asked out of curiosity why he didn't talk to his uncle about it. He replied that he was worried his mother would be too painfully disappointed, and made me promise not to say a word to anyone. During the first term that we shared a bench, numbers and ideograms on the blackboard became a little more blurred for him every day. At the end of term, on the day of our arithmetic exam, I knew he couldn't possibly read the five problems our master had written out. (At the time we didn't have photocopies of the questions, probably to save money.) So I copied them out on a sheet of paper, folded it several times and passed it to him under the table. He read it discreetly, his face impassive, and set to work. Barely a quarter of an hour later, making the most of the fact that the teacher was looking away, he dug me in the ribs and, with a wink, he in turn passed me the piece of paper, folded in the same way. Confused, I unfolded it and, in among my scribblings, I saw his writing, firm and upright, though it had been jotted at speed and was slightly large and uneven, but there it was solving each problem, step by step, right down to the final solution. I could have copied them out in their entirety but, in order to maintain credibility in the teacher's eyes, I settled for copying three and improvising solutions, which were bound to be wrong, for the others, narrowly escaping yet more academic dishonour.

"Throughout Mr. Liu's reign we never knew whether our monarch—whose eye, a portrait painter's most precious organ, always shone with a glint of drink and madness—had noticed our strategy, but didn't want to say so. He regularly cited us as models of cooperation, and for two successive years we shared the same bench near the window through which we twice saw the spring buds of an elm tree transform into clouds of cool green that took up a considerable portion of sky and shaded us from the sun. Now we exchanged not only schoolwork but also marbles, kaleidoscopes, penknives, comics, stamps, solid wooden tops that we spun with a whip and hollow German tops that hummed as they spun, danced across the sky and zig-zagged through the air with a long whine . . .

"At the height of our friendship we pooled our pocket money to set up a fund, with Ma as treasurer. Full of heroic aspirations, we promised ourselves we would increase our capital without spending any of it until it could eventually finance a long trip to Manchuria, where my great-grandfather, a former aristocrat nicknamed Seventy-one, lived in exile. But at the end of the first fortnight we gave in at the sight of some glazed duck with glossy, red translucent skin, hanging in a restaurant window. We bought it and, not daring to sit down, had it cut up and put into a paper bag. Out in the street we savoured a few mouthfuls and it tasted so divine we thought we'd been transported to Heaven; the trees of Peking seemed to float around us and adults swam through the air like famished sharks, launching themselves at us, their noses homing in on our paper bag. We wandered through the streets eating it, no, devouring it, piece by piece, licking the last drops of its exquisite fat trickling down our fingers, before realising our Manchurian dream had gone up in smoke.

"Mr. Liu was succeeded by a strapping young woman who wore a red scarf—the official sign of the young revolutionary elite—round her neck, and a new era, hers, began with a radical reorganisation of our classroom with Ma and myself as the major victims. It was the middle of winter, a few weeks before the end-of-year exams, the worst time to separate us. In her triumphant opera singer's voice she condemned Ma to irrevocable exile on the other side of the classroom. I still remember the moment she passed sentence: we huddled together on the bench, in the black shadows of the bare elm, its branches darkening our desk as well as Ma's enormous head, eclipsing his entire body. He stood up briskly, took his satchel without looking at me, or anyone else, crossed the room with his head lowered and slumped onto the new bench he was sharing with a girl.

"Now Ma could no longer help inflicting the disappointment he so feared on his mother. Once summoned, she came by train from her distant province for a meeting in the headmaster's office, and through the open doorway I saw her—

crushed, as if struck with a mallet. The headmaster was talking, she was crying. That image, captured by the photographic lenses that were my adolescent eyes, was imprinted on my retinas for such a long time that I still find it easy to describe now: in the distance, far in the background, through the window and beyond the dark branches of thuya and cypress trees (the headmaster's office was two floors above our classroom), beyond the school fence, beyond 4th May Boulevard, stand the high walls of the Forbidden City, ringed by the blue-grey of the frozen moat on which the minute figures of skaters flit about like crazed wasps, bending, fluttering, glittering, 'so small they play tricks with your eyes,' as the old poem goes. And in the foreground a woman crying silently. She fascinated me at the time, not for that mute eruption of her maternal heart, but for her brutal metamorphosis: she became ugly! Ugly and old. What a contrast compared to my mother, the most beautiful woman in the museum, if not the whole of Peking.

"My mother's first name, as she herself delights in saying, is made up of just one proud, insolent syllable, a single vowel which refuses alliance with any of its vocalised peers and certainly not with a consonant, giving it a strong ring of protest: E. There are few words in our language with the same pronunciation. My mother's E means 'Mulberry Bombyx,' the silkworm moth, and is made up of two ideograms, the one on the right meaning 'worm' and the one on the left meaning 'me.' She often says, 'I do wonder which one of our ancestors invented my name.' A name like a moth, first a silkworm, a velvety brown caterpillar with antennae straight out of science fiction, which moults repeatedly, becoming lighter and lighter, transparent, spewing out a thread several kilometres long to build a cocoon to wrap around itself. What a perceptive choice of signs, using 'me' to mean 'cocoon.' That egocentric, narcissistic caterpillar never dies. It lives for days and days in the tomb it has built for itself, hermetically sealed, without air or moisture, then metamorphoses one last time into a butterfly, which escapes the cocoon and flies away gracefully, all of which strikes me as something of a miracle. The delicate colours of its wings with their speckled geometric patterns and fanciful stripes . . . Oh! the worm and me . . .

"My mother was such a prisoner of her own work, a slave to daily chores, locked away in endless widowhood, that for a long time she knew nothing about the work I threw myself into heart and soul: constructing a small palace. Near our house, on the edge of the Forbidden City's moat, there was a building site with countless little mounds of pink bricks. I selected one of these mounds for its height and size, then—with Ma as foreman and myself as engineer—we first dug a tiny provisional hole in it, but it grew every day, turning into a narrow berth, which in turn became wider and deeper, brick by brick, centimetre by centimetre, until it was a really gratifying piece of work, a comfortable and spacious shelter with a round opening carefully covered in a mixture of dried grass, rotten planks and branches, which let the sun's silvery rays filter and sift through rather hazily. The light also came through the holes made straight into the walls like spyholes in a real blockhouse. We would have liked to line the floor with a carpet of Bodhi leaves, but the only Bodhi tree in Peking was outside my mother's office, so we abandoned the idea and settled for leaves from the less sacred ginkgo tree in Ma's uncle's courtyard. Leaves in a washed-out green, sometimes pale yellow, their edges browned or sulphurous, slightly irregular but attractively jagged, shaped like four-winged butterflies or birds or the moon, and they scrunched when we lay down on them like old bedsprings, giving off a deliciously soft, earthy smell.

"Ma told me about being separated from his parents and the horror of the first night he spent in an unfamiliar house in a spanking-new wooden bed with bars on it, smelling so strongly of paint it stung his nose. It was right next to the double bed of an elderly couple, two cold, strict creatures who didn't exchange three words during the day but snored together all through the night in perfect synchronicity until it drove Ma mad. He was tortured by the impression, or rather the suspicion, that he had been abandoned, trapped, especially as he was afraid the couple wanted to adopt him. It wouldn't have taken much, that first night, for him to burst into tears. What a concerto that would have been if a Sichuanese boy's crying had snaked its way under the deep, threatening and possibly simulated snoring of the old couple! We didn't realise it at the time, but we both had the same obscure thought: he was being punished because his parents had been punished.

"Oh, our little palace! That was where we first compared the hairs just starting to sprout under our armpits; in that peculiar light he didn't immediately notice, or rather I didn't, that one of my hairs was red. I had to get right up to a source of light to check this intriguing, absurd and touching detail, so exotic it could mean I was unique among my six hundred million compatriots who, with the exception of a few rare albinos, were characterised by their utterly black hair. This clear sign immediately became central to our very existence.

Where did this red hair originate? I thought of the two or three things I knew about family history, of my mother's resistance ever since my childhood to discuss memories, of her tacit refusal to answer the question which constantly buzzed round my head and burned my lips but which I never succeeded in formulating: who's my father? . . . Ma was still lying down, looking at something else, showing no sign of surprise, making no comment, as if he already knew (Who'd told him? His uncle, the museum's Assistant Security Manager?) that flowing through my veins was the blood of a red-headed foreigner, a Westerner—a word which at the time was synonymous with an enemy capable of annihilating the Chinese people, a thousand times more dangerous than the provincial doctors who were his own parents. That red hair was like a mark of infamy stuck to my skin till the end of my days, an unspeakable crime blotting my police record and penalising me in everything I ever undertook.

"Until then the only Western children we had seen with our own eyes were some pupils our age whom we occasionally came across after school on the outskirts of the Forbidden City. They weren't studying at the First of October School (ours, which was solemnly named after the date of the Chinese national holiday) but at the one named after the First of August (a day that celebrated the People's Liberation Army), a primary school close to the Drum Pavilion. They passed our school on a shortcut, which was how we had come across them. There were about ten of them, more boys than girls, nice-looking really with such a variety of colour in their skin, eyes, hair and clothes that dazzled passers-by slowed down to watch them. Some were blond with curly, bobbed hair with little waves rippling in the wind; you wouldn't dare guess whether they were girls or boys. The extraordinary thing was, even in the middle of winter when it was fifteen degrees below zero, they always wore shorts with knee-length socks, as if they were from another planet and the cold didn't affect them. I was fascinated by their socks, wondering whether they would have kept slipping down on my scrawny calves. We were also amazed by their mastery of Chinese, pure Pekinese without a trace of accent, which seemed miraculous to Ma, who was from Sichuan and never achieved correct Pekinese pronunciation the whole time he was in the capital.

"One day we witnessed an argument between the little Westerners and their Chinese classmates, on the path that ran alongside the Forbidden City. We didn't know how or why the row started, but I would never have guessed that those foreign children could muster such insolence and prowess: first they hurled deft acerbic taunts, then a few verbal attacks, before reaching the conclusive phase of insults proper. It was a performance to take your breath away: they called their Chinese opponents every name under the sun in impeccable Pekinese; then the pace quickened, the rate of counterattacks accelerated, the tension cranked up a notch and a flood of swear words in pure Pekinese slang issued from their mouths, always hitting home and each more virulent than the last. Their vocabulary was so extensive that they took malicious delight in varying the constructions and syntax to make their insults all the more striking. Some of their expressions, although vulgar, were so funny and surprising they made us fall about laughing. Those coarse words pronounced by different-coloured children, ringing through the middle of Peking, beneath the walls of the Forbidden City, seemed less ugly than usual, as if their filth, nastiness and mediocrity had evaporated. I'd never heard the language of the capital (which, according to some historians, is simply the product of politics) expressed with such vivacity and charm.

"I also remember a Children's Day celebration organised by our local academy where the little Westerners performed a piece called *The Just War*: dressed as Chinese soldiers, with clothes and caps which mimicked military uniforms, they each had a long stick representing a bayonet. One of them (the leader) shouted 'One, two, three, four!' and they all marched forward, leaping in unison. They jumped right up and, while they were suspended in the air, drove their bayonets into an imaginary enemy's throat, chorusing 'Kill! kill! kill!' Their shouting and the sound of their feet thudding back down on the stage were so powerful that the spotlights hanging from beams overhead swung, making the lights flicker and sending a shiver down our spines. Then they trampled on their first victims' invisible bodies in a simple but powerfully aggressive choreography before leaping again on their leader's orders, shouting out and killing more enemies . . . They were unquestionably victorious. The performance was a triumph. After a standing ovation and thunderous applause, they each introduced themselves to the audience, announcing their nationality and pointing into the audience at their parents, who stood up. They were diplomats' children from Russia, Romania, Poland, Albania—all Eastern European countries.

"As well as my red hair, Ma, son of exiled provincial doctors that he was, found another important thing about me, one that corresponded to Western physiognomy: the depth of my skull. At that celebration of Children's Day, seeing those little Chinese soldiers played by Westerners, he had a feeling something wasn't quite right, although he couldn't say what. Then he got it: the caps! The child-size Chinese military caps, which were very much the fashion at the time, didn't sit properly on the Western children's heads, threatening to fly off and ruin the party at any moment and with every leap. He then grasped that their skulls were differently proportioned to ours. When a Chinese cap was wide enough for a Western head it was bound to be too shallow. And if they chose a cap that was deep enough, it was inevitably too wide. He let me in on this discovery, which, although modest, earned my admiration. I remembered the trouble my mother had endured, trailing me round every shop in Peking, large and small, to find a hat or cap to fit me. With earnest scientific precision we measured the length, breadth and depth of our respective skulls and then, after a series of meticulous calculations, he put his hand on my head like a great patriarch laying his hand on the forehead of an innocent baby, and announced: 'Clearly a product of interbreeding.' But that was all he said; perhaps, I felt, so as not to betray his old communist uncle, who could have driven him out of his house.

"That evening my mother was doing the washing in the courtyard surrounded by single-storey houses, where a tap served a dozen or so families, none of whom had running water at home. Lit by a bare bulb hanging from a gutter, she did battle with a pile of clothes, sheets and blankets soaking in a big tub; sleeves rolled up, she washed each item on a wooden board with a piece of soap, which kept slipping into the water. I had my sentence ready to attack her, I had prepared it, recited it, gone over it again and again. I said, 'Mum,' and she looked up, but I was so gripped by nerves that I stuttered: 'Mum, tell-tell-tell-tell-me, I know-know-who-who-he—' She interrupted me: 'Who?' But my tongue betrayed me: the word 'Dad' stayed stuck in my throat. She asked me again who I meant and I could feel my tears welling up, I tried to stammer but it was no good, impossible to come up with even incoherent babbling like a newborn baby. I laughed stupidly, not sure why, and she said she didn't find my stuttering amusing and went back to her washing.

"Noticing her shoes were wet, I ran to the house and took her green rubber boots from under her bed and, as I carried them out to her, I decided to get round the problem of pronouncing the word 'Dad' by simply asking: 'Am I the son of a red-headed foreigner?' But when I reached her, my tongue, mouth and lips clammed up all over again and I stood there like an idiot, gazing at the long black shadow I cast on the ground. A door or a window was banging in a draught. She suddenly noticed me there, holding her boots, and was surprised, touched even. She finished rinsing a sheet in the tub and asked me to help her wring it out. We twisted that poor sheet like in a tug-of-war; the ground around the tap was slippery with foam and I almost fell, which made her laugh, so I ran to my room and lay on my bed in the dark, furiously angry with myself, crying to think I would never manage to say the word 'Dad,' or learn his identity from E. For the first time in my life I committed the blasphemy of referring to my mother by her first name.

"At the beginning of spring, as the moat of the Forbidden City thawed and swallows came back to sit on telegraph wires, I was offered a distraction: looking through the attic for swifts' nests, a magic remedy for pneumonia, which Ma's uncle suffered from. The dark corner I'm referring to isn't a real attic like in films where resistance fighters, fugitives in danger or illegal immigrants hide, but just a space under the roof trusses, between the sloping tiles and the ceiling of the top floor (in my case, there was only a ground floor), a space that couldn't be used in any way, because it was so low that the two skinny lads we were at the time could barely crawl in on all fours, guided by the beam of a pocket torch, and even in the middle, under the rooftop, a boy of ten wouldn't have been able to stand up. There was a suffocating smell in there: a smell of mouldering wood, damp and bat droppings, peculiarly reminiscent of an old cellar. Even without moving, I could feel the plywood ceiling—barely thicker than the layer of droppings covering it—shifting and creaking beneath our weight. Here and there a bright ray of light filtered between the sheets of plywood, warning us of possible collapse.

"The only route we could crawl along was a wooden beam five centimetres wide, rotting in places and eaten away by termites. We couldn't see the bats, but could hear their squeaks and their wings flapping as they launched into the air like projectiles in response to our intrusion; the tips of their furless wings skimmed past our ears and noses, sending shivers down our spines.

"A few metres further on, like something looming out of the depths of Hell, the torch picked out a nest built in a corner between the tiles and the ceiling: a small pile of straw and twigs which looked like back-combed hair. Ma took out two eggs and handed them to me. They were almost spherical, slippery and dotted with wet clay. Were they swift's eggs, or another bird's? While we discussed it, I made an arc of light through the dark with my torch, only to reveal a shapeless heap about ten metres further on. I was holding the eggs, so Ma summoned his courage and crawled softly over to it with the torch clamped between his teeth; the beam of light zig-zagged through the darkness, wandering haphazardly over panicking bats and crazed insects.

"Eventually he was close enough to touch the lump; he lifted a cover and was instantly surrounded by a cloud of dust, which seemed to hang in the air around him. He picked something up and its shadow was projected onto the sloping roof, something curved, like an upside-down tortoiseshell with two dragons' heads: a musical instrument with a resonance chamber and pegs for strings. My friend plucked one of the strings and it gave a long, melodious note, a strange, deep sound like the moan of an injured crane. Then he strummed the strings and the crane took flight in the half-light of that attic, its wings beating against the tiles. The sound was so opaque, its echo filling the roof space, that it made me shudder. It vibrated for several seconds. My friend announced that it was a *pipa,* and I said my mother had never known how to play one.

"With hardly any light to go by, I wriggled over to him. With the eggs in my hand, my progress was more difficult. I could hear the old wooden beam and the whole roof structure creaking. When I still had about three metres to go to reach him, the torch flickered several times, then its intermittent beam shrank, before going out altogether. The only reaction I could hear from my friend was lengthy muttering, a sort of monologue, during which he mentioned my father, a French scholar (according to his uncle) who, while crossing Manchuria on foot, passed a camp for former political exiles where my mother, E, the granddaughter of a deposed prince nicknamed Seventy-one, excelled in the art of *pipa*-playing. At the camp there was an annual festival for *pipa* players which drew thousands of young girls, and my mother was usually the winner, but that year she was knocked off her throne by the Frenchman dressed as a girl, a man who played the instrument even more beautifully than she did. That was the beginning of a devastating passion (to use the words of my friend's uncle) which led to my mother's marriage . . .

"All of a sudden part of the plywood ceiling gave way beneath my weight and there was an avalanche. A deafening collapse. A searing pain shot through my groin, making me scream. It felt as if my testicles had exploded. A light sprang up at my feet, white, harsh, blinding, like a powerful spotlight theatrically picking out the scene revealed by the gaping hole in the plywood: an aerial view of my kitchen. I was about to fall straight into the cooking pot (which had already swallowed up several chunks of plywood and where our evening rice soup bubbled and steamed, having simmered quietly since lunchtime—one of my mother's special recipes) when, luckily for me, the fatally pointed end of the broken beam which had cut through my trousers and injured my sexual organs succeeded in burying itself in my left thigh, holding me suspended in the air, like a miraculous exhibit in the middle of the hole. Startled and terrified, my friend stopped what he was saying and never wanted to go back to the subject, however much I begged and whatever pressure I put on him.

"I haven't thought about that incident for a long time and

it's reminded me of something else buried deep in my memory, an escapade which radically altered my adolescence and cost me dearly: three years of reform school.

"One evening a few weeks after my aerial castration (as I called the incident in the attic), Ma and I went into the Forbidden City by the Noon Gate, which is the main entrance. Along with a few museum employees and the emperors themselves (who were once the only representatives of the male sex in a place peopled by thousands of women and eunuchs), Ma and I became members of the elite club of nocturnal visitors, setting foot beyond the city's wall after sundown.

"I've mentioned Ma's uncle, the Assistant Security Manager. He was nicknamed Old Deng and was just as small as the other Deng who became the Chinese leader twenty years later, and he, too, was from Sichuan, spoke with the same Sichuan accent and professed the same passion for chillies, cigarettes, opera and bridge. One evening as he came out of the palace, he spotted us playing ball on a poorly lit square outside the main entrance. He came over to us and I told him we were waiting for my mother, who was late coming out, probably kept in by her work. I had forgotten my key, so couldn't go home. Old Deng kindly took us to the gate house and asked the night watchman to let us in.

"Even if we'd been good, timid little boys it would have been impossible to go straight to the building where my mother worked and not take advantage of that heaven-sent opportunity for a detour . . . How many children over the centuries had savoured the pleasure of an evening walk in that place, crossing the vast square paved with age-old stones, hearing the hollow ring of their footsteps on the uneven paving, climbing onto the white marble dais in all its crushing, funereal beauty, where a row of crows on the rail greeted us with their cawing? All at once the biggest building in the palace—if not in all of ancient China—loomed before us: the Hall of Supreme Harmony, which housed the imperial throne and where a few carpenters were still working, perched on stepladders repairing something or other by the feeble glimmer of a few temporary light bulbs. They knew the Assistant Security Manager's nephew and let him sit on the emperor's throne, which made my friend so happy he started spouting nonsense, as if presiding over an important meeting. Meanwhile, I took a couple of sticks and beat out a rhythm on ritualistic musical instruments, punctuating every pronouncement made by the little usurper and accompanying his speeches. It was a set of sixteen gleaming metal bells by the entrance to the hall, under awnings hanging from a portico which had the head of a *Milu*—a sort of mythical stag which was once the imperial emblem—carved on every side with ropes in five different colours between their teeth. Some of the bells had a mysterious muted ring, others a pure, crystalline, more musical vibration, a light, luminous sound like silvery gauze. As I struck them with my sticks, those bronze bells slowly but steadily, note by note, played the tune of a popular Chinese song. Under the spell of this music, the whole vast courtyard became an echo chamber for a melody I had heard my mother hum.

"Then we realised it was late and, worried that my mother would already have left, we started to run. We went round the Hall of Central Harmony, along a three-tiered terrace with a white marble balustrade, jumped down, carried on running, cut through the Back Left Gate and eventually reached the huge area where the concubines used to live, not before going through the Palace of Compassionate Longevity, the Palace of Eternal Health and the Palace of Peaceful Longevity, all of which were reserved for emperors' mothers. Suddenly, as if in a bad dream, we realised we were lost somewhere in a long, narrow, paved passageway, hemmed in on both sides by crushingly tall, dark red walls with the starry sky as our only source of light.

"We didn't lose our heads straight away. According to Ma, all we had to do was keep heading west and it was a mathematical certainty that would bring us out in front of the Imperial Archives building where my mother worked, a building erected by the communists, like a tall screen to obstruct the malevolent eyes of spies (who might stay at the Peking Hotel, an ancient edifice several storeys high and not that far away) desperate to know what was going on in another part of the Forbidden City, which had been converted into a residence for Mao and his closest collaborators in the early 1950s.

"I'll never forget how frantically and desperately we raced through the city that winter's night, which was mercifully clear, with my mother's building obstinately refusing to appear. We ran till we were completely out of breath, like two poor bees lost in an enormous hive, two puppets stranded in a maze infinitely repeating its hard, straight geometric lines. An endless succession of buildings, all on the same level, distributed regularly around a multitude of rectangular courtyards, each deceptively and misleadingly the spitting image of the last. Roadways parallel to the main axis—more harsh straight lines, some of which went on for hundreds of metres—cut across the Forbidden City, which just went on producing the same long red walls. Most of the roads and passages ran from north to south, seeming to force us away from the west, where we were heading, and towards the north into increasingly enclosed secret places, many of them dead ends, that kept on multiplying. It was as if they took pleasure in standing in for each other in the half-light, just to make fun of us.

"And then suddenly a courtyard mysteriously lit up by dazzling lights appeared behind some jujube trees, the outline of their thin, naked branches sharply picked out as Chinese lantern shadows on a grey wall crowned with varnished tiles. This was Yang Xin Dian, the Hall of Spiritual Food. There were two or three crows perched on a metal bar holding a sign which read: *Exhibition of Ancient Chinese Punishments and Tortures*.

"Puffing and blowing, we stepped into a traditional courtyard; it was square, shaped like an imperial seal, and edged on three sides with single-storey buildings each with an opening down one wall and topped with an impressive 'swallow-winged' enamelled roof, which reared up and glittered against the serene night sky, as if set into it. The roofs were supported by squat, blood-red columns. There were two old women in blue overalls pulling out the weeds that pushed up in the gaps between the paving stones. They told us the private view of the exhibition was the following day, and that 'The Chairman'—in other words, the museum's head curator—would be coming at any moment with his staff to give his decisive opinion as the final arbiter.

"We should have left, there was a nasty feeling in the air. Even so, we snuck into the building on the right. I didn't know what was in the ones on the left and in the middle and

I never found out, but everything in the one we went into had to do with implements of death. Methodically catalogued with a historian's attention to detail was a complete collection of real instruments of torture, accompanied by detailed explanations, paintings, drawings, photographs, scale models, sculptures and high-relief carvings in wood or ivory. I was particularly struck by the Technicolor realism of a terracotta sculpture of a man torn apart by five magnificent Thoroughbreds, each taking a share of his living body, galloping in opposite directions, their manes flying in the wind. One of them was more frantic than the others, rearing and whinnying, its head thrown back and mouth wide open. The exhibition allowed itself the luxury of philosophising, presenting a cosmological point of view, and listing the means of torture according to the five primordial elements: water (for example, drowning), wood (beating), metal (the torture of a thousand blades), earth (burying alive) and fire (burning at the stake).

"In one corner of this vast Hell I was disturbed by a particular photograph in the 'metal' category (next to a picture of a man tied to a post with a black, bleeding hole in his chest). I went right up it: it was a black-and-white photo of a decapitation. The executioner had sliced the kneeling victim's neck, the body had slumped and the head was about to touch the ground. Something pale, like a glimmer of light, was dropping from his mouth. I called my friend over. With a shudder he told me he thought it was a cigarette.

"Later that same evening—an evening which already seemed so distant that years might have passed—I had to admit which of us, Ma and myself, had thought of playing games with death. Whatever I said, despite all my twelve-year-old's efforts to defend myself, the police remained convinced I was the one who had set up the hideous torture with the premeditated intention of extracting information about my father from my friend.

"I confessed in order to bring the interrogation to an end, and because a hint of amnesia clouded my mind, but the cause and scope of that amnesia are still a mystery to me. So much happened in that exhibition hall for instruments of torture and death, but all I remember are sentences, or rather a few words, particularly his, and those words brought with them (and continued to do so with terrible clarity through the period of my punishment) a unique sense of disgust which eclipses everything else: confessions made to please the police, incarceration, depression . . .

"In fact, it was Ma who instigated our game. He started by giving me a title, attributing it to me for the first and last time that evening: The Chairman. 'Mister Chairman, would you have a look at this cage, which I'm not sure should be classified in the wood category. Naturally, you don't remember my name, being such a busy man. Everyone calls me Old Deng. I'm the Assistant Security Manager. From Sichuan. If you'd like to watch, I'll give you a little demonstration of how this cage works. I've got everything ready. First, a strong rope. Like this. Could someone tie me up like a condemned man? Thank you. Squeeze a little tighter, please, Mister Chairman. The prisoner's in exactly this position with his hands and feet tied, inside the cage, held up entirely by his head, his neck clamped tightly between the bars at the top. Ouch! My Adam's apple! Do you see? The victim then dies, slowly. Why? In my humble opinion, Mister Chairman, it's intended to prolong his suffering. Look closely. My feet are on the wooden floor. But what a floor! A movable floor, which the executioner lowers one notch every day so our poor man dies of strangulation on the eighth, as the sign I've just read indicates. It's the exact count: eight days for his vertebrae to snap under the weight of his own body hanging in the air. Would you like to have a go? Well done! Go ahead, Mister Chairman, and again, go down one more notch! Can you see my Adam's apple going up and down? Your prisoner's suffering at this very moment, Mister Chairman. No, despite all the respect I have for you, I can't communicate any information about your father. I don't know where he is. No one's told me anything. Stop! Help! I'm . . . suffocating . . . can't . . . breathe . . . Let me go . . . Fucking bastard, that hurt, I nearly died. You're a cruel bastard like your father . . . I . . . I . . . He . . . Help! I'll tell you everything I know. Your father married your mother in order to inherit a manuscript which belonged to Seventy-one, but the old man had already sold it to an exiled poet, who'd since died. The poet's son agreed to sell the scroll to your father, but not for money, or a house, or land, just in exchange for your mother your mother your mother your mother your mother your mother your mother your mother . . . So what if you don't want to hear any more, I'm the one who wants to keep going now. Go on, cry! Your father sold your mother with you inside her for the sake of a manuscript! He was condemned to twenty-five years in prison for trafficking a human being. It was your mother who denounced him, after she escaped from Manchuria, to drag him through the courts.'

"I still remember Ma's last scream. I wanted to kill him. I wanted him to die! I let the wooden floor down to the last notch and ran off, leaving him to strangle himself on his own in the cage. A few hours later some policemen came to arrest me at the house of Mr. Liu, our old teacher. At reform school I heard that Ma was saved at the last minute by the museum's curator; he regained consciousness in hospital and his mother came to take him away to live with her in the country."

4

TIME HAS PASSED. I'VE COME SOME way, but not as far as I would have liked in my research. Teaching Chinese has turned into a full-time job for me; I've been doing it for five years now in a private lycée in Nice. Day after day I swim through a sea of ideograms and—even though I claim not to have touched the floor of this ocean and have stayed quite close to the shore, watching, fascinated, as seagulls circle noisily overhead—I have reached the point where those seas have taken possession of me. I'm becoming more and more Chinese and, like all Chinese people, attach a great deal of importance to years of birth. Tumchooq was born in 1954, the Year of the Horse in the Chinese horoscope. I still remember the calendar for 1978, which he gave me when he was twenty-four, on the threshold of the third decade of his life; the Year of the Horse was illustrated on the front cover by a herd of horses stampeding towards me.

The image of another horse also depicted in that calendar, on the page for the month of May, lights up in the shadows of my memory and glows like a torch floating in darkness. Unlike the horses drawn in Chinese ink illustrating other months, this one was a brightly coloured watercolour, which

I instantly recognised as being by Father Castagnari, an Italian Jesuit missionary. There was no signature or artist's seal, only those of its successive owners, but I had already seen and studied in depth another of his watercolours at the Guimet Museum in Paris, the image of a *Milu* entitled *David's Deer*. His astonishing virtuosity and a style so neutral it was impossible to know to what extent the painter-priest identified with his subject, these were etched on my memory as clearly as the appearance of this mythic hybrid.

Father Castagnari, faithful to the traditions of previous generations of Jesuits committed to evangelising China since the sixteenth century, had adopted a Chinese name in order to facilitate his task (according to inquisitors in Rome, barbarous baptisms like this had a considerable effect on the Jesuits' faith). His Chinese name, Lang Shi-Ling, meant "Peace of the World." He arrived in China at the end of the seventeenth century and lived there for sixty years, appointed as official Court painter by three successive emperors (Kangxi, Yongzheng and Qianlong), and became the only man, with the exception of the monarch himself, allowed to cross the line between the Outer Court and Inner Court, stepping into the enormous imperial harem, where he worked from morning till night painting portraits of countless concubines. The emperor used these portraits every evening to choose his partner, so exemplary were the objectivity, rigorous realism and detailed precision of the missionary painter's work—enough to make a photographer blench with envy.

These qualities all appeared in the picture of a horse chosen to illustrate the month of May. A less grandiose and expressive portrait than those on other pages, with no background of steppes, mountains and vast battlefields, no whiff of gunpowder or violence, befitting the artist's Chinese name. No trace either of those distant landscapes at which Chinese artists excel, melting into a sort of hazy mist on the horizon. Castagnari's picture has a plain, flat background in a very distinctive blue peculiar to him and a key part of his semi-European, semi-Chinese style, a hybrid of cultures that exudes a peacefulness, serenity and limpidity that only true sages can achieve.

At first sight, his horse is like an illustration from a natural history textbook. But on closer inspection you can see that the saddle and stirrup (which is filigreed so as not to be cumbersome) shine with the gleam of pure gold, with unparalleled beauty, and seem to glow from inside. The muscles, which have the precision of anatomical drawings, are animated by a palpable energy, you can feel the blood beating through the invisible veins. The thick, black-grey hooves spattered with mud and grass, the forefeet slightly raised, shod with iron shoes nailed into place, the sheathed penis with its pattern of thick veins, the raised head, three-quarters turned, the eyes studying you, one less sparkling than the other, the dark pupil gleaming in a milky iris . . . nothing escapes the Italian Jesuit, not even the shadow on the soft, pink gums through the half-open jaw. The horse is whinnying through flared nostrils, while a fleeting wind ripples its sumptuous mane; the latter, a striking russet colour, is the most beautiful thing about it. Being a scrupulous observer, Father Castagnari presents us with every nuance of red to admire—glowing, dark and matt, or lighter—in the minute details of the long, waving hairs standing up along the neck and quivering in the wind, while others fall in a slow avalanche along its flanks, suspended in the air as if frozen for all eternity.

Tumchooq handed me the calendar open on the page of that red horse, and said:

"I'm going to write a dedication for you."

His slightly leaking quill formed a series of strokes in the white space above the horse; working from right to left, they slowly created strange, exquisitely sinuous shapes. Some signs appeared several times, like the letters of some alphabet I didn't know, an enigmatic alphabet, abstract drawings rather like a cryptogram or a message made up only of the initial letters of each word.

"What language is it in?" I asked.

"That's Tumchooq, the language I'm named after."

He smiled at me. When he had finished his dedication in Tumchooq, he read it out several times, syllable by syllable; his voice reverberated around the greengrocer's shop and the sound of it reawakened the feeling I had the evening I first heard his name, beneath a veil of fine rain, bordering on mist. The words he murmured sounded like a secret formula full of unfamiliar sounds, producing a vertiginous dizziness in me, a sweet intoxication, like drifting grains of sand bathing all my senses.

"I am a red-haired horse," he then translated, "called Tumchooq."

By nature he always exaggerated a little, but he genuinely was different to his fellow Chinese, and when he took off his hallmark cap I saw, in among his black crew-cut hair, a considerable number of upright hairs that gleamed a pure, fiery red, just as on his ill-shaven cheeks some of the hairs were red; quite the self-portrait by van Gogh!

But he didn't talk about Paul d'Ampère that day, not yet.
And certainly not about why some of his hairs were red.

I need to go back to a family trip during my teenage years to
dig up memories of my first contact with that prestigious
name, which rings round the Ivory Tower of Oriental Studies:
Paul d'Ampère. It was a grey day almost devoid of light and,
travelling in a hire car driven alternately by my mother and
father, we went to the château at Saint-Paul-de-Fenouillet in
the heart of the western Pyrenees, about a hundred kilometres from Perpignan. I don't remember much about the
château itself, except that it was in the Romanesque style,
was open to the public, had a collection of gloves in a glass
display case and the pair I remember best was in white kid
with masses of tiny buttons, and the estate was so vast that,
to visit it, you had to take a little steam train, its trail of
smoke describing a wide curve along a narrow gorge edged
by a torrent plunging down from goodness knows where,
while a man—who was at once driver, conductor and tour
guide—recited through a microphone his inflated history of
the previous owners, the d'Ampère family, their long and
glorious past, and their connections and inter-marriages
with other prestigious families of European aristocrats.

My clearest memory of that visit was a hanging garden on
the side of a cliff; you climbed down to it along a wooded,
little-used path, and when I arrived the sun made a timid
appearance, then swiftly tore through the clouds, building
power until the garden glittered in the middle of dark green
vegetation, like a desert island bathed in light. The garden
had no plants or flowers, but was made up entirely of

minute, slippery-smooth pebbles meticulously arranged to create the illusion of undulating waves, each driven forward by the next, so that I felt I could almost hear the sound of their jostling embrace, like the whisper of seas calling to each other. A tide frozen in time, overlooking the tops of huge trees, beech, pine, lime, spruce, birch and aspen, all quivering in the wind, answering its marine murmuring. Standing on a black rock, a solitary figure in the middle of those pebbles, like a pilot on a boat, I thought I heard a foghorn sound and felt the rock pitching beneath my feet as foaming waves broke over it. Then the sun dropped down, the pebbles darkened, the garden blended into the mountain and the mountain into the sky, waiting for the return of their creator, the last d'Ampère, the orientalist Paul, who— according to the sign—had left for China to devote himself to his research and become a Chinese citizen.

Before leaving, he relinquished his inheritance and handed over his family's entire legacy—which until then had been passed down from one generation to the next through the centuries—to the State. According to some accounts, that garden had once been the place where he meditated. (Did he sit on the black rock? Did he lie in the hammock still hanging between two trees like a net luggage rack on a train, listening for nights at a time as nocturnal birds conversed with crickets, bats, mosquitoes, lizards and tawny owls with astonishingly wide, staring eyes?) Some claimed he had copied the "sea of stones" from a Zen garden in Kyoto; others said the garden represented the graveyard of a long lineage and bore witness to the folly of an aristocratic young intellectual, spoiled by life and behaving extraordinarily irresponsibly.

Years later, before I left for China, I went to the National Library in Paris to consult the monumentally extensive book of this Paul d'Ampère, whose château I had visited as a girl. As a third-year student of Chinese confronted with his *Notes on Marco Polo's Book of the Wonders of the World*, three volumes of one thousand five hundred pages published by the Sorbonne in 1952, 1953 and 1954, I was in turn seduced, dazzled, exhausted and, finally, literally crushed, as much by the enormity of his work as by the miracles or rather mirages Paul d'Ampère created on every page, almost every line. In places I felt I was walking through these mirages, initially made up of words in a particular language, then reconstituting themselves before my eyes in another language, then another, and yet another, all of them vanished centuries ago, some already dead in the days of Marco Polo, who had travelled all over those lands without knowing them. Reminiscences of Pali, Sanskrit, Tokharian, ancient Persian, Turkish, Chinese from before the time of Christ, all exhumed, resuscitated and contributing to his meticulous, endlessly patient investigations of the landscape, carried out one footstep at a time, year after year, for this erudite linguist was also an excellent topographer with a precise eye not devoid of humour.

He was a genius capable of bringing back to life a vanished kingdom, a lost people, heroes and gods with the tip of his pen, just with his footnotes—some of which went on for two or three pages—with no emphasis or subjectivity, simply a scalpel's precision. The illumination this author gave me was not that of great philosophers, nor of quick-witted intellectuals, but the low-angled light of a setting sun, revealing, for example, the upper part of a prodigiously beautiful golden stupa, looming from nowhere, rising up above other buildings, its base bathed in the round pond of a white marble fountain. A door opened for me and, quite without warning, words dropped all around me, stroking and kissing me like flowers in a Buddhist ceremony. But a curse fell on the town, and the stupa—*Ta* in Chinese—was struck by lightning on a stormy night and cleaved in two. The left half collapsed immediately, the right side survived another eight hundred years, then it, too, eventually collapsed shortly before Marco Polo's arrival.

Or he would show me palaces—more enchanting than Coleridge could have imagined under the effects of opium—built for Kublai Khan with gardens populated with stags, greenhouses of rare plants lit up at night, giant trees whose branches streamed with wine and the dark milk of mares with velvety names: Luyong, Limoo, Niya, Wiboor, Vivoor . . . Sometimes, halfway through my reading or as I closed the last page, I could no longer tell which of Marco Polo, Paul d'Ampère or myself had set out to those distant lands, stepped into such and such an oasis, come across a caravanserai laden with spices, precious stones and silks . . .

All these kingdoms which once flourished along the Silk Route ended up, with no exceptions, buried under sand, where their fate was definitively sealed. Paul d'Ampère depicted the horrific death throes of these cultures, the desert, the Apocalypse, Hell—as suffered by the Tumchooq kingdom, that place shaped like a bird's beak which touched me deep in my soul. Those waves of pebbles glittering deceptively, lulling me half to sleep, were eventually swallowed up by shadow. Death. Nothing left, except time immemorial.

I had other literary encounters with Paul d'Ampère at the

library in Peking beside the Northern Lake, in an encyclopaedia of linguistics published in Taiwan in 1975, which I eventually managed to lay my hands on. Even though he was not a pure linguist, part of the article on "Tumchooqology" was devoted to him under the title:

THE PRECURSOR
An exemplary career

Born in France, at Saint-Paul-de-Fenouillet in the western Pyrenees, Paul d'Ampère left at a young age to live in Paris, where he studied Chinese at the Paris Institute of Oriental Languages. He then learned Sanskrit and other oriental languages at the University of Cologne under professor Thomas Müller. He arrived in China in 1945 and began travelling on foot, faithfully following Marco Polo's itinerary. Two years later, so that he could have access to various places recorded in the Italian adventurer's memoirs and closed to foreigners, he relinquished his French nationality and was naturalised as Chinese. This journey, a genuine single-handed desert crossing, took seven and a half years of his life. He was just thirty-five when he finished his *Notes on Marco Polo's Book of the Wonders of the World*, but was already ranked among the most respected scholars of his time. The kingdom of Tumchooq proved decisive for d'Ampère, who crowned his university career by deciphering the Tumchooq language, surpassing all previous attempts in the field.

The discovery of a mutilated text

In his colossal work, the kingdom of Tumchooq appears only in two footnotes and a scale map of the capital showing public squares, city walls, several temples (one of which was cupola-shaped and illuminated at night), as well as unidentified symbols apparently representing signs for small shops, the latter drawn by himself at the time that he exhumed and inspected the site.

In 1952, during a trip to the Manchurian border, he met an exiled aristocrat more than one hundred years old who went by the nickname of Seventy-one, and at the old man's home d'Ampère found a length of silk some forty centimetres by thirty, yellowed by time and, for reasons still unknown to this day, torn either by hand or with teeth, judging by the marks on the fabric. As for the story of its provenance, it smacks of a senile old man's fanciful fabrication: it fell from the sky as an aeroplane flew overhead.

The piece, which has been authenticated beyond question, was once the property of successive imperial dynasties, as confirmed by the constellation of red seals applied by its owners, all of whom were emperors. Among them was the seal of Huizong of the Song dynasty, himself a great painter and calligrapher, and that of the Hall of an Old Man's Five Supreme Pleasures, the name of a collection belonging to Qianlong, known for his passion for antiquities and works of art. These imperial seals cover the upper part; beneath them is a six-line text written in black ink, noteworthy for the horizontal sequence of the writing, breaking away from the verticality of Chinese ideograms. The text is dotted with strange signs never before seen; they are slight, closely spaced, seeming to flow from the sure hand of some scribe, not deviating by one millimetre from such rigorous straight lines that they appear to have been traced along a ruler.

D'Ampère knew intuitively that this was a lost ancient language, from the family of Indo-European alphabetical languages. A few months later he published the conclusions of his in-depth studies: these six lines were written in the official language of the kingdom buried beneath the sands towards the middle of the third century, the Tumchooq language.

Its grammar invites parallels with Pali, an Indian dialect in which Buddha taught, dating back to before the era of common languages. This length of silk, which fell from the sky and was picked up by Seventy-one, was, evidently, a mutilated fragment of a sacred text. According to d'Ampère it was an allegory preached by Buddha himself. After long and arduous efforts of trial and error, he managed to decipher the six lines, but the allegory in its entirety remains a complete mystery since it does not feature in any official version of the Buddhist canon.

The mysterious disappearance

In the years following this discovery a considerable number of documents written in the Tumchooq language were found on archaeological excavations, and since the 1960s the language has become an important branch of orientalist studies. Nevertheless, d'Ampère's deciphering of that short text still astonishes experts in the field for its accuracy and intelligence. As for d'Ampère himself, no one knows what happened to him or where he is. Another complete mystery.

5

17TH JANUARY

I woke in almost complete darkness in the middle of a dream
and for a split second couldn't remember where I was. On
the one hand, there was my body refusing to be roused from
a sleep closer to death than to life, which I sank into moments after abandoning myself to the intense but fleeting
pleasures of orgasm; on the other, there was my brain still
holding on to traces of the dream which had visited me, its
images, colours, sounds, smells and, especially, the cry that
woke me and was still ringing in my ears. I didn't know
whether my body or my mind was further from reality. I
didn't know when it had started raining either. Raindrops
were falling on the roof like grains of sand, and coming
through the gaps in the unevenly spaced tiles, dripping in
the darkness onto baskets of invisible vegetables or—to be
more specific—onto big cucumbers next to the desk, the
administrative and financial heart of the shop hastily

transformed into a bed rather too narrow for two people, so I kept worrying I'd fall out right in the middle of the "meeting of the clouds and the rain," to use the Chinese expression for the sexual act. I was also afraid the desk would collapse under our thrusting bodies, given the deafening creaking sounds it made, which eventually blurred into our heavy breathing in the icy air, there among the smells of beaten earth, vegetables and bodily secretions.

The sound of a car suddenly woke Tumchooq. Neither of us said a word, but the panic gripping us was palpable, even in the dark. Police? Soldiers? Had someone seen me at midnight as I nipped from the deserted street into the shop? (How careless, I scolded myself, making us run a risk like that, knowing it was our last "meeting of the clouds and the rain" in the Year of the Horse, because Tumchooq was going away the following day to spend the new year with his father, who was serving out his sentence in a gem mine in Sichuan.) The sounds of the car drew nearer, as if it were slowing down, and I thought of a young Chinese painter who was arrested outside a foreign diplomats' residence as she slipped out of her French lover's apartment—he worked at the French embassy. She was condemned to two years in prison for dishonouring her country. I wondered which of us would be . . . The car didn't stop, thank God, the engine sound faded, the noise of the rain grew all the louder and Tumchooq, relieved, took me in his arms, kissed me and went back to sleep.

Then I saw him again, the man from my dream a few minutes earlier. In the blink of an eye, when I least expected him, he loomed out of the hazy darkness, slunk between the baskets of vegetables, walked silently past our improvised bed and disappeared behind the cucumbers with the fat raindrops smacking onto them in the dark. I'd never experienced hallucinations before, however brief, and this fleeting vision reminded me of every last detail of my interrupted dream: it was nighttime, as far as I can remember, but I didn't know where I was and I took a while to understand that the silent waves which sometimes seemed clear-cut and sometimes more nebulous, and which I initially took to be the sea, were in fact clouds floating under the feet of a solitary, middle-aged man travelling far in the distance; he was more Western than Chinese and was toiling along a path lit by the beam of a bamboo torch in his hand.

I recognised him, or rather guessed who he was, by two details: first his red hair, which highlighted his handsome face in the most unusual way; then his glasses, which Tumchooq mentions every time he talks about his early visits to the camp where his father is imprisoned. Those glasses matched his descriptions and fascinated me with their lenses, which picked up the yellow gleam of the flickering torch flame (I can still hear the soft crackle of the burning bamboo), and which were fixed onto the frames with pieces of thin wire. As for the side-pieces, every trace of the original material had disappeared; they were bound round with strips of cloth, dirty bits of rag, some of which were very long, hanging down behind his ears and fluttering in the mountain wind.

At first sight, any resemblance to Tumchooq consisted chiefly in that inimitable walk, the body leaning forward slightly, oddly nimble, with big jerky strides so like Tumchooq's you'd have thought it was him I saw in my dream, but twenty-five years older—two and a half decades the father spent in a prison camp and during which his son grew up without him. Paul d'Ampère.

He stayed within view as far as the lie of the land allowed; from time to time he disappeared behind fronds of trees and I lost sight of him, then the feeble glow of his torch appeared again, further away on some rocks, beneath a thick fog; I kept my eyes wide open, pinned on that tiny dab of light in the darkness, which still glows before my eyes as I write these words. That dab of light reminds me of *The Flight into Egypt,* a film I saw as a child, which begins with a very long stationary shot, all but black with this insubstantial glow hovering in the middle while a voice-over talks about the souls of the exiled, condemned to wandering in the desert. Later, I saw that same dab of light captured by a reporter at a refugee camp in a desert in black Africa; it was after a massacre, and dejected exiles—who would never be able to return to their native country and who reminded me of Conrad's characters—told their story over and over again. I saw it again one evening beside Joyce's tomb as I watched the shifting shadows of a tree projected by the last rays of dusk onto the statue of the writer, thin as a skeleton, his elbow resting on one knee, his legs crossed, his huge long head in one hand . . . until there was just one last dab of light on the glasses of that voluntary exile who had fled his own country, like Paul d'Ampère.

The solitary traveller slowed down and started to walk along a path, or rather to advance along it almost on all fours, while his last bamboo stick was consumed by the flames without which he could go no further, growing steadily smaller, one centimetre at a time, heralding the onset of complete darkness. It was a long path, not dug into the rock but formed by a landslip which made the going very dangerous and provoked the eminent intellectual to swear in French: "Shit! Shitting Hell!" The path was barely thirty centimetres wide but seemed to go on for ever, at least fifty metres, every centimetre of the way fraught with risk, because there was nothing to either side, apart from the terrifying drop of the cliffs, the unfathomable abyss, darkness, death.

The small flame of his torch, now reduced to one twig, flickered, a few sparks flew and every glimmer of light went out. As if struck blind, Paul d'Ampère stood still on the path, unable to see anything, defenceless, in all that darkness, which grew bigger and more dense and swallowed him up. I couldn't see him now but guessed his reflex action in the dark: he automatically took off his glasses, breathed over the lenses and, unseeing, cleaned them with the dirty rags wrapped round the side-pieces. He reminded me of his son Tumchooq, who, on the rare occasions that we argue, sits on one of the benches in the shop, runs his hand over his face in an atavistic gesture, irritably rubs his forehead and eyes, seeming to have aged ten years in a flash, and—just like his father—launches into meticulously cleaning his glasses with the end of his shirt or his T-shirt, which may be just as dirty and impregnated with sweat as his father's rags; I'm quite sure he's happy he can't see me any more and, for one furtive moment, has managed to make the filthy outside world disappear.

Low, heavy cloud spreads across the mountain, impenetrable mists crawl over the rocks and along the path where, suddenly, after the sound of several matches being struck, a dazzling flash lights up as Paul d'Ampère's shirt burns; he now stands stripped to the waist, holding this improvised and short-lived torch and entrusting himself to it, not sure where it might take him. Who cares? He wasn't crawling now, as if no longer afraid of falling, as if he couldn't care less, he was hurrying along that path barely the width of two hands, lit by his shirt, which burned like a sheet of paper. Ashes fluttered away, butterflies of black silk so light they floated in the air around Paul d'Ampère, who talked to himself as he hurried on; a flood of words poured from his mouth, sometimes streams of furious syllables, sometimes a fluid melody or an overflowing torrent of eloquence which carried me along with it even though I didn't catch a single word. Was this an epic in ancient Persian? One of Plato's speeches in ancient Greek? Or a sacred writing in Tumchooq?

All of a sudden I was struck by three words in Chinese, "*Cao ta ma!*," their long echo ringing round the mountain, endlessly repeated and merging into one. Not that I was surprised to hear him pronounce them without a shadow of an accent, but those three words that millions of Chinese utter every day, and I do too from time to time, were none other than a synonym for the swearing he had hurled out in French a few minutes earlier: "Shit! Shitting Hell!" Then I understood: he'd just shouted out the expression in every language—Asian, Indo-European, living, dead or dialectal—that he knew, an impetuous river of swear words pouring out in great roaring waves, beating against the rocks, crossing frontiers, roaming across continents, passing through Russia, Germany, Italy, detouring through Spain and Portugal, going back to his native country, taking in Corsican, Breton, Basque and the patois of the western Pyrenees . . . meanwhile, after his shirt, he held his trousers aloft and they burned with a feeble, flickering bluish flame just enough to probe the thick mist and light the other end of the path about twenty metres away, where a dark tree loomed and a bird, perhaps an eagle, called out, promising relief and deliverance.

Submerged by this flood of words, I wondered whether, during the course of his interminable prison sentence, Paul d'Ampère had toyed with the idea of creating a dictionary of swear words, listing them by country and region with phonetic variations, historical origins, linguistic mutations and degrees of vehemence, constituting a sort of "J'accuse" against all the injustices and tortures suffered in his long years of detention.

Then the filthy verbal diarrhoea came to an abrupt stop; I couldn't hear anything, not even the sound of a fall, nothing but total silence in which his still-blazing trousers flew away, hovered for a moment, then went out completely, unleashing such a strong feeling of vertigo and terror in me that I felt I'd fallen off the edge of the cliff myself.

My eyes peered through the darkness, but to no avail, because they were clouded with tears. Then it started snowing in the mountains and I could already picture Paul d'Ampère being found by chance decades later, sleeping naked at the foot of the cliff, a pile of frozen, fractured bones and a pair of glasses with lenses held on by wire, and side-pieces once wrapped in dirty rags long since gone. I can't think of another event in my life which provoked such emotion. There were tears streaming down my cheeks when I suddenly heard him swear again in French and saw him hanging on the edge of the cliff where his hands had managed, in the briefest fraction of a second during his fatal fall, to grab a tuft of grass rooted deeply in the ground. He didn't dare move, afraid the least movement would make the grass give way, sending him into the unfathomable depths. He didn't move but gave a cry, perhaps his last, which woke me from my dream . . .

The greengrocer's shop was steeped in almost complete darkness, with the exception of a ray of bluish shadow between the bottom of the metal shutter and the threshold. It was still raining, outside and inside, dripping on the cucumbers, pumpkins and sweet potatoes with a duller echo than the noise it made on the spinach leaves, chives, chervil, dill and celery fronds, interrupted occasionally by the sound of Paul d'Ampère's harrowing cry, which continued turning inside my head. Still, it wasn't difficult overcoming my initial fear, because the image of that fall, I realised to my own astonishment, was merely the matching piece to another image, the one on a slide that Tumchooq had projected on one of the shop's walls a few weeks earlier, using a projector borrowed from his old teacher, the frustrated painter who had converted to amateur photography. Tumchooq hadn't given me any warning, but I'd known for a long time he had a photo which meant more to him than life itself and which I suspected was a portrait of his father.

I listened intently to the soft purring of the projector; a dazzling beam of light blazed rather theatrically, making motes of dust appear and dance in its path, while the wall with its dirty marks, nail holes and remnants of propaganda posters started to glow, its uneven surface lighting up in the dark like a screen. My heart beat anxiously, I was worried there would be a power cut, which happened quite frequently in Peking and always when you least expected it. I could tell Tumchooq was moved in spite of himself, seeing that image, the only picture he had of the famous mutilated scroll, of which only half remains. The photograph must have been taken around midday, judging by how over-exposed it was, unless that was an illusion on my part, lend-ing it a slightly hazy, fantastical quality like a mirage, particularly as the image wobbled a little because the electric current was inconsistent or under the effects of an impercep-tible gust of wind, a breeze rippling the roll of silk. The scroll, Tumchooq informed me, was held up by one of the curators at the Forbidden City, in other words by the hands of the State, the new owners of this Chinese treasure, this legacy of successive dynasties, torn by Puyi, then the property of Seventy-one, who was by then blind, only to end up causing the downfall of a Frenchman who traded in his own wife for it . . . Or was the image shaky simply because Tumchooq's heart quivered as he pressed the shutter, confronted with his own fate—which strikes me as the most appropriate word to describe the artefact.

As if not wanting to swamp the near-sacred atmosphere of the projection with unnecessary detail, he spared me the account of how she—the curator—succumbed to his suppli-cations and demonstrated exceptional courage in allowing him to take a photograph, within the confines of the Forbid-den City, of a scroll that had not seen the light of day since the State acquired it; in other words, since Paul d'Ampère was imprisoned. Tumchooq's dark shadow moved across the beam of light as the letters of that language which gave him his name appeared on the wall-screen, and as he read them syllable by syllable, in a soft voice, a murmur, utterly trans-formed, almost ecstatic, in a state of veneration, as if presiding over my initiation to some religious rite, or revealing a secret buried beneath the earth for centuries, a favour that would unite us for ever. Behind his glasses his eyes were ablaze with a beatific light I had never seen in them before. He read the text his father had deciphered first in its original version, then in its Chinese translation; each word pierced my heart, and I in turn translated the words to engrave them onto my memory:

> *ONCE ON A MOONLESS NIGHT A LONE MAN IS TRAVEL-LING IN THE DARK WHEN HE COMES ACROSS A LONG PATH THAT MERGES INTO THE MOUNTAIN AND THE MOUNTAIN INTO THE SKY, BUT HALFWAY ALONG, AT A TURN IN THE PATH, HE STUMBLES. AS HE FALLS, HE CLUTCHES AT A TUFT OF GRASS, WHICH BRIEFLY DELAYS A FATAL OUTCOME, BUT SOON HIS HANDS CAN HOLD HIM NO LONGER AND, LIKE A CONDEMNED MAN IN HIS FINAL HOUR, HE CASTS ONE LAST GLANCE BELOW, WHERE HE CAN SEE ONLY THE DARKNESS OF THOSE UNFATHOMABLE DEPTHS . . .*

18TH JANUARY

Every couple of months Tumchooq makes the most of the general anarchy at the greengrocer's shop and does what no other son would do in his shoes: he takes the train, often without a ticket, and travels in the "hard-seat" class for three days and two nights to visit his father at his work camp in Sichuan, five thousand kilometres from Peking. While he's there he stays with a camp employee nicknamed the "poet-ess" (a former prisoner of indeterminate age and marital status), and for the five or six days of his stay he goes to the visiting room where Paul d'Ampère has the right, for twenty minutes at a time, to talk through the double wooden grille and initiate him in the ancient language of Tumchooq, its pronunciation, spelling and syntax, although not actually encouraging him to share in his obstinate search for the missing part of the sutra, a search which for many years has maintained—more existentially than physically—his contact with this world from which he could so easily withdraw altogether. It's a secret garden he has kept hidden throughout his long sentence, except once when he mentioned it in an offhand way, almost as a joke. It was in the winter of 1977, right after the Great Helmsman's funeral, which marked the beginning of a new era. The first sign that spring had arrived, the first crack in the great Proletarian Dictatorship, was a change in the university system. Until then universities had selected their students exclusively on the recommendations of the Party, but now they opened their doors to anyone under the age of thirty who succeeded in competitive exams in mathematics, literature, physics, chemistry, foreign languages, history and politics. Overnight, a great whirlwind blew across the entire nation, a whole generation found new hope and buckled down to preparing for those exams . . . except Tumchooq, whose condemnation to three years at reform school blotted his record. Not that it stood in the way of his profession as a greengrocer, but it cruelly forbade him from enrolling for the competitive exams along with the blind, deaf-mutes, the lame and the infirm all over the country.

"The week after I got the letter of rejection," Tumchooq told me, "I felt a mark of infamy, shame and sorrow weighing on me; I hid all day long in a little tea-house mulling over this destructive, not to say fatal, failure which had struck me down before I even went into combat, and I looked my future in the face with a terrible feeling of impotence at the prospect of being condemned, excluded from society, you could say, for my whole life. I shut myself away in silence. Talking—even to say one word, a simple 'hello'—took superhuman effort. Sometimes I'd open my mouth and no sound would come out. At the end of the sixth day it was the evening before my birthday; I was on the brink of my twenty-third year. At ten o'clock in the evening, with a bottle of cheap booze in my freezing hand, slugging it straight from the bottle, I skated like a drunken madman over the frozen moats at the foot of the imposing walls around the Forbidden City, in the area where I'd spent my childhood. Commercial skates were way beyond my means, so I made do with some holey old trainers onto which I'd attached some metal rods, the way they did in the ancient kingdom of Tumchooq, according to Marco Polo's accounts. This meant I could more or less glide over the ice, like a wandering ghost, pursued by the rather pitiful sparks flying from my Tumchooqian skates on the dirty surface, and tracing two black grooves, one deeper than the other. Those sparks sprayed and scattered, filling my flared trousers, dazzling me like fireworks marking the feast day of a Tumchooq prince, which, I knew perfectly well, bore no relation to my lifelong status as a seller of vegetables. My mind was left far behind by my body as it ran and jumped and danced, carried away as much by speed as by alcohol. For the first time in days I started quoting Holden Caulfield, my favourite hero, talking to a cab driver in *The Catcher in the Rye,* one of the first American novels translated into Chinese and which conquered an entire generation. It was the part where Holden talks about the ducks on the lake in Central Park, wondering what they did in winter. Did they fly away or were they picked up and taken somewhere? But the cab driver thinks it's a stupid thing to wonder about.

"I must have seemed just as stupid, but I didn't come across anyone to talk to apart from invisible fish breathing in that icy water. When the huge clock on the Telegram Centre struck eleven I went under the Bridge of the Divine Army, turned towards the Beach of Sands and arrived beside the National Library, where countless table lamps still glowed, casting an extraordinarily dreamy light through the misty condensation on its tall windows, so that the whole sumptuous edifice with its Western columns and Chinese roofs stood out clearly against the dark sky, conjuring in my mind Kublai Khan's palace as it appeared to Coleridge in an opium-induced vision, a sparkling, glittering palace floating over the ice, while inside guests in the same drunken state as myself drank a mixture of alcohol and fermented mare's milk flowing copiously from artificial trees in which Kublai Khan had hidden his soldiers, just as my father described in his *Notes on Marco Polo's Book of the Wonders of the World*.

"It suddenly struck me with enough force to leave no room for doubt that living without taking university entrance exams wasn't a handicap but rather an advantage, and I could take the academic authorities' refusal as a lucky turning point, a new departure giving me an opportunity to realise a plan I'd been nurturing for some time: to annotate Marco Polo's book using Chinese documentation, doing it in my own way, quite distinct from my father's version.

"I still wonder, if all those circumstances hadn't come

together, if the lights in the library hadn't been on, how that night of drink, loneliness and misery might have ended. I don't know how long or in what sort of state I skated, or which way I went—a tram on route 103 or a bus on route 330?—to get back to Little India Street and my greengrocer's shop at dawn.

"That revelation, which was so salutary for me, provoked absolutely no reaction in my father when, in the visiting room a few days later, I told him what had happened from my receiving the rejection letter from the university right up to my final inspiration. He sat there on the far side of the double grille. His hair, which he'd been allowed to grow since being appointed the camp's pig-keeper, was all tangled, full of filth and mud from the pigsty, a thick red mane standing up on his head in haphazard tufts. He was wearing a worn pair of trousers and a sheepskin jacket, another privilege he owed to his new status, as he no longer had to wear a prisoner's uniform. He listened attentively to my story, took off his glasses all patched with bits of wire and, using the dirty rags wound round the side-pieces, meticulously wiped the lenses, without looking at me or saying a word. When he did eventually open his mouth it was, as with all my visits, to teach me some Tumchooq vocabulary.

"I can hardly remember us talking once about anything personal; Tumchooq has been his only means of escape for two whole decades and I get the impression that—except in Tumchooq—he's forgotten everyday words, and every aspect of real and personal life that goes with them is buried deep inside his memory. He never asks anything about my mother, her circumstances or her life, no more than about mine. I've got used to the enormous barrier he's built out of a dead language, and I carry on erecting it around him, always frightened the truth about his personal feelings might escape through some crack; and yet everyone recognises that, in camps, prisoners tend to cling to their loved ones, and want to know everything that's going on in their lives . . . but not him.

"Our language lessons in the visiting room arouse palpable, virtually universal hostility, judging by the muttering and sideways glances from the other prisoners—most of them common criminals—and their families sitting in the neighbouring booths. Far from being frightened, I take comfort from this hostility, not to say disgust, because it makes me feel not only that my father has his own value but that I too, a humble greengrocer, have mine, and that he's raised it with those Tumchooq words reverberating around that pitiful room, words whose resonant rise and fall the others perceive as mere modulations belched by a solitary camel in the middle of a desert. I pity them, because they're not equipped to admire this language, half angel music, half siren song, even if, when my father speaks it, with his head resting against the wall and his eyes blank, he always looks as if he's suffering some appalling and incurable pain, and his face never shows any trace of the verbal pleasure described by the camp's director, but rather two decades of accumulated unhappiness in each of his craggy features.

"That particular day, because most of the visit was taken up with my story about entrance exams, we had barely ten minutes left to devote to studying Tumchooq and he taught me only two new words: *mokasha,* which means relic or bones associated with a saint, a word whose pronunciation, according to my father, bears similarities with certain central

Indian languages, particularly Prakrit and Pali, both languages in which Buddha preached and which are as soft and transparent as pearls and corals beneath the limpid waters of the Indian Ocean. The second word, *alaghaci*, means massacre and has a brutal, warlike ring to it, clearly indicating Persian or Parthian origins. My father, who's a connoisseur of the subject, couldn't help telling me its roots (*ala*—killing, and *alaca* or *alaja*—assassin), as well as its nominal and passive forms; and it is thanks to these two forms, he claims, that a Tumchooq sentence maintains all the versatility and variety of Sanskrit constructions, despite the absence of inflexions and declensions. To finish, as he usually did, he gave me a syntax exercise using the two new words, putting together a sentence which he uttered so unbelievably slowly I was completely bemused: 'I wouldn't be in the least surprised were you to end up like me with a massacred relic' (that's a rough translation, given that the Tumchooq language only has present, future and conditional tenses, and has no subjunctive form).

"At his request, I repeated the sentence until I knew it by heart, although I didn't understand its exact meaning or logic. His voice grew deeper and deeper, petering into a silence in which he might have been picturing the future he had just drawn for me, until the guards shouting to say visiting time was over brought him back to reality. He left with them and the door closed once more on his unimaginable suffering.

"The true significance of his comment in the form of a grammatical exercise had escaped me. I didn't understand what either of us had to do with a 'massacred relic.' The following day I set off for Chengdu in a lorry laden with stones, from there I took the train to Peking and my father's enigmatic remark faded as my mind was steadily exhausted by that ordeal of three days and two nights on a hard, cramped seat, an ordeal that always ends up erasing every kind of suffering and unhappiness, and even the most memorable words . . .

"But two weeks later, back in Peking, in an underground train at the stop for the Temple of the Source of Law, the doors of my carriage opened and I heard a boy singing in the language of I have no idea which minority, with a refrain in Mandarin. His voice was heavenly, resonating as if in a church, with a tremulous celestial grace. When the train set off I saw the boy sitting on a bench next to a monk; they were at the far end of the platform and the passengers were slowing down to admire him as they passed. The monk was wearing bright yellow Burmese robes and the young singer, who was ten or eleven, wore a very fine length of linen wound around his waist, like a long white skirt falling to his feet, attached with a black silk belt, Thai style; and his top, which buttoned up to the neck and had wide sleeves, was so white it shone under the lights. He was a novice of extraordinary beauty, head shaven, round eyes, straight nose and shining teeth. When my carriage passed him, in spite of the deafening noise the wheels made on the rails, I couldn't believe my ears when I heard him sing: 'I love the Lotus Sutra, which taught me that the sutras are Buddha's relics, his supreme relics.'

"In a fraction of a second the mystery surrounding my father's words disappeared and I understood for the first time that I would end up like him, searching for the missing part of a manuscript, a mutilated sutra, in other words a massacred relic."

26TH JANUARY

The first day of spring is nearly here and with it the holidays, the university deserted, the student residence almost empty. I don't know whether my exam results or my friends' invitations make me happy or unhappy. I don't know who I really am. Either way, a feeling of emptiness put a lump in my throat earlier when I went along Little India Street, past the greengrocer's where the coral pinks of carrots, the matt ivory of parsnips and the tiny green marbles of peas made bright splashes of colour under the red lanterns set up for the celebrations, celebrations without Tumchooq, who's gone to spend them with his father, and I gauged what an infinitely long time it takes for a week to go by in his absence. Outside the shop the only feeling I had was of emptiness, of missing him; I should have bought lotus roots, sweet potatoes and red-hearted turnips to eat raw this evening, chomping into them as I sit alone in the courtyard listening to the firecrackers that will be going off, but all I could think about was slinking away.

I associate Tumchooq less with sexual pleasure than with the taste of the various vegetables he's taught me to eat raw; the first steps towards a radical re-conversion for someone like me, who grew up with boiled green beans and mashed potatoes. It started, if I remember right, one Sunday in the middle of summer when the two of us set off by bike to visit a temple on the outskirts of Peking, which was once very famous but is now in ruins. On the way back, the sun, like a vibrating ball of lead setting the rhythm for Tumchooq's pedalling and our beating hearts, was so hot it had melted the tarmac; in other words, we were pedalling through an oven with our throats on fire, so we made a beeline for an isolated house by the side of the road where Tumchooq succeeded in making a friend—a natural gift for him, he's equally at home with princes and beggars. In this instance it was a farm labourer of about forty, a thin man with very tanned skin and one arm missing so his shirt sleeve flapped limply, who took us to a well in an inner courtyard, beneath a large ginkgo. Using his one arm, with a deftness and grace all his own, he lowered a bucket on a long rope into the depths of the well. We heard a dull impact right at the bottom and the muffled echo of the bucket smacking the water, sinking into it and filling up. The man tugged sharply on the rope, the bucket came back up, he grabbed it by the handle and, without a word, poured it over Tumchooq. Gasps of surprise, laughter. Then he lowered the bucket back down and it sank into the water again and came back up; when I screamed, half the bucketful was already streaming over my hair, shoulders and body—pure, cold, refreshing water; I took a big gulp of it, shuddering with pleasure while the other half of the bucket gushed down inside my T-shirt and my trousers, and I felt them billowing out around my waist, stomach and legs.

After this restorative shower, Tumchooq took some long lotus roots (probably stolen from the shop the day before) from his rucksack, washed them assiduously with help from our new friend, who filled the bucket again and slooshed the roots to remove the mud from them, revealing fragrant, creamy, almond-coloured skin. Like the two of them, I picked up a long root and bit into it: it turned out to be so juicy, fresh and crisp that it later became my favourite vegetable, always associated with our "meetings of the clouds and the rain," either as a prelude, or at the end.

As for Tumchooq, he knows no greater pleasure than

biting into a turnip from the Zhangjiakou region: the skin on the bottom half buried in the ground is the colour of jade, an almost transparent green, on the top half it's ivory-coloured; the flesh is white as snow, with a pattern of purple veins shot through with a ruby-red thread. Holding a turnip in his hand, Tumchooq likes imitating street vendors, bellowing a sing-song "Zhangjiakou turnips, better than Guangzhou pears . . ." Then he throws it on the ground, the turnip splits into pieces and he bites into one, chews it, then passes it to me, mouth to mouth, like feeding a baby bird. The sugary, exquisitely refreshing juice pours over my tongue and down my throat, and spreads through my whole body for an immeasurable length of time; it sometimes feels as if the taste will stay with me till the end of my days.

Tumchooq left a week ago and after three days on the train—"listening to the hammering of the wheels," as a popular song goes—he must have arrived in Chengdu on Monday evening, set off for Ya An on Tuesday morning, that's the day before yesterday, and spent another whole day on the bus on a rutted mountain road, "a snaking, silvery ribbon climbing to the clouds," if his greengrocer's funds allowed. Sometimes lack of money means he has to get to the prison camp by hitchhiking and he spends hours by the side of the road. When he's been refused by several lorry drivers he hides behind some trees on a corner where the lorries have to slow down before a steep slope. He's described it to me so many times I can picture him running behind a lorry, launching himself at the back, gripping onto iron bars or a rope that holds down a tarpaulin, then, in a dangerous manoeuvre, heaving himself up to this access point, freeing one of his hands, untying the rope, opening the tarpaulin and climbing inside; then the lorry gets smaller and smaller and I lose sight of it. But that's not always the end. Often, somewhere along the four hundred kilometres he still needs to cover, he has to jump out of the lorry at the last minute and get into another one, because the driver changes direction without any warning and heads for somewhere else— Luo Shan, Emei, E Bin, but not Ya An—usually accelerating, hurtling off at top speed, thundering along, as if to express his pleasure, his eagerness to deliver this trapped man to justice. A real nightmare. Tumchooq knows he'll have to retrace his steps, but first he needs to escape the possessed vehicle. He closes his eyes and jumps, and sometimes he lands in a rice paddy by the side of the road and sinks into mud and shit full of worms no one's ever seen in any biology textbook, Sichuan worms covered in white down, which squirm and writhe, until one of them settles under the skin on your forehead or in the pit of your chest.

Ya An, "Exquisite Peace," is the name of a mountain town which is now small and poor with barely sixty thousand inhabitants, but, if the regional annals are to be believed, it had a glorious past as the capital of the province, complete with bustling streets, a cinema, the governor's palace, two decent hotels, its opium trade, its vegetable and spice market (where the heads of decapitated criminals were displayed), and its Tibetans and Lolos who made up part of the population. In 1955 Ya An was demoted, reduced to the status of principal town in a region of eight districts, each more dependent on the mountain economy than the last . . . in other words, extremely poor. An area from which Westerners were banned. Over several decades under communist rule this region achieved fame across the whole of China for the number of people who died, nearly one million between 1959 and 1961—that's forty per cent of the population—anonymous victims carried off by famine, most of them dying long, slow deaths, too weak to stand upright, crawling on the ground like animals breathing their last. So Ya An became synonymous with a giant mass grave. After that scandal no one mentioned the sinister place again, the shameful wart erased itself from collective memory and all that remained were prison camps, lost among the dark silhouettes of its towering mountains, which curved bizarrely through the fog. One of these camps, on the River Lu, is known by millions of admirers of Hu Feng, a writer and great intellectual condemned by Mao himself, who always appeared extremely jealous of this particular prey, though no one ever knew why. (Hu Feng has been imprisoned there since 1955, a detention, I notice to my horror, which—give or take a couple of years—coincides with that of the French orientalist Paul d'Ampère, also incarcerated at the River Lu camp.) His sister Hu Min describes the camp in her memoirs, which were recently published in Taiwan:

When the main road from Chengdu to Tibet reaches Ya An it carries on climbing westwards for fifteen kilometres, and comes to the Pass of the Immortal Steering Wheel, a name which perfectly emphasises how perilous the topography is and reminds mortals how dangerous and difficult it is to pass. There the road forks. On the right is an uneven track of beaten earth, not to say mud, scored with deep ruts carved out and churned up by lorries laden with stones, a barely practicable eighteen-kilometre stretch along the River Lu, which carves its own bed at the foot of tall cliffs and is in fact not navigable because it has so little water and an infinite number of massive, dark rocks that have tumbled from the top of the mountain—rocks so macabre and ugly, so loaded with menace, they look like the bodies of the infirm, the deformed and the mad subjected to unimaginable tortures, screaming in pain, struggling, squirming and finally petrifying in the tormented shape of their final punishment, of death by fire or iron. In geographical terms, choosing this place to set up a prison camp on the side of a mountain is a stroke of genius because the Pass of the Immortal Steering Wheel need only be closed for it to be cut off from the world, and any attempt at escape would be bound to fail.

The substantial river becomes narrower and narrower until it is little more than a stream, running dry most of the time, as it crosses a tiny plain one kilometre long by two wide, thrown up in the heart of the mountains, surrounded by cliffs and painstakingly sealed off with high walls of barbed wire. At fifty-metre intervals along the fence there are watchtowers guarded by armed soldiers and equipped with searchlights, which sweep their powerful beams over every corner and recess of the grounds.

The camp is divided into two areas: on the right bank of the River Lu are the administrative buildings, residences for prison staff, an infirmary, a shop, the warders' canteen and a strange concrete edifice built in the 1960s to house the directing staff of the provincial police force, should there be an American invasion, a sort of shapeless lump partly buried underground with a vast dome camouflaged under artificial trees standing on a three-storey quadrilateral with walls also smothered in ivy and climbing plants, which are stirred by the slightest wind, the slightest breath of breeze, turning the building into a monster, a peculiar species of hedgehog.

As the American invasion never came, by the early 1970s the edifice was lived in by the families of the head warders who, even on their days off, keep a watchful eye over the other part of the camp on the more steeply sloping left bank of the River Lu, the part reserved exclusively for prisoners: first, the work camp proper, a mine exploited using medieval techniques where each gem shaft is indicated by a heap of earth around an opening a couple of metres in diameter, gaping holes dug at random into the bank or beside the river bed. At first light an army of ghosts—how many of them? a thousand? two thousand?—winds its way down to the river bank in single file in detachments of twenty or so individuals, each stumbling and swaying to a separate shaft. Fifty light bulbs come on one by one along the river, each lighting its own shaft, where a warder does a roll call of his uniformed, shaven-headed prisoners (only cooks, pig-keepers and barbers are allowed to keep their hair), who line up like soldiers while he bellows out their numbers, which echo around the mountain. The warder then repeats, as he does every morning, the punishment each of them exposes himself to for the least breach of discipline, before the prisoners—one by one, each laden with heavy tools, packs of explosives and bamboo baskets—silently climb down an infinitely long bamboo ladder to reach the bottom of the shaft, a dozen or so metres below ground. One of them, often the most experienced, lights three candles in a basket, lowers it gently to the bottom and sets it at the mouth of the gallery they have to dig. This is the only security measure available to them in that, if oxygen runs low, the three candles will go out.

Just one prisoner stays on the surface (he might once have been an engineer or a great opera singer, who knows?) and he takes a mouthful of fuel and spits a thin stream of it onto the carburettor while pulling the cord, and the motor shudders with heavy spasms, which make the ground shake as it comes to life. A pump spews out black water drawn from the bottom of the shaft as the sound of other motors carries from shafts further away. The racket from these thrumming witches' cauldrons heralds the beginning of a long day of forced labour in the shadows, with the members of each team staying underground for six hours, barefoot in mud and water, standing and digging or kneeling and digging into the clay that falls away in blocks, fingering and prodding the walls in the hopes of finding a trace of gemstones, but knowing from experience that there is a one-in-ten-thousand chance of success. They fill baskets with clay and indicate when they can be hauled up by blowing a whistle so deadened by the damp that it sounds like a long moan, a lost cry emanating from a dark tomb. The man on the surface pulls the rope, raises the basket, pours the clay into a sieve and, using water from the pump, sorts through it minutely for precious stones.

It is this same dirty muddy water that sprays over the naked prisoners a few hours later at the end of the day. The first man up washes his hair and shoulders while his teammates are still climbing the ladder in a state of near exhaustion. One after another they pause as they reach the surface, as much to take a lungful of dry air as to readjust to the light of day. It is not unusual for one of them to be unable to heave himself out. He then has to be dragged by the arms and pushed from behind before he can collapse by the edge of the shaft, prostrate on the ground, struggling to exhale, more dead than alive.

The gem shafts stay with their slaves once the work is over. On nights when the wind blows and the moon is bathed in a sort of yellow nimbus, the shafts keep their hold on the prisoners' minds in a different way as they lie on their bunks in vast sealed hangars with corrugated iron roofs:

through the tall, high windows they can hear strange noises coming from the shafts, a hundred of them in all, if the camp's nickname is to be believed, each transformed into an enormous echo chamber, a deep abyss swallowing the mountain wind, which wails and cries: plaintive, tormented cries, shrill, piercing cries hurtling up to the sky and whisked away or metamorphosing into mournful muted exhalations, like a long sigh hovering in the air for a moment before slumping in a corner of the dormitory or dissolving into the darkness above what might have been the bed of a prisoner carried off by dysentery, malaria, jaundice, hunger or exhaustion. Sometimes it sounds like ghost voices whispering for a few seconds, and some think they hear their own names or the names of lost companions.

On terrifying stormy nights, when the wind swoops unbridled through the mountains, these sounds develop into a drum roll as if an army of vengeful spirits were launching an attack on the camp. On quiet nights, so quiet they can hear the corrugated iron cracking as it shrinks in the dropping temperature, having expanded in the heat of the day, a gunshot sometimes shatters the silence, followed by a burst of three further explosions coming from the summary executions site, not far away in the same valley. Always four shots, four related but different sounds, most likely from four rifles to leave no glimmer of hope for the bound and gagged escapee who has just been stopped—yet another one—and now kneels before a hole in the ground into which his body, shot through by four bullets, is to fall.

The camp prisoners are arranged in two distinct categories that never intermix: the common criminals and the "thought criminals." Each group of twenty prisoners has a leader who must belong to the first category, creatures still more sinister and cruel than the warders who appointed them, and more dangerous since warders do sleep at night, whereas these leaders, equipped with the title of guard helpers, are absolute masters of their groups, both physically and psychologically, and can exploit the other prisoners' weaknesses without having to account for their actions to anyone. A group leader might, for example, organise a meeting about escaping the moment a shooting is over, asking each individual to admit to his own errors and delve into the deepest recesses of his mind to find the merest shadow of longing to escape. The leader has the right to decide whether a nocturnal meeting like this takes place with or without the lights on, and, when it happens in the dark, it often turns into sessions of common criminals beating up the "thought criminals," because as soon as one of the latter opens his mouth, he can barely get three sentences out before he is assailed by black shadows that spring from every direction, his fellow prisoners in the first category jumping onto him, covering his head with a sheet, punching and kicking him, then going back to their places and, safe in their perfect immunity, carrying on with their own confessions and sincere promises to mend their ways. And all the while their victim bleeds and cries in pain, aware that his suffering only enhances the pleasure of this collective barbarity, which was either ordered or encouraged by the leader and thus by the whole staff and the entire penitentiary system. The only "thought criminals" to escape this brutality along with the slavery of forced labour in the depths of the gem mines are prisoners held in the other sector visible in the distance, beyond the Pass of the Immortal Steering Wheel, on the rare days when the mountain is not shrouded in mist and when the air is transparent: eight dazzlingly white buildings in two straight lines on the side of the mountain, set apart from the main dormitories; a little separate world no one knows anything about except that the rooms there are individual or double, never communal, and that its residents—mostly major Party figures who once reached pinnacles of power—may well be prisoners but they enjoy the wonderful privilege of reading *The People's Daily,* the official organ of the Party.

Tumchooq has a black-and-white photograph from the early 1970s, in the small eight-centimetre-square format of the day, given to him at the same time as *The Secret Biography of Cixi* by his childhood friend Ma when he came to Peking. The fact that their unfortunate nocturnal outing cost Tumchooq three years of reform school did nothing to change their feelings; quite the opposite, particularly as when they were reunited each had come a long way, one through reform school and then a greengrocer's shop, the other having been "re-educated," and they had both gained in confidence and a degree of experience in life.

Ma was eighteen when he took the picture. A year earlier, when he left school, the state had sent him for "re-education" to live with poor revolutionary peasants on the Mountain of the Phoenix in the Yong Jin district, one of the eight miserable districts in the Ya An region. Thanks to his "minor virtuosity as a violinist," as he called it, a reputation that spread beyond the mountains, he was spotted by a local semi-professional propaganda group who "borrowed" him from his village. He was not remunerated—although his board and lodging were free—but this absurd temporary employment meant he could escape hard toil in the fields and rice paddies. For many months the group travelled all round the region by bus putting on revolutionary shows, and Ma became friends with a little genius of a flute player by the name of Chen, the son of a warder and a nurse at the River Lu camp. The day this boy asked him to spend the 1973 New Year celebrations at his parents' house, "I jumped at the opportunity," he later told Tumchooq. "I even had trouble hiding my joy. It wasn't to visit the camp, which disgusted me, but to try to lay my hands on a priceless treasure that anyone familiar with the black market in forbidden books dreams of getting hold of by whatever means possible: a manuscript which, according to rumour, Hu Feng had secretly written during his long period in solitary confinement. It was called *Storm on the River Lu,* and some passages, for lack of ink, were written in blood pricked from his finger with his pen."

It was the first time Tumchooq had seen a picture of the place, an overall shot of the River Lu camp in the middle of winter, and the palpable shaking of the photographer's hand as he hastily, secretly took the photo gives the place a Siberian feel, like a Sichuan *Gulag Archipelago.* Seen from above, the dormitories look like burnt matches, black carcasses tracing geometric figures on the snow, the prison buildings forming rectangular courtyards surrounded by the circles of the mine shafts, all cloaked in cold and infinite indifference. Above was another inhabited area, the white buildings of the privileged inmates, also geometric but with ephemeral patches of reflected snow making them look like a lunatic asylum, a place dominated by endless boredom, another form of incurable evil.

Further up still was an isolated house, visible only as a sloping tiled roof, since the rest of it was masked by a very high wall, no doubt also very smooth, very thick and impossible to climb. It was here, if the flute player was to be believed, that Hu Feng, "the emperor's prisoner," as he was known, was kept in isolation, but the only evidence of his presence was the dark foliage of a mandarin orange tree he had planted at the beginning of his imprisonment and, at the time the photograph was taken, the top of the tree was taller than the top of the wall, standing as isolated and proud as the man who planted it.

"I looked at that mandarin tree for a long time," Ma told Tumchooq. "A vibrant green shimmered over its monochrome leaves, but I don't know how long it had been since the sun had made even the shyest appearance through the clouds or the light of dawn had skimmed the tops of its foliage. I wondered whether birds came and perched in it to keep the writer company in his incarceration that dates back such a long way it almost stands outside time."

He took this photo on his first visit. He had spent an unimaginably long time looking at the camp, until he knew its topography by heart, picturing himself getting past the armed guards on their rounds to climb up the thin, narrow almost shivering line which, on the photograph, represented the only pathway up to the isolated house. In the three years after his first visit, even though he'd already left the propaganda group (whose new leader thought the violin an instrument designed to express only bourgeois sentiments), Ma went back to the River Lu camp several times, still entertaining the hope of acquiring Hu Feng's secret masterpiece.

He lived with Chen's parents, showering them with presents from the Mountain of the Phoenix—eggs, chickens, medicinal plants, terracotta dishes, etc.—but the isolated house with its mandarin tree remained as inaccessible to him as a star, the moon, the sun or Kafka's castle. Eventually, he admitted defeat and decided never to set foot in the camp again and shortly before leaving he confessed his regret to Chen's father, who, in the meantime, had climbed a few echelons in his long career as a warder and was now one of the six assistant directors of the sector for ordinary prisoners. They said their goodbyes in the kitchen.

"You, and you alone, have a way of doing that," Ma told Tumchooq. "Even though we were separated by an impossible distance, you have this ability to pop back up out of nowhere; it knocked me speechless, struck me dumb. A resurrection isn't something you explain, it just happens. Ten minutes after saying goodbye to Chen's father I was still there with the smell of cooking oil and chillies, not because I was thinking over what he'd just told me but because for the first time in ages I was wondering where you were. I thought back to that night so long before in the Forbidden City, in the hall with the exhibition of instruments of torture."

According to Chen's father, Hu Feng's secret work was pure legend, based on nothing at all: at the beginning of his incarceration the writer had a phobia of paper, the source of all his troubles, given that he was arrested and incarcerated because of a letter he had addressed to Mao. Before 1957 there were few "thought criminals" at the River Lu camp—as in the whole of China at that time—so the prison staff had little experience of this new category, and the Hu Feng case was beyond them, at least for the first few years of his incarceration, because he was a national figure who had made his mark on Chinese history. His family were, therefore, allowed to bring him books, particularly his own published works of literature, as well as his notebooks and private diaries. But one night he burned them all in the courtyard of the isolated house (to prove that his faith in literature had been destroyed just when he most needed it, perhaps, or to punish himself for losing the ability to write?), and people whispered among themselves that this gesture marked the beginning of the madness into which he descended. He was seen holding completely imaginary conversations with Mao from morning till night. One day, prison guard Chen saw him with his own eyes standing out in driving rain arguing with Mao, his eyes turned to the skies as he gesticulated and explained at length his opinions on democracy, censure, education and religion. From time to time, drawing level with his young mandarin tree, he would bow his head, incline his body and plead with the invisible Great Helmsman, quite unaware that the rain was beating down ever harder, his shirt clinging to him, his trousers flapping in the wind and water streaming over his hair (which he was allowed to wear long at the time because of his privileged status), running over his face and into his eyes, mingling with his tears and filling his mouth, which went on emitting snatches of words and icy breath, fading to moaning and mumbling—but never an obscenity or insult—until he was reduced to silence.

During this period people noticed an increasingly rapid decline in his memory, as if his brain were somehow ossifying. He could no longer remember recent events—clean clothes, for example, the meagre meals he ate alone or the nurse's name—then he stopped recognising the warders and

the camp director until the day, during one of her rare authorised visits, when his wife wondered whether he even recognised her. She begged him to say her name and wept when
she realised he could not, his ravaged brain was just a space
filled with shadowy mists and shapeless, nameless monsters;
she broke down on the spot, for no one knew better than she
how phenomenal her husband's near-legendary memory
was. One thing is sure: at that point, in spite of his youth, the
writer was closer to descending into senile dementia than to
writing a novel; he no longer had the physical or intellectual
means to do so.

   No one ever knew whether it was a surge of pride, a lucid
moment, a way of escaping the isolated house which had
become his tomb, or an accident in a fit of hysteria that made
him hit out at one of the guards, resulting in his expulsion:
his head was shaved, he was moved to a communal barrack,
slept on creaking wooden planks and began life as a common prisoner, taken to the gem mines like all the others in
the morning, and climbing down into them, never knowing
whether he would come back out safely. In the depths of a
mine shaft he crossed paths with a man who was, in some
senses, as mad as himself and who from his first day at the
River Lu camp had never spoken in anything but Buddha's
language, a dead language which cut him off from all communication with the world, except for a fly tied at the waist
with a very fine thread and attached to the side-piece of his
glasses, flitting around him with a constant buzzing sound.
All reports confirm that he was always perfectly, worryingly
calm, even when he was attacked by his teammates, who
were common criminals, a band of devils, rapists, thieves,
paedophiles and sadists who homed in on him during their

political meetings in the dormitory in the dark, punching him and taking pleasure in tearing the hairs growing back on his head and in more intimate places, "reactionary imperialist" hairs, to use their actual words, which weren't black like Chinese people's, but red.

"Tears sprang from my eyes," Ma told Tumchooq, "before he'd even said the word 'French.' I couldn't say why, but those few red hairs made me cry like a baby, a blinding pain shot through my head, almost breaking it open; it felt like the same pain I had as a boy in that strangling cage when you tortured me, because you would do anything for information about him. That same Frenchman was suddenly so close to me, two or three hundred metres away, at the bottom of the black hole of a gem mine where he had already spent nearly twenty years, and during that time a huge underground network had spread in every direction, so complex he must have felt he would never get out."

Ma could no longer remember how the conversation started up again in that kitchen, but what the old warder told him left a dark image stamped on his memory, where he could see neither the Frenchman nor even a bamboo basket, but could just hear a fly buzzing in darkness. He was talking about the first time Hu Feng went down a mine shaft. Towards the end of the morning the candles that served as lighting as well oxygen detectors went out, and the prisoners raced for the wooden ladder up to the surface, stepping over anyone who fell, their panicked screams echoing through the tunnels, fighting to be first. Although conscious of the imminent danger of asphyxiation, Hu Feng, as he told his wife later, just sat motionless at the entrance of the gallery, convinced in his paranoid state that the whole scene was actually a plot devised against him and that, whatever happened, he would sooner or later be the victim of a murder disguised as an accident, so he might as well die straight away.

While he waited for death in total darkness he heard a buzzing sound approaching out of nowhere, coming from a winged creature, probably an angel, given the circumstances. The noise circled round him, constantly drawing closer, then pulling away, always to the same distance, making the surrounding silence feel all the more impenetrable, so he was startled to hear a man's voice close to him murmuring a strange word with an unfamiliar ring to it, and, although he didn't understand it, he guessed what it meant: fly. Hu Feng struggled in vain to see the man in the darkness, and kept repeating the word, like a coded message, until all of a sudden that simple, gentle, airy syllable gave him confidence: he realised the candles had gone out because of the rising humidity and if the air had really been lacking in oxygen the fly wouldn't have been able to dance like an angel or a wandering soul, a dance as light as the sound of that unfamiliar name given to it by its master.

At the end of the day, once freed and back up on the surface, the Frenchman metamorphosed into a goldsmith, gently untying the fly from the fine, almost invisible thread with his dirty, blackened but magically adroit fingers, and orchestrating a silent symphony for his only spectator, his new fellow prisoner, as he released it beside the River Lu. Hu Feng watched it gently beat its wings as it gathered its wits before flitting away. Much later he came to understand the word the Frenchman said every day during this deliverance ceremony back up on the surface, thanking the insect for perfectly fulfilling its role as a guardian angel, or simply to celebrate their survival. Hu Feng was immediately filled with curiosity for the ancient language his teammate spoke, and this developed into an increasingly consuming passion. He even proved surprisingly talented for a beginner in his ability to decipher the words the Frenchman said or wrote out on the clay walls of the mine shafts, words that acted on him like a cure for amnesia, miraculously anchoring in his brain as his memory began a slow resurrection. ("Each new word gives me an extraordinarily uplifting feeling," he later confided to his wife in the visiting room, according to a warder's report.) In the space of a year he accumulated a sufficiently rich vocabulary to be initiated in Tumchooq chess, which archaeologists had discovered shortly before the Frenchman's arrest. "All games were strictly forbidden and entailed an extension of your sentence," Chen explained, "but however closely the prison authorities looked into this case, there was little they could do against the two men, because they played chess mentally and orally without any pieces, without drawing out a board, and certainly not actually touching anything. Were they being provocative? Was this a kind of revolt, a display of their intellectual superiority? Or, in spite of their erudition and talent, were they just like a couple of children who wanted to play and made do with very little? Either way, they took things too far."

The aim of these bouts fought in the dark, as Hu Feng explained to his sister during a visit, completely escaped the authorities' vigilant eyes: it was nothing more or less than an exercise to reinforce the writer's resuscitated memory. They launched into the game at every opportunity, either in the dark underground passages where they could be heard parrying words, which made other-worldly echoes in the depths of the mine; or in the dormitory against the howling wind, the piercing whistling from the mine shafts and the gurgling of the River Lu, which became quite a torrent during the thaw, making this probably the best time for them to indulge in their complicated game.

First one of them would announce the subtle move of a particular piece; his opponent considered it, smiled and retaliated with another word, which disguised a carefully elaborated and constantly changing strategy, and that was how they fought out each round, which went on indefinitely, sometimes right through until dawn. And when, without realising it, their concentration flagged and their thoughts and words lost their edge, the other prisoners in their group tried to interpret the expressions on their faces and the least nuance in their voices. Now it was the others whose blood was up, their eyes sharp, breathless and tense as they, too, were caught up in a game, the more clandestine prosaic game of betting on the winner of the next round, which the writer would announce on impulse—or perhaps because he had a generous nature. (In a camp where food was terribly restricted, bets consisted of a little scrap of fat—which could usually be exchanged on the camp's black market for a new pair of trousers—or a slice of meat, a mouthful of soup, a piece of sugar or a few vegetable leaves; sometimes, though very rarely, the betting reached astronomical heights: a bowl of rice.)

When someone lost a bet he naturally paid what he owed, whatever the price, but he could be so sickened by the loss that he harboured implacable hatred for the Frenchman or the writer. This is what happened with the team leader, the absolute master of the barrack room, even though no one ever dared claim the debt when he lost. When the chess player he had named as loser won the round it struck him like a physical blow, his face flushed red, his heart skipped a beat and he ordered his opponents to double the stakes for the next round, but the result often went against him once more. One evening his debt, which he never paid, multiplied so many times he suspected the two intellectuals were doing it on purpose to make fun of him. They didn't have to wait long for his revenge: in the morning the Frenchman and the writer were condemned to the harshest, filthiest, most dangerous work.

In one of his reports the team leader informed the authorities that the writer had wept tears of happiness as he performed the apparently banal gesture of picking up a scrap of old newspaper, which acted as wallpaper in the dormitory. It had come away from the dusty wall and now lay crumpled and dirty on the ground. He picked it up, he later admitted hastily in Tumchooq, to record the rounds won and lost against his opponent. ("I suddenly realised what I was doing," he added. "It brought an end to my phobia of paper and writing. For that purely literary reason I couldn't hold back my tears of joy.")

Even though the writer tore the piece of newspaper into tiny shreds on the spot for fear of leaving any trace of their forbidden game, the team leader picked it up, pieced together this proof of their offence with the patience of a clockmaker and glued it to another piece of paper. The flautist's father still keeps this exhibit in a drawer, a page covered in indecipherable signs, "which looked like shit from the huge rats at the River Lu camp," he told Ma.

It was a dazzling victory—the first of a language over a phobia—and the writer confirmed this in a conversation with his wife in the visiting room. According to the transcript of the recording, Hu Feng felt he was "in a state of grace," "in love with the Tumchooq language," especially now the Frenchman had introduced him to a sacred Buddhist text written in the language and copied word for word onto the inside of the sheepskin jerkin he wore day in and day out, summer and winter. "Venerating a text like that," the writer confided to his wife, "being in permanent physical contact with it, touching his skin, is all the more astonishing in a Frenchman who, apparently, ought to be the archetypal Cartesian. I've touched those words written on sheepskin with my own hands and they were as warm as living things. Some of the strokes have been distorted by the Frenchman's sweat and look like veins—sinuous, palpable, almost quivering. And over time some of the dots have turned into minute lotus flowers, reminding me, as it says in the text named after that flower, that the sutras are Buddha's relics."

The poor quality of the tape means some passages are inaudible, but this was a more or less accurate account of Hu Feng's first contact with the text of the mutilated manuscript. The recorded document also includes a long description of his deciphering of the text in which some words, despite his staggering progress and mastery of basic vocabulary, were still unknown to him. His French instructor, as he called him, would sit on his bed in silence, patching up his glasses with wire and wiping the lenses with the rags wrapped around the side-pieces, lost in thought. Whereas he, stimulated as much by the mystery itself as by the hope of finding the key to it, felt like a child alone in a huge forest, overwhelmed with happiness at being reunited with particular trees, grasses and plants, as if he knew them intimately, calling each by name, touching them, stroking them, smelling them, while others, unfamiliar to him, loomed out of nowhere, coldly blocking his path so he had to flatten them and clear them aside, only to admit that, between the endless intermingling of truths and deceptive appearances, he was actually lost.

The writer compared himself to a sailor of old navigating a river in an unknown continent and coming across as yet unexplored stretches where rapids unleashed themselves over the riverbed, clutching a map with no place names attributed to the blank spaces, just images of animals: lions, leopards, cobras, giraffes. Night after night Hu Feng explored those fabulous animals, carefully tracing them, tentatively pronouncing their names, analysing them, dissecting them, performing morphological and phonetic autopsies on them, and comparing them to those he knew already. After a while he felt he had lived with them all his life, penetrating the thoughts of their creator, a faithful companion to their evolution.

In his dreams he sometimes saw himself on the platform of a small station with a dozen or so children he had delivered from a goods train whose wagons were locked with metal bars. But he had forgotten one poor child who was now setting off again in the train, and, still full of their successful escape, the saviour didn't notice the spewing steam and the carriages beginning to move. The train drew slowly away, gathered speed and hurtled into a tunnel while Hu Feng started running after it, so nearly catching up . . . Then the orphan would appear to him as he truly was, as the ones he had saved were too: a word in Tumchooq—one he had struggled with for a long time without succeeding in deciphering—disguised as a child who wanted to escape with him. Much later, when the word was no longer an obstacle for him, when he knew all its derivatives, compounds and conjugations like the back of his hand, he would still remember the image from his dream every time he came across it, as if each stroke of that simple word carried within it the terror in an abandoned child's eyes.

"Bit by bit the text emerged from the shadows," he explained to his wife. "When I read it from beginning to end for the first time I felt as if I were in a plane—what unimaginable luxury for a prisoner—which had been delayed on the ground an unbearably long time, then lurched and slid along the runway, but was now taking off at last. I was slowly rising up to the silent heights of all the beauty that was Tumchooq. Overhead island clouds floated by, some dark grey, others brilliant white, and here and there I could make out a patch of forest, a frozen pond, an area of rice paddy, and I started thinking, although the idea itself is ridiculous, I was gliding over islands of the languages I had landed on in the past: Chinese, Japanese, Russian, French, English. Then I recognised what they were: my own works in Chinese, their solid pedestrian prose constantly shackled by society, by banality and more particularly by [inaudible word] dictatorship. While my Chinese writing only very occasionally takes flight, Tumchooq prose, now that dances."

History, in this instance the transcript of the recorded visit, does not elaborate on the reaction of the writer's wife. It may well have been like that of a woman whose husband is missing and presumed dead but who still waits, watching out for the slightest sign of his possible return. Now that her husband's memory was resuscitated it would truly be a miracle if his writing—even in a language she didn't understand at all—were also resuscitated, more powerful, more ethereal and more admired than ever. To her, Tumchooq was the Saviour, a God whose mythical power was further reinforced by these words from her husband: "I can't allow myself to recite the text to you, not because it's incomplete, but because the beauty of the language can't be translated. It's almost too beautiful to survive in this world. In my opinion, neither I nor any living Chinese writer would be able to convey half its charm, we could only translate it word for word, giving the bare bones without the flesh and life. It reminds me of my unfortunate experience translating Gogol: despite my best efforts and however much my work was praised, the beauty of the original slipped through my fingers. It hurt so much I wept, and I think of all those unfortunate people in the world—God knows how many of them there are—who don't read Russian and will die some day without ever experiencing the beauty of Gogol's prose. How appalling!"

The camp directors eventually made a collective decision to separate the Frenchman and Hu Feng after receiving a report denouncing these two thought criminals who, one Christmas Eve (this was confirmed using a Western calendar), went too far by treating themselves to a taunting, provocative celebration, which deftly insulted the camp's food regulations and defied the rules of their incarceration. It was a windless night, the hundred mine shafts were silent and the inside of the barrack room was bitterly cold; during a pause between two rounds of chess played in the dark, the Frenchman carried on chatting to his opponent. No one knew whether this was totally improvised, a premeditated act or whether he was talking in his sleep, but the writer, whose voice had a very distinctive ring to it, was suddenly heard translating his partner's words sentence by sentence. A peculiar dialogue, one speaking in Tumchooq, the other in Chinese, like a medium interpreting a barely audible, incomprehensible voice from another world in the shadowy hut.

"It's a recipe from the western Pyrenees, the land of my glorious ancestors. I tasted it as a child but forgot all about it until I came across it in Marco Polo's writings in a passage describing how to make a concoction which Europeans were still unfamiliar with in the Venetian's days and which we now call by a name taken from Aztec: chocolate."

As the word doesn't exist in Tumchooq he said it in English, mouthing it so softly in that silent dormitory you could almost hear it melting on his tongue: it resonated in his fellow prisoners' ears, but most if not all of them had no idea what chocolate was, and the writer, touched by their ignorance, paused for a long time as he delved into his distant memories to give them this explanation:

"When I was a student in the late 1920s, partly because I was short of money but also because of the exuberant cultural scene there, I rented a room in the heart of the French concession in Shanghai. There was a Belgian chocolatier on my street and every time I went past the shop I would close my eyes and run, even if just for a second, drowning in the hot fragrant exhalation from inside. I could hear the last few coins, which I was meant to use for my one meal of the day or my rent, clinking in my pocket, begging to be let out, because those wafts of milk, sugar and grilled cocoa smelt so good, pursuing me right to the end of the street, sometimes even into my dreams as I tossed and turned on my stifling bed. More than once I woke in the middle of the night and went down into the deserted street, and, even though the chocolatier had closed up shop hours ago, the magic still hung in the air, the atmosphere seemed thickened by the daytime smell of a country that would never be accessible to someone like me with no money, and I would stand there fascinated by the brightly lit window display filled with lions, eagles, doves, tigers, fish, chickens, rabbits and eggs, all in chocolate, alongside silver cups and saucers, teaspoons, porcelain butter dishes and still more chocolate in boxes piled up in pyramids tied with silver and gold bows . . ."

The Belgian chocolatier's shop with its glittering interior was making the listeners salivate, and when the Frenchman started talking again they were dazzled by Marco Polo's description of Kublai Khan's palace, which seemed to suspend them in mid-air, ready to take flight. Refusing to tell the story in his own words, he recited the Italian's text so fluently that his faithful translator marvelled as much at the clarity of the words as at his friend's phenomenal memory. In places he wondered whether the Venetian adventurer himself had come to the camp with news of his friend Kublai Khan or whether the Frenchman was simply his reincarnation.

"The Great Khan does indeed have a stud of stallions and mares as white as snow and countless in number: more than ten thousand mares. No one dares drink the milk of these white mares unless they are of the emperor's lineage, the Great Khan's lineage. It is true that another kind of person may drink it: these are called the Horiat, and this honour was granted to them by Genghis Khan for a great victory they won with him.

"In the middle of a vast hall where the Great Khan sups there is a magnificent, tall, ornate pedestal shaped like a square chest, each side three feet long, intricately worked with very beautiful gilded sculptures of animals. It is hollow and inside it is a precious vessel, shaped like a large pitcher, made of fine gold and filled with white mares' milk. From this milk a delicacy that the Great Khan considers his favourite sweetmeat is made in the following way: ten portions of milk to one portion of musk, some sugar, myrtles, mastic gum, lavender, thyme and so on, slowly caramelised in the little pitcher . . ."

The criminal who wrote the report doesn't remember at what stage he stood up. His hands were clenched, he had never felt so overwrought: it was the Frenchman's words and voice, he felt sure. Some sentences had made the image of his wife appear to him from nowhere—a fleeting image of her hips rocking and her dark vagina welcoming a glistening bar of chocolate flitted across his mind several times, making him forget his status as absolute master of the barrack room, where just one word from him would have been enough to end it all and have the Frenchman punished without his lifting so much as his little finger. The ground grew softer, elastic, seemed to dilate beneath his weight as if he were walking on cheese, a familiar sensation which reminded him of that distant night when he killed his wife, whose dark staring eyes were now more beautiful than ever, mingling with Marco Polo's words, creating a hypnotic effect, an inaccessible world which was a concentration of all the fine things of this earth, everything man has found to be great and beauti-

ful and which he would never be able to enjoy. He resented
the Frenchman for giving him a glimpse of that universe
and, had he had a knife, would have slit his throat to
silence him.

"You should also know that those who served this delicacy to the Great Khan were themselves barons. And I can
tell you that their mouths and noses were veiled with beautiful silk and gold cloth, so that their smell and breath should
not reach the food and drink and this wonderful . . ."

The Frenchman was heard screaming in the dormitory, a
scream of terror followed by silence and a few gurgling
noises from his throat, throttled between the leader's iron
hands. Long afterwards the latter remembered hearing a
man bellowing in his ear, clutching at him to tear the
Frenchman from his strangulating grasp: it was Hu Feng.
The leader struck him in the pit of his concave chest, he
swayed and fell to the ground. Someone lit a bulb, which
swung overhead, spreading a harsh light in which the leader
appeared as a dark shape getting back up to his feet. Picturing his wife again, dead from his knife thrusts, he spat in the
Frenchman's face, making him squirm as he groaned on his
straw mattress. He spat several more times, aiming at the
Westerner's nose, but missing his target so that the nauseat-
ing, viscous filth fell on his victim's cheeks, eyes, mouth and
the high forehead topped with its shock of red hair.

The flautist's father drove Ma to a lorry parked in the
middle of the River Lu's dry bed, close to a mine shaft, and
asked the uniformed driver to take this "great violinist of the
future from Ya An region," his son's friend, back home to
Chengdu. The warder nodded, still keeping an eye on a
horde of ghostly figures, exhausted, half-naked and covered

in mud, loading a huge blue-grey stone onto the lorry; it must have weighed at least a ton and was shaped like a wart torn from a monster's back. They dragged it centimetre by centimetre, cried out as they heaved it up with the help of ropes and thick wooden poles, but mainly with their bare hands, shoulders, backs and arms, so that their bodies bore the stigmata of vicious scratches, black bruising and deep cuts, hideous tattoos left by the cruel, harsh rock.

Ma went up to one face, then to another without finding the Frenchman or the writer, whom he had already seen in a photograph on the cover of a collection of short stories bought on the black market. The former must have been down in the depths of a shaft. As for Hu Feng, his host told him that after the incident at Christmas the directors had moved him to another group, because they wanted to cut off all contact between him and his mentor.

"In my long career as a warder," he added, "I have never seen or heard anyone describe a more difficult separation. I wonder whether Hu Feng suffered as much when he was arrested in front of his wife of several decades. This time, he was destroyed. Every journey down into the mine shafts without the little fly attached to his friend's glasses to watch over his safety unleashed hideous fits of hysteria in him, and these so terrified his teammates that he had to be kept in the infirmary, where, on the strength of his notoriety, they summoned an important psychiatrist from the University of Medicine of Western China, Dr. Lin. The doctor made his diagnosis and prescribed electric-shock treatment, a hundred or so sessions over several weeks, a therapy aimed at progressively eradicating the ancient Tumchooq language—the source of his mental disturbances—from his brain.

"At the cost of terrible pain and at the risk of causing total amnesia or the loss of his entire personality, this eradication of Tumchooq was meant to mark the first step towards normality, a sort of docile state first indicated by an infallible sign: thinking in Chinese. Hu Feng was sent away in an ambulance, tied to the stretcher like a dead prisoner ready to be thrown into the river. He left with an enthusiast in the use of electrodes, a specialist in bodily convulsions and grimaces of pain, in other words an advocate of torture. He was never seen again."

CONTINUATION OF MY PRIVATE DIARY

FEBRUARY–MARCH 1979

8TH FEBRUARY

Even as a child, bent over my schoolbooks with a perfectly sharpened soft-leaded pencil, I liked bringing things back to life—people, lives, stories I had read or heard—in my private diary or my notebook, which I guarded jealously in a locked drawer. I delighted in watching as the curved shaving of wood coiling around the pencil grew longer, hung in the air and eventually spiralled down onto a sheet of white paper next to a tiny pyramid of glinting black dust. It was my private ritual. My daily prayer, a sort of confession.

To make this humble exercise even more sacred I set myself a rule: finishing that day's writing when the pencil was no longer useable, and never sharpening it a second time, come what may. Many years later, when my schoolbooks were replaced by diaries, I continued to apply my childhood rule to the letter, faithful to my brief, fragmentary sketches, captured in haste, brought to an end as much by the state of my pencil as a sort of weariness. This is the first time I've written so many pages at once and I can't get over how many of them there are.

I don't want to read through these fragments of notes, not for fear of their tremendous length, but of rediscovering the distress hidden behind the words, the distress of a girl barely twenty years old who noticed the first signs of pregnancy the day after Tumchooq left, shortly before writing these notes. It was still dark when I was woken by a reflux of slightly stinging acid rising in my throat. A power cut turned my confusion into panic. I was soon up, fumbling in the dark for the few candles I always kept as a precaution.

Resisting the urge to be sick, I took out my diary and started writing (even though I was not at first sure what about) by the flickering light of the candles, which kept stubbornly falling over. Eventually one of them fell on the floor, and as I picked it up I felt a hot torrent rushing through me, ready to burst from my mouth; it was so violent that all the candles flickered and went out one after the other. I was on my knees, as good as blinded, gripping onto the table, clearing my throat till I saw stars, but, oddly, I wasn't sick. The surge of acid had subsided; just a warning. But it left such a horrible sensation that, in order to get rid of it, I had the ridiculous idea of throwing myself body and soul into writing down memories, and these soon turned into an endless stream, a great succession of French words as soft as my mother's breath. I didn't dare stop, even to smoke, for fear of being assailed by the mysterious acid reflux again, or having to face reality. Acting on this impulse, I made sure not to miss a single detail and looked up from my writing only to sharpen my pencils, worn down at impressive speed as the pages went by.

For two weeks the terrifying symptom didn't re-offend. I carried on writing, interrupting my work only to eat a mouthful or sleep for a while, so that I could stay in Tumchooq's world, maintain contact with him—he's been gone three weeks, that's twenty-one days with no news—and keep him company day and night, wherever he may be.

On the 28th of last month, the day before Chinese New Year (which Tumchooq celebrated with his father, who, since Mao's death, has been promoted to the rank of pig-keeper and finally freed from working in the depths of the gem mines), for reasons I don't understand, I declined invitations to parties organised by my university and the French embassy, and spent the New Year alone in the company of my private diary, locked in my room out of mute solidarity with this "devoted son." Bent over my paper, writing about him, his father and his prison colony, I felt I was with them in that part of China banned to foreigners.

Pig-keeper! How ironic for the eminent Western scholar, who should have had a chair at the Collège de France or been elected to the Académie française long ago. I think Paul d'Ampère would have preferred to be appointed a shepherd (after all, we call the evening star the "shepherd's star" in French, but, as far as I know, no pig-keeper's star shines in the firmament). There's none of that nobility of pastoral care, sovereignty or leading the flock about the term "pig-keeper"; instead it conjures an image of a poor, skinny little child darting between hunks of wobbling flesh as his pigs sprawl in the mud with their small, mistrustful eyes. That same child hoping to steal a share of the dirty, fetid food they bury their muddied snouts in, grunting; he swallows it straight down, only too happy to find anything to cheat the appalling hunger that grips his innards.

In comparison with a prisoner digging in the mines, though, pig-keeper is the most sought-after position after working in the canteen, given its food-related benefits. Should we read into this the effects of his faith in Buddhism, which respects all creatures, or his joy at leaving his previous team, synonymous as they were with the Underworld if not with death itself? But, according to Tumchooq, even the most jealous of his new fellow prisoners acknowledge that Paul d'Ampère is the best pig-keeper the River Lu camp has ever had.

At break of day he stands dreamily chopping grass with a knife, setting a regular, unchanging rhythm like a monk beating a stone instrument. Then he lights a wood fire and boils up the chopped grass with bran in a huge cast-iron pot. Meanwhile he cleans the floor of the pigsty, centimetre by centimetre, using water drawn from the River Lu; then he calls one of the pigs by the Tumchooq name he has given it, and the animal grunts and nudges through its companions, making its way towards the gate like an obedient soldier coming to his commander. Paul d'Ampère cleans the animal so competently he might have been doing it all his life. He pours water on its skin and brushes it until it gleams like black silk. He gives them all the same treatment, and last of all comes the queen, a solid, no-nonsense, magnificently fat sow with dark silk patches on her back and lighter ones on her belly, and teats that fill out when she has piglets—which the directors hand out to the warders' families. Waddling, reluctant, she has the privilege of a bath in the River Lu, and she buries her short legs in the mud and flicks her snout to splash herself with water before coming back to the pig-keeper for her morning wash, snuffling and gurgling, her whole body seeming to swell with voluptuous abandon.

Paul d'Ampère is genuinely distraught in the lead-up to a celebration, when one or several of the pigs have to be killed for the warders' feast. As soon as he sees the canteen director with a dozen prisoners-turned-butchers coming over to the pigsties, he wants to run away, to hide as far from there as possible to avoid witnessing the scene. But he has to stay and watch the creatures, who seem to hold their breath, not grunting or making a sound, to hear what the visitors are saying. And when the director points out the victim, it backs away of its own accord, right to the far end of the pigsty, as if guessing its fate from what the man has said. Then the butchers head over to the corner, hauling out the animal as it digs its pointed trotters into the mud and gives great long squeals, almost like the cries of a dying man, wails that go on and on endlessly, until the poor pig-keeper's eardrums are fit to burst. The squealing becomes even more frantic when its throat is slit, which is often done in the canteen kitchen.

"Perhaps I've never really been sensitive to sounds, except for the human voice," Paul d'Ampère confided to his son, "but from their first cry I feel I can hear them begging me in Tumchooq to help them. My whole chest constricts with pain and I can't tell whether the butcher's knife is going into one of my pigs' throats or my own."

10TH FEBRUARY

Yesterday I was overwhelmed by mounting anxiety or rather a premonition. It's more than ten days since New Year now and a week has passed since Tumchooq was due back. I went out, not sure where to go, walking so heavily that, at one point, I realised I was trundling along the street hunched over like an old lady under the weight of that premonition. It was dark but I recognised Little India Street, which seemed to have turned into a never-ending tunnel. The shop signs were still lit up and I thought—though it was just an illusion—they said the names of the towns along Tumchooq's route to the River Lu: Chengdu, Xin Jin, Qiong Le, Ya An, Yong Jin and the last part of the journey, the Pass of the Immortal Steering Wheel, ghostly ideograms spinning before my eyes and seeping into my mind, even after the shops had closed, lowering their metal shutters one after another.

The last shop left open was the traditional pharmacy. A man of about sixty sat next to a porcelain lamp, bathed in mellow light and a distinctive smell, milling dried herbs and tree bark. I hesitated for almost ten minutes before asking whether he could tell fortunes, as most of his colleagues can, and whether I could ask him about Tumchooq, whose name I changed, of course, because the pharmacist is bound to know him, given how close their shops are to each other. I watched him mixing the plant powder with alcohol, grinding it and blending it, as if hoping to find some good omen in those slow, meticulous gestures.

As he picked up a paintbrush and prepared some ink, probably to write out the name of the medicine on a label, he looked up and stared at me with apparent astonishment. In that fraction of a second I thought I could see in his eyes—would I have imagined something like this?—that he knew my fate and Tumchooq's and that of the embryo deep inside my womb. But I left before we'd exchanged a single word, partly because I was too shy to confide in him and partly for fear that, even with one little word, he might confirm my premonition.

I came very close to losing my mind outside the greengrocer's, which had been closed for a while, kicking the rusted metal shutter so hard I hurt my toes, each kick giving off a dull, listless echo. Next I launched myself at the rubbish baskets, tipping them over in the street, spilling their fill of rotting, unsellable cabbage leaves, pumpkins, aubergines, marrows, chicories, carrots and cucumbers. Then I saw a man with a cart coming round the corner of the street and heading towards me; he was a pedlar selling grilled sparrows, something I know Tumchooq loves, they have a distinctive taste, thanks to the nutmeg which forms the basis of their diet. I bought everything left on the cart, hoping Tumchooq would make a miraculous reappearance in the middle of the night. Then I headed back to the campus and waited on my bed till dawn, quite incapable of closing my eyes.

Would our child—if the Heavens granted us one, to use a Chinese expression—have red hair? The question buzzed around inside my head as I half slept. When I got up to make some tea the wooden floor creaked slightly beneath me and, for the first time in a long while, the dawn light skimmed over my teapot, as it does in a poem by Du Fu, my favourite poet, also from Sichuan. For no apparent reason and without warning, tears streamed from my eyes and I was properly sick, twice, in quick succession.

16TH FEBRUARY
Where are you?

Met Tumchooq's mother at her house. Didn't achieve much. Mutual mistrust.

In an envelope posted from a small town on the Chinese-Burmese border, I found this letter in Chinese:

Paul d'Ampère is dead. The pig-keeper is dead. The Frenchman is dead. My father is dead. The river is dead. The mountains are dead. China is dead. The sky is dead. The earth is dead. The world is dead. Everything's dead.

On the 26th of January, two days before I reached the camp, some prisoners started a rumour that there was a newborn piglet with red hair. My father was accused of raping the sow, a completely aberrant fabrication, and he died in a scrum of frenetic prisoners descending upon him in a collective lynching.

I'm in mourning for him and will be for the rest of my life. I've sworn I'll never go back to Peking, the capital of the country that assassinated my father—even to see you. Writing to you will be the last time I use the language of my father's assassins. I will never utter another word of Chinese. I'd rather die. I'm not yet ready to give up on everything and resort to suicide in a final act of protest, but that's mainly because the fable told by Buddha in Tumchooq on the scroll is incomplete. I'm prepared to travel all over Burma, Vietnam, Laos, Cambodia, Sri Lanka, Nepal . . . because my father, who never succeeded in finding the text in the Chinese Buddhist canon, was convinced that the complete fable did exist in the canon of the Hinayana school of thought. Oh, Buddha! I long for this so achingly and sincerely! Only you can fulfil my wishes and grant my father gentle, peaceful rest as a final offering from his son.

I buried him beside the River Lu. I would have liked to build a vaulted tomb like a gothic cathedral, but his status as a prisoner and my pitiful greengrocer's finances meant all I could do was add another ordinary gravestone to the ones already there, in a vast desolate necropolis stretching several kilometres along the river under the cliffs; a place covered in yellowing brambles, strewn with graves, which mostly have no stone and no name, a hotch-potch of rubble, half-buried under the earth.

For now, his grave still looks new, but soon it, too, will be over-run by weeds, Death's timekeepers, and it, too, like all the others, will become part of the landscape. In a few years, if that part of China is opened to foreigners and if you want to make a pilgrim-age there before it crumbles, don't go in the rainy season but the dry season, when the waters that flood the graveyard have ebbed away. You'll recognise my father's grave; there's nothing engraved on the stone, in keeping with his last wish, which he swore me to respect: nothing, not a word or his name or a date, just a rough, white stone and its wavering reflection on the surface of the water, along with the reflection of the clouds, the sky and the trees, like in a dream.

30TH MARCH

Weeks later Tumchooq's letter still causes me pain, especially as his words are now associated with a smell of medicine, formalin, disinfectant, the gynaecologist's and nurses' breath, the smell of the hospital, where, after he'd left, I had an abortion, and during the operation, in between snatches of his letter, which I recited to myself, alongside the snap of rubber gloves, the clink of scissors, scalpels and other metallic instruments, I heard, or thought I heard, a whimper from the foetus—the endearing but contradictory excrescence of our dead love, ripped from my body. Every time the memory of that whimper resurfaces I try to persuade myself it was pure hallucination, produced by the physical pain, but even though this soothing hypothesis is plausible and eases my suffering, some nights I still think I can hear that feeble cry.

Because of haemorrhaging, the gynaecologist kept me in hospital for a few days. I shared a room with seven Chinese women, all of whom had turbans tightly bound round their foreheads, and this, according to their customs, would protect them from the stealthy onset of evil postnatal energies, which could subject them to chronic incurable migraines for the rest of their lives. The door to the ward kept opening as the parents of newly delivered mothers came to visit; when they finally left, the door would swing open again, this time for the colleagues of another patient. I found these constant visits, punctuating our days until late in the evening, unbearably moving, not for the human warmth or family solidarity they demonstrated, but because I saw newborn babies being shown off, a scene endlessly repeated, as if on purpose, bringing tears to my eyes and making me shake with envy. Even if the baby wasn't particularly beautiful or contented, it only had to look randomly in my direction to unleash a surge of vicious jealousy in me, a jealousy that neither Tumchooq nor any other man before or after him had ever or would ever ignite in me. I would have suffered less in a prison cell than in that ward where a demographic sample of married women, all of them at least ordinary if not downright stupid, already had a foothold in Heaven. That ward was their paradise, but it was Hell for me.

I remember an anecdote my father told me: for a long time he was troubled by a tumour on his prostate and the whole time he was ill he didn't dream, but a week after his operation, which was more or less successful, he had a dream. I had the same beginnings of recovery on my third night in hospital when, for the first time since Tumchooq left, I had a dream. It was a dream I'd already had a few months earlier in the greengrocer's shop on Little India Street, but I didn't immediately recognise it. The mountain path was covered in thick fog through which I could barely make out a faltering glow of light, which grew gradually brighter as it drew closer, eventually turning out to be a torch made of bamboo canes, as in my previous dream. This time I was the one holding it. It was attracting a cloud of moths, invisible until they reached me, milling from all sides to dance about, captivated by that one splash of light in the mountains, describing thousands and thousands of trajectories around me. Some were enormous, the most extraordinary shapes, with stripes in such fantastic colours they blurred my sight, which was already struggling to make out the sides of the path through the mist. Even though I was edging forwards like a sleepwalker, I had a vague sense of déjà vu, a sort of recollection, like when you sit at a piano and play a Beethoven sonata you've heard someone else play. It amplifies the emotion, each note has a different ring to it under your fingers, putting you in a sort of trance. With this dream I knew the script, I knew there was a fall lying in wait for me, but all my vigilance and precautions proved pointless, I couldn't avoid the inevitable: putting one foot wrong. I let go of the torch and clung to a tuft of wild grass by the side of the path to try to stop myself from crashing to the base of the cliff. The moths were invisible again now, humming around my ears, their wings flitting over my nose and skimming past my lips, as if trying to get inside my mouth. I can remember when I woke up feeling a kind of euphoria, like when a close friend you've almost forgotten because they're so far away suddenly reappears. That torn roll of silk was the only thing Tumchooq had left me. At the time I felt an almost deeper affection for that fable, which had surrendered itself to me so entirely, than I did for Tumchooq, while the person who introduced me to its mystery had decided to distance himself and make it impossible for me to share in his suffering.

After that dream I walked out of the hospital ward and scuttled down the stairs like a fugitive. There was no one in the reception area for the gynaecology unit, but there was a cold smell of milk, an aggressive smell of nurseries, which made me reel in disgust.

I cut across the cycle park, then a huge deserted court-yard. The night watchman was asleep. I found myself out on a cold, dark, grey street. A road sweeper in blue uniform, armed with a long broom with a bamboo handle, was picking up rubbish and dead leaves. The icy wind made me shiver, and with every step I took I felt a slight pain deep inside, but I set off on a long solitary walk, driven partly by a tentative new energy, partly for other reasons I can't explain.

All at once I understood from the distinctive smell of the street I was walking along that I was in the middle of the Muslim quarter of Peking. The shops were closed, but the deserted street was permeated by a stale smell of mutton and beef. I walked past the mosque and along the perimeter wall of the Buddhist University which was once very famous—for instructing high-ranking monks—but had been closed since the beginning of the Cultural Revolution, and still was, even after Mao's death. Through gaps in the crumbling wall I caught glimpses of buildings under construction, bamboo scaffolding, twinkling with frost in the glare of spotlights.

After the university I went past the headquarters of the Chinese Buddhist Association, considered throughout the country as the supreme authority of this religion. It was still dark. There was something touching about that night-time walk, which plunged me into a state of melancholy: the cold of Peking, its gloomy half-light . . . soon I would be leaving them for ever, I knew that, out of love for Tumchooq. "I'll do what he's done"—that was the determined decision I'd made during the abortion.

There was a fragrance hanging in the air, exquisite yet light and one I couldn't immediately identify, but eventually recognised: incense. Like a taste of what lay ahead, that delicate smell filling the streets steered me to the Temple of the "Source of Truth." I hesitated outside the doors, guarded by two stone lions, but had hardly touched them before they swung open silently before me and I was instantly bathed in so much heat, so much candlelight, the smell of chrysanthemums and of incense, that I stayed on the doorstep for a long time, feeling as if a gentle blessing had touched my forehead with that waft of warm air.

A group of monks—how many of them were there? thirty? fifty?—came into the main hall, knelt down and began intoning a prayer chant so beautiful I started praying with them and singing, not in Chinese like them, but in French; first for my aborted baby's soul or its ghost, then for its grandfather's, Paul d'Ampère, for its father, Tumchooq, and also for myself.

To this day I don't know whether at the time (things are so different and indefinable when you're young), given the barbarous gang murder of Paul d'Ampère and Tumchooq's irrevocable departure, whether there were any options other than the hasty decisions I made, which, like Tumchooq's, were more a protest, a cry from the heart, than an actual choice: leaving the country and never speaking its language again. Did I consider for a moment that such a decisive act was a waste of long years of study and work intended to achieve a doctorate, and would arouse anger and disappointment in my family who financed my studies? I don't remember. The only elements engraved on my memory were packing my bags and the terrible wrench of having to leave behind my books in Chinese, a condition of my commitment. I took a long time deciding what to do with them, stood gazing at them for hours, particularly the ones that Tumchooq and I had unearthed at the flea market in the "Pan Family Gardens" (a market only open at dawn, where treasure hunters rummaged through mountains of paper under the feeble halo of street lamps, a hazy, dreamy light filled with dancing motes of dust).

The courtyard outside my dormitory was silent and deserted. Like a thief, using just the tips of my fingers, I opened a book with a stitched cover, the once white thread now blackened with age, and leafed through it for the last time; it was a book of notes made by an erudite member of the Qing dynasty on ancient books he had read. The paper was thin, made of hemp, and the ideograms—printed in vertical lines not using lead characters as they are now, but from engraved wooden boards steeped in black ink—seemed to me to have a life of their own. Each page quivered in my fingers, as if the scholar had transmitted his very soul into the book. His words, I could tell, had jealously harboured this soul until that very moment and were now distilling it in me. On the brink of abandoning my radical decision to sever all links with Chinese, I bent closer to read what he had written, but, unbelievably, even though I perfectly understood the structure, punctuation, hidden meanings, syntactical subtleties, etc., I couldn't pronounce a word out loud. My tongue froze, my lips refused to move, not a single sound came from my mouth. Disturbed by this perilous, almost nightmarish experience, I watched as the sentences dissolved before my eyes into isolated ideograms, unconnected signs in which all I could read were the insults and whoops of joy bellowed by the prisoners who had lynched Paul d'Ampère. Murderous words. Once again, imaginary or not, I heard the muffled cry of the foetus, filling me with shame and terror, which drove me on. In a hysterical outburst, shedding tears that were as uncontrollable as they were liberating, with brash, almost masculine movements amplified by the cold, I lit a fire in the deserted courtyard and threw all my books onto it. Licked by the flames, those precious works began to turn red, yellow, black, eventually reduced to cinders. Watching the flakes of black ash, light as goosedown, wafting up, hanging in the air, drifting off in the darkness and falling back down on my head, I realised just how much I loved and how closely I identified with Tumchooq.

"I am Tumchooq," I told myself.

PART TWO

WANDERINGS

1979 — 1990

I

IN APRIL 1979, ONE YEAR AND FOUR months after arriving in Peking—where I had acquired not only a perfect Chinese accent but also a rich vocabulary, including the city's own vernacular with its distinct, palatalised sounds—I broke off with China (no, you can't ever break off with China, only run away from it) and went back to Paris, to the Latin Quarter. I moved into Concordia, a student hall of residence close to the Rue Mouffetard.

Though typically French, this pedestrian street with medieval paving stones is not without similarities to Little India Street. It is just as narrow and slightly winding with a long, gentle slope edged with souvenir shops, perfumeries, chemists, a post office, Greek restaurants, bookshops, newspaper kiosks, butchers, cheesemongers, shops selling orthopaedic shoes, children's clothes, leather bags and, where it crosses the Rue de l'Arbalète, a street market for fruit and vegetables which exhales the same odoriferous (a word Proust often used) smells as Tumchooq's shop. Apart from two or three items from Africa, it sells more or less the same things, perhaps in better condition, in brighter, more commercial colours. The salesmen are mostly of Arab origin and as they holler the names of the vegetables and their prices they remind me of Tumchooq's colleagues, lame and in poor health, shouting with little real energy, but who adopted me without any political prejudice, thinking of me as part of the shop's family. What I should have done, and I regret not doing, was to go and say goodbye to them or at least witness one last time the collective theft from the State's tills in those few seconds of deliberate darkness.

In my frequent bouts of nostalgia I spent a lot of time in that market on the Rue Mouffetard, not buying anything, happy just to gaze at the vegetables, touch them, smell them. Sometimes my old friend White-Tuft—my Peking rabbit, another victim of assassination—popped into my mind and I remembered him nibbling my hand when I offered him the vegetables Tumchooq had given me. A few years later, when I moved to the Rue Daguerre, I found an almost identical market. Little India Street was definitely following me around.

Returning to Paris was a pleasure and I got back into the rhythm of more harmonious times. I was lucky to get a room at Concordia, once a delightful private home, now converted into a students' hall of residence, with a huge reception room on the ground floor complete with domed ceiling, immaculately waxed parquet floor, an untuned grand piano and a pair of double doors opening onto the garden. To the right of the reception room was a cheap canteen, perfectly suited to my limited means—a loan from the Banque National de Paris, which I eventually finished paying off many years later. To the left was the television room, where we had a democratic vote every evening to decide which channel to watch, and the reading room, where every inch of wall space

was covered in bookshelves laden with general encyclopae-
dias, Larousse dictionaries, every sort of language dictionary,
etc. On the imposing marble-topped reading tables were
porcelain lamps with green shades, giving a soft, pleasant
light, which soothed my painful memories of China. I discovered almost the exact same lights in the library at my college (where we sat between the bookshelves), the National
Institute for Oriental Languages and Civilisations, where I
enrolled in the first year to study Tibetan.

I decided to take this new tack in my university education
with Tumchooq's tacit agreement, at least that was what I
imagined, hoping he hadn't forgotten our past discussions
about Tibet. In intellectual terms, Tumchooq was one of
those Chinese (was he really and is he still?) who lived in a
state of disillusion with his own culture for a long time and
then, in the 1980s, hoped to find new inspiration from the
Tibetans. In personal terms, in his search for the missing part
of the sutra, Tibet fired his imagination, because its culture
was so imbued with Buddhism he assumed that the integral
text from the torn scroll should logically be somewhere
among all the sacred works accumulated over the centuries
by the Tibetans—at least a Tibetan version if not actually a
Tumchooq one. Who knows? I once read a book by a German author that told the story of a scholar looking for the
oldest map of Tibet: in a nomad's tent in the middle of the
Mongolian steppe he came across a hundred or so pages of
text written in an unknown language, which the owner considered to be a "relic from Buddha," refusing to let him have
it whatever price and whatever terms he suggested. The German scholar only secured the right to photograph them. As
the inside of the tent was too dark, the shots were taken out-

side in windy conditions and, despite their precautions and best efforts to keep the pages relatively if precariously still, when the photographs were developed on his return to Europe they all proved to be failures, out of focus, condemned without question to the dustbin. Learning Tibetan had been our common aim, for Tumchooq and me, and by doing this I felt I was involving myself in his late father's unfinished undertaking.

When I made this resolution a suspicion I had harboured for some time floated to the forefront of my mind: Was I deluding myself that this was love? I was trying to give so much to Tumchooq, unbeknown to him, but would he give me any sign of gratitude or affection in return? The fact that he had excluded me from his suffering was a bitter pill I swallowed out of solidarity and unconditional love. But it still tormented me so much I felt I was swallowing it all over again each time I woke alone in bed with sheets drenched with sweat. I swore that if life helped me find him again I would allow myself the satisfaction of establishing—out of a simple desire to know the truth—whether or not he thought of me on the day that he decided never to speak Chinese again and to leave his country.

What is left now of those three years of arduous study and constant enthusiasm? Tibetan words often crop up in my mind without warning, and from time to time I find myself coming out with unexpectedly beautiful sentences, and they have a ring to them which reminds me of the Tumchooq language. Sentences like that, sometimes even single words with no more significance than any other, delighted me back in the days when I was learning them. Sitting in the classroom, I thought for a few seconds I could see them glittering like a cloud of pollen, grains of fine sand, equipped with special Tumchooqian powers, borne on the breeze to my tutorial group, where they fell on me like gentle rain, especially when they were spoken by Mr. Tarakesa, who taught us Buddhism. He was a blind Tibetan monk, tall, thin and in his sixties, with a face like a medieval ascetic and an ability to recite sutras from memory, which gave him near legendary status among the students (by an ironic twist of fate, the first four letters of his name, *tara,* meant *eye* in Sanskrit and Tumchooq). He started his course with this sentence, which I like to think is still engraved on all his students' memories: "The scope of sacred Buddhist books, called sutras, is as vast as an ocean on which each of us is a small boat edging forwards, losing its way, then edging forwards again."

One day in mid-October, after asking us to read extracts from Tantric texts, he handed out photocopies of the last chapter of the *Gtandavyuhasi-Sutra* in both Tibetan and French. I started to read the Tibetan version but, struggling with a word, glanced at the French. My eyes then fell on a text with such distinctive syntax that I immediately felt only one person could have written it—because no one else wrote like that. I had read all his books and his articles published in scholarly reviews and I recognised his inflexions, his very individual tone, his style, the unique way he constructed a sentence like a silkworm drawing a longer and longer thread produced from its own juices, weaving that thread, forming a structure and eventually a cocoon in which to take refuge, protected from the outside world, his long sentences characterised by terse, unexpectedly enlightening conclusions, which alter the meaning of the words that have gone before. (The only work of his to escape this rule is his *Notes on Marco*

Polo's Book of the Wonders of the World, in which his style is more neutral, less individual.) I asked the professor whether Paul d'Ampère was the translator of the text. Mr. Tarakesa confirmed that he was and showed me the book: *Teachings of the Gtandavyuhasi-Sutra,* translated and annotated by Paul d'Ampère, University of Louvain, Institute of Oriental Studies, 1962.

The last chapter of this sutra relates the eventful travels of an intelligent and modest novice monk who roamed the world in search of fifty-eight "bodhisattva"—his fifty-eight instructors who each adopted a deceptive appearance as a monk, a nun, a tribal patriarch, a doctor, a monarch, a sailor, an immortal, a heretic, a beggar, a thief, a prostitute, etc. Drawing on their experience of all human passions, they reinforced their own sanctity; those whose lives were full of sin relied on their vices to uncover the profound inanity of existence, thereby establishing a universal moral rule. It was Mr. Tarakesa's favourite sutra and his lesson would turn into a theatrical performance where, by altering his voice, he acted out the discussions between the novice and his good teachers disguised behind their different masks, sketching in the setting, adding descriptions of their social background, their clothes (probably only from his own imagination), offering philological analyses worthy of a linguist, making comparisons between the Tibetan and French versions, and emphasising the subtlety of their choice of words.

If only Paul d'Ampère could hear this from beyond the grave, I thought, could hear his translation recited from memory by this erudite, blind scholar whose eyes, covered with a translucent white film, shimmered on the days the sun appeared through the window, but turned a hazy, pearly grey and closed altogether when he lost himself in one of his recitations, chanting the text non-stop and giving a running commentary, as if in a dream. The more I heard Mr. Tarakesa delivering Paul d'Ampère's French text—he spent two months teaching us that sutra—the more I felt his words were secretly linking me to d'Ampère's son. The French translation cast a spell like an enchanted island; it was a steamboat stripped of all its weight, gliding silently round the room, so that none of my fellow students suspected it was there, looming out of nowhere, tall, majestic, with me as its only passenger, the happy, chosen stowaway whose privileged status no one else could guess. In those few moments how much I regretted having that abortion, not being able to keep our child and bring it up on my own to perpetuate the ancestral genius of the d'Ampères, or at least, as a grandmother might say, to carry on their name. When Tumchooq and I no longer exist, there would still have been a d'Ampère in the world to embody our affection for Paul, and to love him.

Mr. Tarakesa was quick to become an ally after I sent him a long letter in which I gave him a two-page résumé of d'Ampère's life and confessed I was searching for a sutra, half of which he had translated. He couldn't remember being aware of this sutra and spent sleepless nights pacing up and down his studio, gazing out of the window for hours, trying to prise from his memory—which was a living library—any recollection of a similar parable in an Indian sutra or an analogous allegory that Buddha might have used in his frequent teachings, but in vain. He promised he would ask other Tibetan scholars, exiled—as he was—in various corners of the world, and specialists he knew in Cambridge, Oxford, Heidelberg, Harvard, Stanford, etc.

This investigation went on for almost all of my second year of Tibetan study. It was led, with great generosity, by Mr. Tarakesa, and from time to time it opened up leads which at first seemed interesting, but which proved on closer inspection to be false. None of his colleagues' suggestions escaped the law by which each new possibility eradicates its predecessor, and none of them unearthed anything definitive about the sutra itself. The documents coming in from the four corners of the world, each more valuable than the last, were mostly about the Tumchooq kingdom, where recent archaeological finds had revealed its origins, its silk production and its totem-pole-based religion prior to its conversion to Buddhism.

To mark my gratitude I offered to go to Mr. Tarakesa's house once a week and read to him, either in Tibetan or French. He accepted, to my considerable surprise.

"I would like to hear," he said, "the language which Paul d'Ampère was first to decipher and of which I don't understand a blessed word."

I couldn't refuse him this pleasure even though I was aware that my knowledge of Tumchooq, in which I had been initiated by a greengrocer, would not match his expectations. And so our weekly trips to the kingdom of Tumchooq began. On Saturday mornings I would go to his studio in the Rue du Cherche-Midi, a place which in many ways was like a hermitage, perched on the seventh floor (the red stair carpet stopped at the sixth), a former maid's room under the eaves, transformed into a sort of sanctuary, with the tray and plastic curtain for an electric shower plonked crookedly across one corner. There was hardly any furniture, but a statue of Buddha had pride of place on a purely decorative mantelpiece

and above it hung a large mirror in which, on each of my visits, I watched my reflection prostrate itself before the golden
statue, while my prayers were accompanied by a rhythm
beaten out on a ritual wooden instrument by Mr. Tarakesa,
in ceremonial dress beside me. Then he took off his robes
and, in his shirt sleeves, lit the gas stove to make Tibetan tea;
the nozzles made a soft whistling sound, the bluish flames
flickered over the Buddha's face . . . and I started reading
extracts of Tumchooq texts, most of them published in historical and archaeological reviews and orientalists' mono-
graphs, which I had read and reread over the course of the
week, until I achieved a degree of fluency.

I still don't know what frame of mind he was in as he listened to me reading. Did he let those unfamiliar words carry
him away on a sort of cloud, taking him on a journey back
through time until he heard the voice of a loved one in that
foreign language? Did he see it as a kind of meditation echoing a higher state, which allowed him to pray and bless all
humanity, if not actually to save it, a meditation undermined
by my poor pronunciation and strong French accent? I
kept wanting to ask him whether the world was as empty,
as pointless and as incomprehensible as the words I spoke.
I sometimes even suspected he was simply reliving Paul
d'Ampère's life, one episode at a time; the oval of his cheek
would stretch obliquely, filling out with the intensity of his
emotions as he let slip a barely perceptible, knowing smile.
Occasionally, without any apparent connection to what I was
reading, his face would tense, his features harden, screwing
themselves up and then relaxing again, and no alteration to
the rhythm or resonance of my voice could do anything to
change what he was feeling. Who was inspiring these feel-

ings in him? The French orientalist? It was as if he had known him, as if they had been the greatest friends in the world. Quite often, after a couple of hours' reading, we would go out to have some lunch, almost without exception in a Vietnamese restaurant on the corner of the Rue du Cherche-Midi and the Boulevard de Montparnasse, where he would sit in his usual place behind a huge aquarium of goldfish and always eat the same dish, a vegetarian noodle soup, even though the Tibetan school of Diamond Way Buddhism—which states that anyone can achieve enlightenment and become Buddha—allows its monks to consume meat in moderation, the Tibetan climate making it a necessity.

After our meal we went and had coffee in the little café opposite called Le Chien qui Fume, then he would go home and I would catch a metro from Duroc station to get back to the Latin Quarter. I never allowed myself to insist on seeing him back to his studio, for he loathed being an object of pity, except when he suggested I read to him in the afternoon. Those afternoons sometimes went right on until the light failed, both of us enjoying a sense of calm and delight as we bathed in the charm of the Tumchooq language. I felt at peace with myself at last, as if nothing could threaten my newfound equilibrium. Well, almost.

A curvaceous young woman, who lived in the building opposite in a studio also under the eaves on the seventh floor facing the one belonging to the Tibetan monk, appeared in the window at regular intervals and undertook a shameless seduction scene intended for my instructor's neighbour— a young Greek doctor doing time as a houseman in Paris— who was also at his window. Separated from each other by the street, they embarked on an aerial conversation, clearly discernible as it batted back and forth. Their exchanges, which became more provocative with every passing minute and were delicious in their simplicity, grew increasingly audible as my weary reading voice feebly mumbling Tumchooq words eventually constituted nothing more than background noise to their vaudeville performance, and we were reduced to the status of privileged spectators in the front row of the stalls. At some point the question was settled, the young woman left her window and the action moved to the future Greek surgeon's studio on the other side of a party wall thinner than a sheet of cardboard, plunging my tutor and me into a state of appalling embarrassment, defenceless against an auditory onslaught of excited laughter, undressing noises, exclamations and female comments about the size of the Hellenic medical student's member, encouragements, filthy words, creaking bedsprings, groans of ecstasy—my God, it went on, every second felt like an eternity! Their moans came through the wall without any loss of intensity, taking the statue of Buddha by storm, coagulating in the air between the Tibetan monk and me, smothering my voice so that, in spite of the heroic stoicism I displayed, my sentences in Tumchooq lost their resonance, their musicality, their rhythm, becoming as bleak and monotonous as bare mountains, bare beaches, a bare horizon in that bare studio, ready to collapse when the two neighbours' cries accelerated faster and faster until they eventually exploded into Greek monosyllables that the Olympian hero hurled in our faces in all their enormity as his exploits reached their climax.

Of all the Tumchooq texts I had laid hands on, Mr.

Tarakesa delighted most in the one from the mutilated scroll and would regularly begin a morning session by asking me to read and reread it; and, if he wanted me to carry on reading in the afternoon, it was always to devote the time to that text, either in the original language or in the French translation, or even in the Tibetan version that he himself had established and dictated to me. That portion of text was his chosen one, it seemed to be part of his furniture, on a par with his gas stove or his teapot. He accumulated different commentaries on it, frequently making comparisons with *The Jatakas,* accounts of Buddha's previous lives, which form an important part of the Buddhist canon in Pali and which he knew by heart. I sensed that he secretly hoped to bring his learning to bear on the unknown and, in his meditations, to find the end of the fable, even if its conclusion turned out to be just a single sentence.

Our weekly sessions carried on for nearly a year with a few interruptions during school holidays, then Mr. Tarakesa left for New York, where the Dalai Lama had entrusted him with an important responsibility. It was a Thursday when I learnt from another tutor that he had resigned from the Institute of Oriental Languages. I couldn't wait until that Saturday morning's session, our last, and went to see him the same evening. He welcomed me in, surprised to see me. I had barely sat down, while he—as usual—prepared the tea, before I burst into tears. I knew he was embarrassed by my outburst, but I found it impossible to contain, overwhelmed by the sorrow of separation from the last person who connected me to everything I loved, to the Tumchooq language and, therefore, to Tumchooq himself. I was filled with fierce depression and a feeling of loneliness; until then I had been bolstered, sustained and brightened by the hope that I would one day see the mutilated scroll completed by Mr. Tarakesa, a hope he was now burying for ever. I recovered my composure as best I could, and when he started talking it was to ask me, as if he, too, were obsessed by the missing part of the manuscript, to let him know if the other fragment of the scroll or the integral text of the sutra were ever found. He himself, he admitted as much, had tried to imagine the ending, but in vain, even though the character in the fable—the man hanging on the edge of the cliff—had often appeared to him in his little studio, suspended in mid-air, a few inches above the floorboards, for longer than the laws of gravity allowed, but each time the image had vanished almost the moment he saw it.

"What I need," he told me with a sigh, "is a pair of those golden wings like founders of religions, great philosophers, Buddha himself and some of his disciples, wings that allowed them to 'take off' and fly over the world. Without them, a mere mortal like you or me can never hope to be up to the task."

"Even Paul d'Ampère?" I asked him.

He looked embarrassed by the question, repeated Paul d'Ampère's name several times, then, after a long silence, said:

"I know him only from his work and from what you've told me about him. An individual as exceptional as him—erudite, sensitive and with his experience of suffering—would probably have acquired those wings and been able to fly. And I wouldn't have been surprised if he had found the end of the parable, except that he was a Westerner."

"I don't see the connection." My voice had a slightly shaky quality.

"Our imagination is dictated by who we are. It seems to me that finding the end of a teaching like that requires an entirely oriental mind, far beyond dissertations on the outside world, explorations of human conscience and earthly passions, beyond the unpredictable beauty of an isolated sentence or image . . ."

I brought an abrupt end to the visit, not even letting him finish what he was saying. I even ran to get away, because I was so exasperated by the way he talked about Paul d'Ampère. Whatever we do, we're still just "Westerners" to them! Among themselves they can have hatred, wars and massacres, but they know each other, understand each other and never think of each other as foreigners.

I can't remember whether I slammed the door or how I got out onto the street, but I do know my whole body was shaking, on the brink of hysteria, and I had to sit down at the bottom of the steps for God knows how long. Then I went home on foot, dragging my feet beneath icy rain, which reminded me of that sad night coming out of hospital in Peking when I wandered like a sleepwalker in a state of immense loneliness. When I reached Concordia, tortured by an appalling migraine, I locked myself in my room and stayed in bed for three days, more dead than alive. Since that day I've never set foot in the Tibetan department again. At a stroke, I sloughed off the three languages (Chinese, Tumchooq and Tibetan) that I had learnt for the sake of someone I loved, someone who had disappeared in the meantime; languages which had come to be—and would remain—prisons in which I shut myself away.

My renunciation of three Asian languages began a slow eradication of my memories of Tumchooq, perhaps even a decline in my love for him. The fact that he was not with me hurt less: my heartache was abating. The only thing that survived was my pleasure in learning languages. That is why, in late September 1983, with what was left of my bank loan, I went back to the Institute of Oriental Languages, this time to enrol in the African Studies department, where I started learning Bambara, a perfect contradiction not only of my parents' expectations for my future life but also of my own.

2

TO BE HONEST, AT THE TIME I HAD NO concept of what an African language might be, even less of the workings of humanitarian organisations, but I signed up as a volunteer to one barely a year after I began studying Bambara. Out in the field I threw myself wholeheartedly into a project to build a school in northern Mali, three hundred kilometres from Bamako, near the former capital of the Songhai Empire.

With a naïvety which now brings a smile to my lips, I could already see myself as a schoolteacher surrounded by dozens of orphans of all ages, staying on after lessons to take them down to the Niger and watch them have fun, jump, swim and play hide-and-seek while the great red disc of the sun dropped slowly into the river, where bare-breasted washerwomen stood waist-deep in the water, singing and laughing as they beat wet clothes over stones with wooden sticks that made a dull, slightly muffled thud. I myself would bathe the youngest children (Would I have known how to? Is being born a woman enough for that skill?), supporting the toddler's streaming back with one hand and soaping him with the other. Then I would tell him to wriggle his arms and legs in every direction in time to the washerwomen's jubilant song, or do a slight variation on this the way African mothers do: bunching the child's arms and legs over his tummy, then suddenly letting them go and smothering his silky soft naked body with kisses, as if he were my own baby, my child from Peking who, as he grew up, had changed skin colour—a frequent phenomenon in dreams, where physical appearances go unnoticed, can be modified and are often interchangeable. As I cared for my little orphans I would wash myself of the last stains I felt still deep inside me and which still hurt. I imagined they would dissolve like refracted prisms in the Niger.

Because most people live with constant anxiety about finding their place in society, few can afford the luxury of healing a broken heart in Africa. I was exceptionally lucky, I realised that. I was a chosen one, greeted each new day by this preferential treatment, which smiled down on me like the sun above the mists of the African bush. By coming in contact with life in its raw state (absent in Western societies so well organised they have frozen rigid), the hitherto inconceivable idea that love isn't eternal and can die no longer frightened me. On the contrary, I discovered to my stupefaction all the beauty of a lost love, a melancholy liberating beauty, a sort of macabre dance in which I twirled and spun like a madwoman. I threw myself at strangers, meeting my one-night stands in the bush and Bamako's kitsch restaurants, and eventually they all looked like a familiar ghost, Tumchooq.

The experiences I had then were salutary. Is there just one single love in a lifetime? Are all our lovers—from the first to the last, including the most fleeting—part of that unique

love, and is each of them merely an expression of it, a variation, a particular version? In the same way that in literature
there is just one true masterpiece to which different writers
give a particular form (taking the twentieth century alone:
Joyce, who explores everything happening inside his character's head with microscopic precision; Proust, for whom the
present is merely a memory of the past; Kafka, who drifts on
the margins between dream and reality; the blind Borges,
probably the one I relate to best, etc.). I imagine that if they
met they would each apologise for stepping onto the shared
stage too soon.

Perhaps it's in my nature, but in Mali I had no more success than anywhere else in forging peaceable relationships
with my compatriots within the humanitarian family. It
really was stronger than me, I couldn't help giving my opinion about everything going on around me, saying what I
liked and what I found shocking: for example, the colossal
amount our organisation spent on communication, which
matched what was spent on work in the field; the difference
in wages between white "managers" and black employees;
the fierce competition—worthy of privately owned compa-
nies—between different organisations, etc. I therefore had a
feeling of relief, almost of deliverance, when I could finally
spend my time in a dug-out canoe on the river Niger. This
started in June 1985, when the first delivery of school equipment arrived after my long campaign to acquire it through
repeated letters and endless intercontinental calls to French
establishments. The equipment was intended for Ansongo in
the Gao region, where I had been trying for several months
to set up a school for the Songhais. The railway does not go
beyond Bamako, so wood, animal fodder, cooking pots,

dried fish and every imaginable sort of produce is transported along the Niger in large hand-built boats. I had mine constructed as follows: an impressively thick beam ten metres long and five wide was hoisted and fixed onto several canoes connected together to form a sort of platform, and equipped with an old engine, which could be heard banging and spluttering several kilometres away, worse than a pneumatic drill.

I recruited two crew members, a retired boatman and his wife, who would work as our cook, and I had the equipment, sent from goodness knows what prehistoric hangar, loaded on: desks and benches which looked pre-war if not from colonial days, two or three blackboards with flaking paint, and boxes of exercise books, chalk, pencils and pens. I called my vessel *Tumchooq,* and in black ink in the mysterious letters of that ancient language—despite the waning spell they had over my heart, I still thought them beautiful and irreplaceable—I wrote the name on a yellow flag, which I attached in the middle of a pile of desks to the bridge of my African craft. When anyone asked what my banner meant and I replied that it was the name of the greatest greengrocer in Peking, people eyed me suspiciously as if I'd gone quite mad.

Like Marlow in *Heart of Darkness* and like Conrad himself, both of whom travelled up the Congo on a small steamboat, I went down the smaller Niger on board the *Tumchooq,* from the clear waters at Bamako, through a series of rapids at Satuba, across the Mandingo Plateaux, taking four days to cross the vast Macina plain with its network of tributaries, lakes and swamps. At times my boat, its engine screaming, toiled through putrefying weeds that undulated below the surface like hair. My boatman stood at the prow, prodding the riverbed with a pole, while I held the tiller, which left a wake through the mud and weeds, stirring up a swampy stench and prodigious quantities of mosquitoes. But none of this dampened my mood and, after that difficult stretch, we came back onto the winding but clearly defined main channel.

I turned off the engine and everything was quiet again; all we could hear was the sound of the water, as old as the world. The exhausted boatman drank some dolo and fell asleep, blind drunk, over the rudder, and *Tumchooq* drifted. It was such a pleasure seeing the boat abandon itself to the whims of the current that night, where, just like in the mutilated scroll deciphered by Paul d'Ampère, the moon, masked by dark, low clouds, did not appear. The boat was no longer navigating but gliding over that ebony surface, occasionally bumping into the bank and setting off again in the right direction.

After midnight the moon appeared, illuminating a few meagre huts along the way, dark, silent family homes. In places there were nameless aquatic plants with purple flowers, their stalks and roots mixed in with wide flat leaves and slender reeds. Further on, small islands of flowers floated on the water, paler, more grainy and crumpled. Overwhelmed by sleep, I climbed up onto the cases of stationery, lay down on a desk, perhaps the very one my grandparents used, and fell asleep, just like that.

I was woken by a noise: swaying and lurching, the old boatman was making his way towards the back of our square vessel. Moving almost with the virtuosity of an acrobat and the slow stealth of a sleepwalker, he climbed down to the rudder, the upper blade of which was half submerged in the water. Once there, he paused, took down his trousers, squatted and stayed motionless in that position for as long as the procedure took. I couldn't help laughing out loud when he almost lost his precarious balance and fell into the river as he bent right down to water level to wash his buttocks.

After Mopti, a major trading centre with a fishing port where the Niger is joined by the Bani, one of its main tributaries, *Tumchooq* set off across the limestone and sandstone plateaux of the Bandiagara region in Dogon Country. Villages became increasingly scarce and we could travel for hours without glimpsing a human presence as far as the eye could see, apart from columns of smoke rising in the distance over the vast bush. Towards midday we suddenly heard the sound of an engine in the sky and, apparently swooping out of nowhere, a drumming helicopter appeared overhead, extraordinarily low and slow-moving, its powerful draft flattening the weeds along the banks and making our bodies vibrate so much they felt drained of all substance. Painted in yellow on the cockpit door beneath the blades were the words: EMBASSY OF USA. *Tumchooq* was paralysed, quivering in every limb, and its flag flew off in the air when the mechanical monster whirred away, gleaming in the blinding sunlight.

Three hours later we came across it again in a Dogon village, with a team from the American embassy, Malian soldiers and local policemen who had come by jeep. They were outside tall, round straw huts with thatched roofs and were surrounded by naked children and the silent intensity of a crowd of locals in rags. The body of an American missionary, with hair so dusty it looked like an albino's, was carried to the helicopter on a handcart. The body had been found in the bush, about ten kilometres from the village. According to the Malian policeman I spoke to, it was going to be difficult to identify the perpetrator of this appalling crime, because the wounds and marks found on the missionary were unusual, and the body was in an advanced state of decay. The local Dogons claimed the culprit was a bull giraffe roaming the area, a solitary creature six metres tall (a whole metre above average) and known for his violence during the rutting season.

We continued on our way and, two days later, reached the Timbuktu region, the starting point for Saharan caravans where the river, which until then is angled from south-west to north-east, begins a long eastward curve, forming a pretty loop, narrowing through the gorge at Tosaye and curving out towards the south-east at Bourem. We finally arrived in Gao, the former capital of the Songhai empire, crossed the Tilemsi Valley and made our way down to the Ansongo Valley through a series of rapids.

Savouring a moment of relaxation, I looked at my surroundings with the eye of a schoolteacher who would spend the rest of her life there: a quiet valley where they grew rice, cotton, groundnuts, millet, sorghum, etc. *Tumchooq* was warmly welcomed by the Songhais; the school equipment was unloaded, admired and transported to one of the major villages, where it was put into attractive buildings with domed roofs. After resting for two days I set off again on my African boat, heading back upriver for a second delivery of equipment from France due to arrive in Bamako.

Although released from the weight of the equipment, *Tumchooq* suffered more on the return journey, finding it harder to resist the river's assaults: water seeped into the canoes supporting the platform of my unusual-shaped vessel; we had to bail constantly, with calabashes, only rarely exchanging the odd word. I decided to stop off in the Dogon village where we had seen the American embassy helicopter, because it started raining and the menacing black clouds indicated a violent downpour. As I ran through the rain I caught sight of a strange object attached to the top of a post at the entrance to the village. From a distance this thing, which appeared hazy through the raindrops, looked about the size of a small box of sweets dangling on the end of a rod; swaying beneath the box, fragile as a ribbon, was an endlessly long thin shape, which fell right to the ground. As I drew closer the box grew bigger until it overflowed my field of vision: it was a wooden cage with a head imprisoned behind its bars, not a man's head as in *Heart of Darkness,* but a giraffe's. I had to touch the ribbon hanging beneath the cage with my own fingers to grasp that it was the gigantic animal's spine.

A villager who spoke Bambara told me that after the American helicopter left, Dogons from all over the region set out to hunt down the giraffe rightly or wrongly accused of the missionary's death.

"A white man's life is priceless," he told me. The hunt seemed vital to the villagers, who were afraid of the Americans—although the embassy had formulated no concrete demands on the subject—and whose regional governor had threatened to withhold all international aid if the culprit went unpunished. The hunt had mobilised about a hundred men and two police jeeps. The scapegoat, pursued across the bush for two whole days, took refuge in the mountains, but in the end, hounded on all sides by men shouting and firing shots as they drew ever closer, it was so exhausted a breath of wind would have mown it down. In the small hours of the morning it was found dying at the foot of a white limestone cliff. It was then transported to the village, where a witch doctor finished it off.

The region had seen no rainfall for two years and Dogon children stayed out in the rain, letting it whip their naked bodies as they expressed their happiness with whoops of joy. They paddled in the mud, jumped, played, laughed and danced. One of them ran towards the post bearing the cage, but he slipped and fell in a puddle halfway. He picked himself up and, I don't know what made him do this, threw a nasty look at the cage, picked up a handful of mud, shaped it into a huge ball, which he moulded with great care and then threw with all his strength, his muscles quivering with childish glee. The soft, heavy projectile rose up through the air straight towards the giraffe's head, but missed its target. Rain streamed over the pelt of the decapitated head with its distinctive markings, dripped from the animal's long ears, filled its pinnae, ran over its forehead where a perfect tuft of hair conferred grace and nobility on its features, which looked as innocent as a newborn baby's.

Soaked from head to foot myself, I retraced my steps to *Tumchooq* and set off again. I regretted coming to that village. I regretted it bitterly, because a feeling of guilt, which had been lulled to sleep by my long stay in China, woke and descended on me with thunderous force. For the first time in my life I felt guilty for being white, or even guilty for being human, guilty for my presence in that village, or even on that continent. I now understood that I could go to impossible lengths, set up a hundred more schools for the Songhais, Dogons, Malinkes, Bambaras, Bozos, Sarkoles, Khassokes, Senoufos, Bobos, Fulanis, Tuaregs or the Maures, but I would never be free of that guilt. These thoughts churned round inside my head as *Tumchooq* toiled back up the Niger, its engine sound deadened by the rain.

It was difficult to see much. The swampy, sparsely populated plain stretching from Mopti to Segu seemed even emptier, even more desolate than on the way down. We could see nothing in the river waters (we were covering under three kilometres an hour) except, here and there, a circular eddy, a vortex, a grassy islet.

At nightfall the rain stopped at last and *Tumchooq,* struggling with the counter-current, cut through the banks of aquatic plants we came across on the way down, the ones that seemed so magnificent, but now felt hostile. They skidded swiftly towards us, cruelly barring the way to our vessel, and, in order to make any progress, we had to battle constantly, pushing them aside with our long poles. I was at the end of my strength when a swarming black cloud of mosquitoes—they seemed to have multiplied now that the rain had stopped—surged out of the darkness, attacking me from every direction, surrounding me so that I almost couldn't breathe. Real kamikazes, greedy and mindless, homing in like arrows on the tiniest patch of exposed skin. I killed quite a lot of them, and for a moment the others would abandon my veins to suck the blood-filled corpses of their companions, stuck to my skin like one large viscous scab.

By the following morning I was suffering from a terrible fever, my body on fire, blazing. As my temperature soared, my eyelids grew heavier and heavier and my ears buzzed, even though the mosquitoes had disappeared at dawn. Confused ideas collided inside my head. Huddled in a corner and racked with icy shivering, I wondered whether I was going to die. The fever still burned me from the inside like poison and spread into the hollow of my left hand, where it formed a concentration of sharper, more intense pain, while my left leg stiffened, then the whole left side of my body, with a sort of cramp which I tried to release by changing position.

From one end of that plateau to the other I ambled like the giraffe I saw as a child under the big top of a circus; fired up by the music, it danced around the ring under a garland of coloured lights. In my feverish agitation, that distant memory marked the beginning of a transference which came to a head when the boatman brought me a bowl of a dark-coloured drink, probably a decoction of medicinal herbs, and I thought I heard an animal squeal coming from my own bitter mouth. It wasn't me crying out, but the giraffe dying at the foot of the cliff, sacrificed by the Dogons, who then put its head on a pillory; unless it was the cry of the man in the sutra who, once on a moonless night, fell from a cliff.

Niger, never-ending Niger! My African boat was deteriorating as pitifully as my own physical and moral state with every metre of the river it covered. I didn't get up for a whole week, staring at the sky and constantly reciting the text from the Tumchooq manuscript. Its simple words—strange, tender, often monosyllabic—resonated like a gentle incantation, giving me the illusion that I was flying up to the clouds, diving into the water, sliding between the aquatic plants, where my body dissolved and my flesh fell away. From time to time the old boatman intoned a Malian song, our voices overlapping, our two ancient languages in harmony.

He tended me with his traditional infusions, with varying degrees of success, until we reached Segu, where he took me to a hospital, which immediately transferred me to Bamako, and from there I was repatriated to France, bringing an end to my short-lived humanitarian career. Perhaps that was written in my fate.

I DIDN'T KNOW WHAT SORT OF TROPI-
cal disease I'd contracted and the doctors had no clearer
idea. My recovery was as swift as it was mysterious, and its
only after-effect was a long period of depression following
my hospitalisation in Paris.

Still this phase was punctuated by various achievements
and broken up by bouts of enthusiasm, but the depression
was always latent and reared back up from time to time,
as regular as the breathing of the unknown demon that inhabited me, paralysing me for days on end. I was pinned to my
bed, shut away in my "glass menagerie," as I called my modest
one-bedroom apartment, whose walls I had entirely covered
with gilt-framed mirrors. (Buying a flat would have dispelled
my constant anxiety about eventually dying on the street, but
property ownership was far beyond my means and I had to
make do with renting.) My own diagnosis was that my depres-
sive state was due just as much to my unfortunate experiences, one in China and one in Mali, as to my obtaining the
highly competitive *agrégation* teaching qualification and being
given a job at a lycée in Nice, two events I felt, more or less
consciously, were betrayals of Tumchooq.

By now I was thirty-two and could already see what I would be like at sixty, or even on the eve of my death: shrivelled, fragile, toothless, almost bald, surrounded by shoe boxes full of payment slips from social security, tax invoices, pension statements, insurance certificates, bills for the phone, electricity, plumbers and travel agencies, rent receipts, bank statements, warranties and guarantees, all neatly sorted and filed in chronological order. My ossified life was set to the rhythm of weekly phone calls from my family, disastrous Christmases, unsuccessful presents, weekly shopping, constantly postponed pay rises, arguments with colleagues or neighbours, in a word all the complications of human relationships. My glass menagerie was on the Rue des Terres au Curé (a bleak name evoking an impecunious curate's measly plot of land), and I saw its apparently anodyne number, 77, as a premonition of the venerable age I would reach before breathing my last.

My windows overlooked a fish market and every morning the rumble of delivery lorries, the vendors' cries and above all the fetid stench of the sea infiltrated my bedroom, where the countless mirrors in their gold filigreed frames flashed and shone in silent competition, bouncing back multiple images of me, huddled in my bed, small and inanimate as the puppets hanging on the walls: puppets on strings representing Chinese emperors and empresses, courtiers, scholars and concubines, their long sleeves wafting in the air, swaying slightly on the end of strings connecting their shoulders and hands to two crossed rods; two or three Indonesian glove puppets, their wooden heads attached to golden costumes with hands also made of wood at the ends of the sleeves; a few traditional French *guignol* puppets, a policeman, a baker and the like. I felt like them, connected to the world by a few invisible threads, my morning cup of coffee, my work and most of all the two volumes of my Hebrew dictionary, which I had had specially bound: a silk cover lined with moiré, decorated with a clasp and corners in gold. Ever since my return to France I experienced voluptuous pleasure in touching them, handling them, turning them over, opening them and closing them. Giving in to my natural tendencies, I had set my heart on these volumes which, for a couple of hours each day, helped me in my semi-autodidactic quest to conquer those unfamiliar words, to step over the sacred threshold into the temple, to embark on a new journey of indeterminate length and to an unknown destination. The peculiar need—that I experienced several times a day and sometimes even at night—to touch the dictionary, the need I had already felt several times in my life to cling to a foreign language, proved the most effective anti-depressant. I felt genuine love for the Hebrew language. Its right-to-left writing, its words written only in consonants, the vowels staying buried inside the reader's head like a family secret . . . it all inevitably reminded me of the manuscript on the Tumchooq sutra, whose opening sentence, "Once on a moonless night," still occasionally echoed around inside my head.

Time passed. In 1988 I published *Being a Jew in China,* a history book, but also the first work I succeeded in completing. Two years later, although I didn't know why, perhaps guided by Paul d'Ampère's ghost, I began work on another book about two great translators of the past—his precursors, you could say—who travelled the length and breadth of China as he did and became Chinese citizens. This was the synopsis:

The story takes place in fifth-century China and retraces the
lives of two great translators of Buddhist sutras. The first,
Buddhabhadra, was born in Kapilavastu, Buddha's home-
land, and was a follower of the strict Theravada discipline,
Hinayana. He brings the Pali canon to Changan, then the
capital of China, where the other protagonist, Kumarajiva, a
native of Kutcha and a follower of the Mahayana tradition,
reigns as absolute master of all religious activities. The latter
owes his celebrity as much to the quality of his oral translations of Sanskrit texts into Chinese (each of his performances
presided over by the emperor himself in the presence of hundreds of faithful disciples and scholars writing down every
word he utters) as to his reputation for lax morals, particularly, if historians are to be believed, in his relationships with
the fairer sex.

The differences in their doctrines rapidly create enmity
between the two men, setting the court ablaze and dividing
not only the court itself but also its intellectual following,
while confronting the entire country with a dilemma as to
the choice of a national religion. Buddhabhadra is appreci-
ated for his erudition and talent and for the rigorous restraint
of his behaviour, but his contempt for the great of this world,
particularly with respect to the emperor, hampers the spread
of Hinayana in China (in the same way that, a thousand
years later, the Jesuits would miss the opportunity to convert
that vast empire to Christianity).

Kumarajiva emerges triumphant from the dispute. The
emperor, who dedicates what amounts to a religion to this
great translator's qualities, even comes up with the idea
of perpetuating these by ensuring the monk has descen-
dants, setting him up in sumptuous apartments with ten

wives of unmatched beauty, while the loser, Buddhabhadra, is forced to leave the capital and trail around southern China as a simple beggar, dressed in the rags dictated by his beliefs.

Nevertheless, driven by personal desire—the source of all our misfortunes—he decides in a final spasm of pride to challenge Kumarajiva with his written translations, given that the latter translates only orally into Chinese, aiming less at faithfulness to the original than at clarity and elegance. And so it is that Buddhabhadra, while begging in the street and living on alms, translates the twenty volumes he still has of *The Jatakas* (the complete *Jatakas* comprises fifty volumes, but thirty had been stolen from him along with all the other sutras in Pali that he took with him). *The Jatakas,* or "nativities," consist of some five hundred accounts, in a mixture of prose and verse, relating the former lives of Buddha. All specialists in the field agree on one point: Buddhabhadra's translation is a masterpiece of Chinese literature, a veritable miracle if its translator's foreign origins are taken into account. Nothing more beautiful has ever been created before or since those twenty volumes of *The Jatakas* in Chinese, volumes in which Buddhabhadra evokes every hardship suffered by the future Buddha, whether in animal, human or divine form, his sentences stripped of all weight, unremarkable in themselves yet dazzling when put together, like simple bricks which together make the edifice of a magnificent shrine.

These two adversaries die within a day of each other. Kumarajiva, whose lack of children thwarts the emperor's wishes, sees his popularity decline and is increasingly challenged by Chinese scholars who openly accuse him of mixing his own ideas in with Buddha's in his oral translations.

Feeling, at his more than respectable age, quite ready to breathe his last, he begs Buddha that justice be granted to him after his death by ensuring that, during his incineration, his whole body should be reduced to ashes except for his tongue, as sacred proof of the fidelity and veracity of his oral translations. Perhaps we should see this extreme spectacle as a final bit of spin from Kumarajiva, the great master of communication, but also as a sincere need to justify himself. Kumarajiva's wish is granted. In the largest temple in the capital, before the emperor and his entire court, the pyre is set alight and eventually delivers a verdict in favour of the late great translator. The emperor immediately declares the Mahayana doctrine China's official religion.

In response, Buddhabhadra sets off for Ceylon in pursuit of the remaining *Jatakas* in Pali, intending to translate them in their entirety. But that same evening he is assassinated by a fanatical disciple of Kumarajiva's in a miserable inn near Prome, an ancient kingdom in Upper Burma known at the time as Pyu. After committing his crime, the murderer rips the filthy patched robes from his victim's body and, screaming frenziedly, slices them with his knife, cutting them into pieces no larger than a fingernail, a symbolic gesture representing the annihilation of Buddhabhadra's beliefs.

It seems to have been at the mention of the name Prome, or Pyu, that in late July 1990, on a night when my "glass menagerie" was plunged deep in silence, I decided to make use of my long summer holiday to set off in search of historical documents at the scene of the crime, in Burma. But the most likely determining factor, as I acknowledged on my way there, was my reading a footnote by Paul d'Ampère who, in order to check the name of Prome, which was barely mentioned by Marco Polo in his book, had gone to see the place for himself:

Having walked for nearly two weeks without seeing anything except for jungle trees and the course of the Irrawaddy, suddenly a huge rounded hump, several dozen metres in height, I would think, loomed out of the river mist. It was an imposing sight, which drove everything else into the background. This was Bebe Paya, the temple of Sriksetra, so like its Indian forerunner in name and physical form: monolithic, solid, tall—so tall I was almost afraid to look up—sculpted and hollowed out of blocks of granite, topped with a tiered pyramid embellished with miniature pavilions populated by sculpted figures, alone or in twos, and narrative bas-relief designs, symbolically representing the universe; and at the top stood an elaborately carved polygonal cupola, which can be seen shining from far away on land or sea.

Later the visitor discovers the complex of eighty-three stupas, Buddhist reliquaries, each constituting a complete microcosm: a square base rising in increments and representing the divine residence analogous to the mountain at the centre of the cosmos; a central staircase inside, signifying the central pivot of the world; and the secret chamber housing the relics, identified as the receptacle for the embryo of the universe. Finally, faithful to the Indian model, beside the entrance to each stupa stands an isolated column topped with a capital shaped like an upturned lotus or a group of animals standing back to back, reminiscent of the pillars erected by Emperor Ashoka to be carved with his moral edicts. The royal palace and capital are enclosed within a wall of brick covered in green enamel, ringed with a moat, punctuated by twelve doors and fortified with towers at each corner.

4

IN A LUMBERING YELLOW BUS GROANING with chickens, pigs and human passengers, some of whom clung in clusters to the door like dark caterpillars on the skin of a ripe mango, I made my way to Prome, where a scooter taxi took me on to Maungun. From there I continued on foot with a local guide. It had rained the night before and my dainty ankle boots sank pitifully into the muddy path between fields of sugarcane. Later, when we cut through a crop of maize, most of which had been harvested, the boots became so bogged down in the soil that I had to keep making jerking movements with my whole body to heave myself out as, step by difficult step, I drew closer to the last vestiges of the capital.

Everything had disappeared: temples, stupas, walls, moats and palaces. All that remained of the entire city was the huge raw hunk of rock rising up in the middle of the fields, a block of pink sandstone of the most magnificent shape and colour, forming an alcove two and a half metres tall by ten wide in which a Buddha carved from the rock lay resting. It was a representation of what Buddhists call "Total Extinction," the last of the four miracles of his final earthly existence (after "Birth," "Awakening" and the "First Vow").

The Buddha's profile stood out against a delicately carved background, and I was struck not only by how beautiful he was, but by the breath of life which seemed to emanate from that resting body, a good proportion of which, perhaps a quarter, was already buried in the ground, having sunk lower and lower over the centuries. His clothing exposed his right shoulder, and where the cloth draped over his left arm it was carved in a series of folds, spaced apart to afford glimpses of his palpably supple, recumbent body. Life quivered in every fluid contour of his body right up to his head as it rested on his right elbow. His round face with its closed eyes expressed a contemplative serenity, while a tuft of hair between his eyebrows appeared to ripple in the breeze. His mouth had the barely perceptible hint of a smile and, like so many other details, I recognised the bulge on his head, where flames seemed to spring up between the flat coils of hair (according to legend, Buddha had two brains). Lastly I found a dozen or so ancient letters carved onto a background of clouds. They were so close to the Buddha's left hand that, in his dreamlike state, he seemed to want to touch them.

I started to photograph them, but they wavered slightly in my viewfinder. All at once, in the blink of an eye, I thought I saw the Buddha's left hand move, as if giving me a sign, but there were too few of those archaic words in Pyu for me to form any sort of opinion, least of all on the subject of an assassination which dated back all of fifteen centuries.

Once back in Rangoon I carried on with my investigations for a few more days, taking rickshaws through streets and neighbourhoods in search of traces of old trading links with Ceylon or legends about monks who translated sutras. One day when I was waiting for some administrative documents in the foyer of the French Embassy, I happened to go into the library and leaf through Auguste Pavie's memoirs, although I was not sure what I hoped to find there. Granted, this telegrapher who became a hero for single-handedly and peacefully conquering what is now known as Laos warranted attention, but I found little of interest in his writing and was about to close the book when a passage leapt out at me and it felt as if clouds were breaking open to allow the sun's beams down onto me:

> In 1907 negotiations to determine the borders between Laos, Burma and Thailand brought together delegations from the three countries in Mandalay, the largest city in Upper Burma. In the pause between two exhausting sittings, I tried to go down the Irrawaddy by boat. To this day the river's name alone conjures the sheer size of its muddy bulk. We stopped off at Pagan, a town accessible only by boat. This former capital of Burma, which prospered between the ninth and thirteenth centuries, is indisputably the most impressive site for Buddhist temples after Angkor, though they are all already in ruins. There is a printing house run by monks for sutras in Pagan, and I vied at length to buy a particular stele; I desperately wanted to take such a treasure back to France, where, I was quite sure, it would have delighted our museum curators, for it bore an inscription of a long text in Pyù, Mon, Pali and Burmese, relating, according to the translation I was given, a grim assassination committed in the fifth century. The victim was one of the most famous Buddhist scholars of the time. But the head of the monastery proved intransigent and refused to let me have it, whatever my price.

The name Irrawaddy may have made the adventurous telegrapher's ears ring to the sound of the river sweeping through high mountains, but that of Mandalay had been charming—even fascinating—pilgrims through the ages. From the nineteenth century onwards, Mandalay had the same effect on English writers and poets who covered the length and breadth of the British Empire, under the spell of its name. I myself took the Mandalay Express and, sitting on a narrow seat between sleeping passengers, I read Somerset Maugham's *The Gentleman in the Parlour*. Maugham travelled across Burma on a pony between 1922 and 1923. Mandalay, he wrote, is above all a name. There are towns like this whose names have their own magic. He thought that a man might be wise not to visit such places for fear of disappointment: like Trebizond, which might be just a miserable village but whose name carries the weight of an empire, or Samarkand— the word alone makes the pulse race and fills one with a sense of unquenchable longing.

Even before Somerset Maugham, towards the end of the nineteenth century, Kipling himself had written a poem called "Mandalay" in his collection *Barrack-Room Ballads*, earning him comparisons with Byron from the critics of his day. Although Kipling wrote it after his one brief stopover in Burma, and his talent as a poet doesn't match his abilities as a short-story writer, the fascination exerted by Mandalay is here, conjuring its nervous energy as it quickens the heart:

> "If you've 'eard the East a-callin', you won't never 'eed
> naught else."
> > No! you won't 'eed nothin' else
> > But them spicy garlic smells,

An' the sunshine an' the palm-trees an' the tinkly
temple-bells;
On the road to Mandalay . . .

For me, personally, the road to Mandalay, the very name Mandalay, is more inclined to evoke the gloomy apprehension that gripped me when the tropical fever—which I'd congratulated myself for avoiding for more than five years—suddenly took hold again without any warning in a carriage on the Mandalay Express after seven hours of travelling, when I was still only halfway there. I stayed pinned to my seat by the hefty threat implied by this gratuitous recurrence. Scalding hot flushes, each hotter than the last, then bouts of icy shivering, each colder than the last, swept over me, growing more powerful, more furious, overwhelming me when I was already dazed by the constant stream of local music spewing from loudspeakers.

As the train began to climb an incline I felt myself descending into a sort of trance and, unable to bear the music another second, I opened the carriage window; a cloud of white mist blew in and through it I could see neat lines of crosses in a military cemetery, stretching as far as the eye could see, probably the graves of soldiers who fell in the battle of Mandalay in 1945. I saw ghosts looming out of the fog and glimpsed scattered bones from skeletons, strangely clear but swallowed up immediately by the dark night. I couldn't say how long the hallucination lasted. A minute? Thirty seconds? I was afraid this fleeting moment was only the prelude to an even more violent attack, an imminent catastrophe, but nothing disastrous happened.

We stopped briefly in a small station before crossing the

viaduct at Goktek and, in an effort to shake off my torpor and return to reality, I gazed at the gigantic arches of the bridge rising up from the shadowy gorge cloaked in jungle. I noticed, although I didn't really believe it, that my temperature was stabilising. The train swayed, juddering over some points; the hammering of the wheels changed cadence and accelerated. When we crossed the only bridge built by the Americans in the days of the British Empire I cried, not because I was moved by the beautiful scenery, but because I noticed to my surprise that my temperature had returned to normal. My body was no longer burning, I had stopped shaking with cold or with terror, even though I still felt weightless. Light from street lamps filing slowly past outside reached into the carriage, lingering over me, scrutinising my ashen face and my hands gripping the seat, then disappeared. I sat beside the window, which gleamed in the dark, with tears rolling down my cheeks, though less from relief than a sort of homesickness, a searing feeling of exhaustion, loneliness and general disappointment that settled over me. If this is what freedom has to offer, I thought to myself, then it's horrible, dismal even.

At various points in our lives, or on a quest, and for reasons that often remain obscure, we are driven to make decisions which prove with hindsight to be loaded with meaning. The moment I arrived in Mandalay I hailed a taxi, but—instead of looking for a hospital or hotel or going and visiting the palace with its seven hundred stupas, its statues and markets—I asked to be taken straight to the port, where I caught the first boat for Pagan.

5

Now it should be known that after travelling on horseback across far-flung places for the two weeks I have recounted above, one comes to a city called Mien, a very large and noble place, which is the capital of the kingdom. Its people are idolatrous and have a language all their own. They are subjects of the Great Khan.

NOTES MADE BY PAUL D'AMPÈRE: Mien is the Pagan of today, a village on the banks of the Irrawaddy. It has a school of lacquer-work famous throughout the region, and a printing press–monastery. It has been the capital of Burma since the ninth century. (It is not without significance that, shortly after its independence in 1950, the country rejected the name Burma given to it by the British colonial administration and called itself Myanmar, a name derived from the ancient city of Mien, which, although less familiar to us than Burma, is the name by which it is now officially recognised worldwide.)

Pagan is first referred to in 1106 in a work regarded in China as authoritative, *Archival Studies* Volume 332:

In the fifth year of Xi Lin of the Song dynasty, Pagan sent an ambassadorship with a tribute for the imperial court. These were the instructions given by the emperor: "Pagan is now an important kingdom and no longer a dependent state. It deserves the courtesy granted to Arabia, Tonkin, etc. Henceforth, all imperial missives addressed to its king should be written on a sheet of white paper backed with gold paper, printed with flowers, sealed in a wooden coffer covered in gold plate, locked with a silver padlock and wrapped in silk and satin cloth.

Contrary to accepted wisdom about the *Book of the Wonders of the World* (by which I mean that it is considered to be more or less a collection of the Venetian's personal memories), what he tells us about the road that apparently took him to Mien was not based on his own experience; he must have heard or read it somewhere without ever setting foot in Burma. One sentence alone betrays him: the fact that, according to him, he had to ride for a fortnight to reach Mien-Pagan, when the only access to it—to this day and from whichever direction—is along the Irrawaddy River.

A careful reading of the preceding chapters, where he claims to have stayed in Yunnan very close to the Chinese-Burmese border, proves the even more regrettable fact that he never crossed that border nor saw the Irrawaddy with his own eyes, even though in his writings he describes the river as magnificent and unforgettable. The name might be famous the world over, but at least Marco Polo could have left us a first-hand account describing the river's course, which would have equipped us to respond to theories put forward by some English geologists who claim it used to flow into the valley of the Sittang, another much wider river that flows from central to southern Burma. If that were the case, then its major western tributary, the Chindwin, and the upper Irrawaddy itself would have been the outlet for the Brahmaputra, and the history of Tibet, China, Burma, India and Bengal—all of which the Brahmaputra flows through—would probably need rewriting.

NOTES MADE BY TUMCHOOQ: It's so hard to know how to start! Not because these are notes about notes but because I don't know what name to give the author of these notes, a man whose surname—with its seven letters, its apostrophe and its accent—could have been my own. (I remember the first time I ever saw that name. I was twelve and living in the reform school I'd been sent to after the incident in the Forbidden City when I nearly killed my best friend in that strangling cage. A guard took me to an office, where my mother was allowed to visit me. She wrote the name on a piece of paper without a word. I was just a child at the time, and I gazed for several minutes at those unfamiliar, foreign letters with their graphic signs above the vowels, and, even though I would have had no idea how to pronounce them, like the letters of a dead language, I still knew they made up your name. She tried to pronounce it, several times, and did succeed, although her voice was almost stifled by sobs. The word was barely audible, uttered so tentatively, like a distant echo, and I was bowled over, not only by the strange sound of it but also by its dramatic, not to say tragic, quality.)

Now, as I try to write these notes with my thoughts going round in circles and my pen still hesitating, a text from the Satyasiddhi-Sutra has come back to me. It's a fourth-century text published by the printing press–monastery in Pagan around the twelfth century; fragments of it in Pali were found in the vestiges of a stupa in Pagan and were carefully preserved, like a saint's sacred bones, or his teeth, his coat or his alms bowl, for which a king would pay an astronomical price only to put them in a reliquary, bury that deep underground and build a stupa as extraordinary as a pyramid over the top of it. I've often thought about the theory put forward by Hari-varman, the author of the Satyasiddhi-Sutra, who was a Brahman before his conversion to Buddhism, a theory which can essentially be summed up in this sentence: "All that it takes to achieve Nirvana is to recognise the unreality of things and the unreality of self."

Being an old Buddhist, as you have been for decades, I would be surprised if you hadn't read this text in its original Sanskrit version, and probably in the Pali version. You are also likely to know the Chinese version with which I wanted to make a comparative reading and which is infinitely longer because it's interspersed with the personal interpretations of its eminent translator, Kumarajiva, who introduced the Mahayana doctrine to China and translated some forty sutras from that school of thought. The fact that he worked on a Hinayana text shortly before his death, and the miracle of his tongue resisting incineration, helped increase the fame of this magisterial work. Here is his translation:

Things do not really exist, neither do knowledge, the possession of things, physical form, the body, nor the representa-

tion of an individual, but what does have a real existence is the name denoting its abstract unity, for a name is, in fact, the absolute that exists in the intimate heart of man, as it is at the centre of the universe. And all that it takes to find salvation is to recognise that fact. Anyone who, understanding this, turns for support to the extreme intelligence of the Bodhisattvas is then freed from his name and, from that moment on, is delivered not only of his own body, but also from the order of time. He attains total annihilation and is therefore, so to speak, a Buddha in a state of utter "Awakening."

This reminds me of your last wish, a sort of farewell that you dictated to me when you were gripped by a final surge of energy and suddenly emerged from the deep coma you had been in, following your lynching at the hands of the camp prisoners. "Listen," you said, "I don't want anything on my grave; nothing but a blank space, a gap, not my name or any dates."

Why that denial of your name? It strikes me as much as a sign of protest as a philosophical principle, which meant you were already rejecting the world you were leaving behind. The world was reduced to what was left of your memory; in other words a name, yours, the last pale reflection of a process that had come full term; and, by erasing it, as the Chinese version of the Satyasiddhi-Sutra states, you were putting yourself beyond the past and, eventually, beyond the order of time altogether.

To get back to writing these notes, in the academic sense of the word, the thing that encourages me to take this liberty is the fact that there indisputably is a printing press–monastery (and that's a term you must have coined for the purpose, given that the establishment calls itself a "temple where the monks print Buddhist sutras") in Pagan. They've been printing books there since the eleventh century, as indicated by the date of completion on the cover of the Satyasiddhi-Sutra: fifth year of the reign of King Anawratha (Aniruddha). I'd also like to point out that the reliquary in which the work was found, the one cited and commented on above, is in lacquered wood which has been extremely well preserved, and that the tradition of this particular kind of lacquer-work goes back at least as far as King Anawratha's reign.

I would like to say a few words about the lacquer, because I feel an irresistible rush of pride to think that, unless I'm wrong, I'm the only person to know of the secret love you felt for a Chinese lacquered box sculpted with figures and landscapes that your grandmother gave you for Christmas when you were ten. You yourself told me about it when I visited you in the camp: you couldn't take your eyes off this newfound friend and the tiniest scratch on it would have broken your heart. Then you recited a Rimbaud poem that you'd translated into Tumchooq, although you were so disappointed with the translation you said it spoiled the precious memory you'd just shared with me. Then you left. That memory returned to me recently when I came across the same poem, "The Orphans' New Year's Gift," while teaching myself French from a book I was given:

> —Ah! what a beautiful morning, this New Year's morning!
> During the night each had dreamt of his dear ones
>> In some strange dream when you saw toys,
>> Candies dressed in gold, sparkling jewels,
>> Whirling and dancing a sonorous dance . . .

Buddha teaches us that everything is as if it were nothing, or rather as if it were pure non-being, not that this means an individual's actions are in the least way subject to chance. Quite the opposite, they are laid down as part of a grand design from which, I believe, even your predilection for Chinese lacquer isn't exempt. It was a sort of sign from destiny, which deals out the cards: it only remained for you to use them. Zhuangzi was the first to compare a scholar's life to that of the lacquer tree, *Rhus vernicifera,* an elegant tree some twenty metres high, but which, from the age of eight to forty (the twilight of its life), is exploited, incised and regularly bled of its precious fragrant sap, thick and white as curdled milk, oozing gently from the monstrous open wound on its trunk. It is collected, filtered, purified, dyed and applied layer after layer onto wood or another background, to become a work of art, a symbol of refinement.

The Pagan reliquary in question bears a long inscription which gives the names of the craftsmen and workshop managers, and the date it was made as well as testifying to the time and application taken to turn a simple object into a unique treasure: lacquer was painted on in thin layers, each one dried and sanded before the next was applied. As this exquisite substance coagulates only in humid conditions, the drying process was carried out on the Irrawaddy in a boat taken onto the water a total of fifty times, the exact number of layers of lacquer needed to create this one item. Then the scene of Buddha's Extinction—depicted in three different tableaux—was sculpted on it, carved through the thickness of the layers: first there is an atmosphere of fear as the pyre built by the Mallas refuses to catch light until Kasyapa, his most faithful disciple, has come to kiss his master's feet one last time; then, in a mood of intense emotion, Kasyapa almost swoons with grief and has to be supported by another disciple to say his final farewell to Buddha; lastly, Kasyapa presides over the funeral ceremony and the pyre catches light of its own accord. Every time I think of those scenes carved in lacquer, another funeral scene comes to mind: yours, beside the River Lu, whose murmurings still reverberate in my ears; a misty, almost insubstantial image, except for your feet, which I touched with my forehead and kissed, as a reflex action, not because I knew the Buddhist tradition. I seem to think they were still warm.

CONTINUATION OF MARCO POLO'S BOOK: In this city there is a noble thing I shall describe to you. For in this city there was once a rich and powerful king. When he was about to die, he ordered that on his tomb or, to be precise, on his monument two towers should be built, one in gold, the other in silver, in a way that I shall describe. One of the towers was made of beautiful gems that were then covered in gold, and the gold was at least a finger's thickness, and the tower was so well covered with it that it appeared to be made entirely of gold. It was a good ten paces high and as wide as befitted its height. It was rounded on the outside and all about its curving surface it was covered with small golden bells, which rang every time the wind blew between them. And the other tower I spoke of above, made of silver and in every way like the golden tower, was made of the same materials and to the same height and in the same way. And, similarly, the tomb was partly covered with gold leaf and partly with silver leaf. And the king had this built for his grandeur and for his soul. And, I shall tell you this much, to see them was to see the most beautiful towers in the world, of immense value. And when the sun touches them, they are resplendent and can be seen from far, far away.

NOTES MADE BY PAUL D'AMPÈRE: Constructor kings like this run through Pagan's history between the eleventh and thirteenth centuries, right up to the Mongol invasion. Anawratha, its founder, and the next two generations are reputed to have built Buddhist monuments of titanic proportions, and Pagan still has more than eight hundred of them over a stretch of about four hundred kilometres, not to mention those that have fallen in ruins, making it a gigantic sacred city, which has nothing to envy Angkor in Khmer country. The famous Temple of Ananda, to take just one example, is a vertiginously positioned shrine shaped like a long-handled bell, perched on a huge tiered pyramid which looks like a perfectly white hill, a great glittering mass, surrounded by two cloisters and topped with a dazzling, almost frighteningly tall point, rising higher and higher, so far into the sky it disappears in the clouds. This monument borders on the fabulous, but, in the end, my investigations served only to highlight a fundamental and widely known truth, which is that Marco Polo never came to Burma and, therefore, couldn't know that in a sacred Buddhist city like Pagan there isn't a single non-religious edifice, far less a royal tomb. Take, for example, what's known as the Shwedagon Pagoda, commissioned by the first king, Anawratha, in 1509 and completed by his son (or the man recognised as such) King Kyanzittha: it is a vast plinth made up of a succession of platforms, rising in tiers from a square base with inverted corners; mounted on it is a rounded silver tower with, on top of that, another tower, this one in gold and shaped like a bell, with a roof which, it was claimed, was covered with genuine diamonds, and—if the colonial archives are to be believed—these stones ended up in the coffers of the Bank of England. This stupa and not a royal tomb, as the Venetian thought, plays an important role in the country and is to this day the national shrine of Burma, for it was here that a replica of the famous Buddha's tooth was placed, the tooth preserved at Kandy and sent by the king of Ceylon, Vijayabahu (1059–1114).

NOTES MADE BY TUMCHOOQ: In 1975, the year of the monkey, Pagan was struck by the worst earthquake in its history. The edifices mentioned above, those truly ancient architectural masterpieces bordering on the fabulous, were now a spectacle of total devastation: Shwedagon's stupa crumbled and still lies by the banks of the Irrawaddy today; others, half-buried in the ground or submerged underwater, still exude the grim confusion of a field of ruins the morning after a bombing. All at once their star was no longer a lucky one, a cruel setback inflicted by history. The famous Temple of Ananda, which you described in all its beauty in your note above and which was once fifty-six metres high and sixty wide, is now just a handful of dust, a stretch of wasteland where, in among a few vestiges of bricks barely suggesting the niche that sheltered him for almost eight hundred years, stands the decapitated statue of Sanakavasa, Ananda's giant disciple.

Peculiarly, in this ghostly setting, the nine-metre-high sandalwood torso of the statue has remained intact; only the ochre colour of the monk's robes has disappeared over the years, but in places you can still see the artist's careful work in trying to represent realistically what is known in Sanskrit as a *samghati*, the ragged, dirty, hemp robes that were the pre-scribed clothing for a monk visiting a king's palace, begging in the street or preaching before an audience. According to leg-end, Sanakavasa was born with a disproportionately large body, already wrapped in a length of cloth, which grew longer as he developed into a true giant, eventually becoming a *samghati* after his conversion by Ananda. When the moment of his Annihilation came, he announced his wish that his dishevelled robes should remain in this world as a reminder of the miraculous power of his faith, and should turn to dust only when Buddha's law no longer served a purpose on earth.

I actually still have your personal *samghati*—the rags you wrapped around the side-pieces of your glasses, the lenses and frame having been destroyed by your assassins—and I keep them like a precious relic.

The ruins of Pagan fill me with joy, because they remind me of the year 1975, when I first met you in the visiting room at your camp. The large hall divided in two by a wooden grille wasn't yet there because not many prisoners had visi-tors. I was taken to an office, where I sat or rather perched on a wooden stool so tall my feet didn't reach the ground, facing another stool, which was incredibly low—a fitting place for an enemy of the people—and that was where you had to sit and look up to me. I waited an eternity until the door was eventually opened and then, forgetting the visiting rules, I jumped down from the stool and made for the door, half in a dream and half in the real world, not even hearing the warders shouting at me to get back to my seat. You weren't yet a pig-keeper at that point, and had just come up from the gem mines; you were so muddy, broken and drained that I mistook you for Chinese and almost confused you with the old plain-clothed screw escorting you. Instead of "Dad," different words—"Mr. Liu"—popped out of my mouth and rang round the room, rooting the warders to the spot. The name Liu didn't correspond to your Chinese name Baolo (a transcription of Paul in Chinese) or my mother's name, and therefore mine, which is Zhong. At the time neither of us reacted. We each sat in our intended places, exchanged a bit of small talk about my journey and then, speaking in a perfect Sichuan dialect, you suddenly asked:

"What did you call me?"

You'd barely finished the question before we both burst out laughing so loudly, despite the warders' intervention, that I fell off my stool—the one reserved for the population at large—unable to control myself. You laughed so much the dirty rags around your glasses came undone and dangled from the side-pieces, swaying with every move of your head while your cheeks were wet with tears.

Tradition and respect for the hierarchy of generations meant I'd never dared ask Mum about the circumstances of your arrest, even less about the reasons for the life sentence to which China had condemned you, but on that day, during that first visit, I felt more doubtful than ever that the little man sitting facing me on his low stool could have traded his wife for a manuscript.

And even if you could have loved a piece of text more than a woman, did you know at the time of the transaction that she was pregnant?

Perhaps not. At least I hope not.

It's strange, but I followed in your footsteps, many years later; I too have left a woman I love for the sake of a text, the same text. Like father, like son? Two spectacular bastards?

(One question smacks me in the face as I write this, and I wonder why I didn't think of it sooner: Didn't I leave Peking at a time when . . . like you, perhaps without your knowing . . . I haven't got the heart or the strength to formulate the question—about my offspring, another Tumchooq, another manuscript-hunter?)

These notes, which followed on from Paul d'Ampère's, were jotted down roughly in Chinese on the squared paper of a Burmese schoolbook, written in pen, its nib gliding from left to right and accelerating in places, as if chasing its own shadow, chasing fleeting memories or a scene that came to mind with no warning and had to be captured straight away without rereading. Were these few notes the beginnings of a book or just a sketchy introduction to the frequent internal conversations he held with the late Mr. Liu, a Freudian slip he maintained, as far as I know, all through the years when he regularly visited his father at the camp in Sichuan?

I discovered that schoolbook when I arrived in Pagan, in among other books and papers strewn over a low table in the house of the superior at the printing press–monastery, a two-storey bamboo building on stilts on the side of a steep hill, protected from behind by the towering Achan mountains and facing out onto the mirror-like surface of the Irrawaddy as it flowed across a plain, irrigating rice paddies and disappearing along the valley. The monastery superior was travelling abroad and the main room in his house—which acted as an office, reading room and bedroom—was spacious but empty of furniture; sober, even austere. Visitors took off their shoes before stepping onto the floor of plaited bamboo, a cool surface that moved backwards and forwards underfoot, and they sat on a rush mat on the floor to take tea. Hanging from the roof at the far end of the room was the superior's bed, a simple mat, clean but old with holes in places, repaired with pieces of faded blue fabric. Above this hung a white nightshirt and an ochre-coloured tunic with only one very long sleeve, which reached right down to the floor. Neither of these, according to the monastery's deputy who welcomed me very courteously, was a *samghati* (the robe of rags), because the master had taken his with him.

He added (his words translated by Min, a young Sino-Burmese girl acting as my interpreter) that, of all the masters who had presided over the monastery, the present one, although still young, had the greatest reputation for his tremendous erudition, and that monks and followers came from the four corners of the country to listen to his teachings. One day he was visited by a delegation of Japanese monks and they had been so impressed by him that, on their return, they invited him to Kyoto to preside over an international symposium, and this explained his absence.

I put my glass of tea down on the low table and was about to ask him to show me the stele in four languages which had brought me to Pagan when, completely by chance and for no apparent reason, I thought of Tumchooq for the first time in a long while. As I waited for the deputy to finish praising his master, I leafed through a schoolbook on the table. You know the rest. Before I even grasped what I was reading, I was shaken to the core, the words dancing before my eyes, the pages quivering in my hands as I trembled from head to foot. What a journey I've been on, I thought, to reach this moment which finally gives some meaning to my life, to these long years of drifting between different languages and different continents! Thank goodness.

6

TUMCHOOQ ARRIVED IN PAGAN IN THE early 1980s, the monastery deputy explained, retracing his story for me. A real vagrant: no one knew where he was from, because he remained utterly silent and had neither a passport nor any other administrative papers. At first he was employed in the kitchens, where he chopped vegetables from morning till night, not talking to anyone, so that for a long time he was thought to be mute.

A few years later, when the paper mill needed another worker, he was sent there, although no one expected great results, because the process of making paper for sacred books requires exhausting, monotonous work as well as exceptional attention to detail. But people soon realised that the paper pulp obeyed him better than anyone else, from ageing monks to young novices. For three whole years he worked in silence, his hands permanently in water as he made paper, sheet by sheet. Then he was sent to the xylography workshop, where he became an unusually good engraver of texts.

It was here that people realised he understood Pali, had a phenomenal memory, remembered every text (even the most complicated) he engraved and was able to translate them into Burmese, as if born with a Pali-Burmese dictionary in his head. Then one day he finally spoke, expressing himself in elegant, literary Burmese with a rich vocabulary, but also a slight accent and the occasional mistake, which betrayed his foreign origins.

He made his vows after a six-year probationary period spent in the kitchens, the paper mill and the xylography workshop, where he had felt his vocation while observing all the rules of the monastery. He chose Tumchooq as his monastic name, a name which, according to him, appears in one of Buddha's sutras or *jatakas*. The magical circumstances that accompanied his recitation of "The Path to Purification" (a classical work of the Hinayana doctrine) before the assembled monks was enough to convince them altogether, and the master of the monastery entrusted him with the key to the Cave of Treasure, where they kept all the engraving plates ever made since the establishment began. He shut himself away in there for many years to record and list the five hundred thousand plates and, according to more malicious sources, to look for the sutra that features his own name. A sutra that no one in the area had ever heard of. When the monastery's patriarch embarked on his journey to the beyond, to everyone's surprise, it was to Tumchooq that he handed over his ragged *samghati* and his alms bowl, asking him to preside over his funeral. And so Tumchooq became the new master of the monastery.

7

AFEW HOURS AFTER I ARRIVED, THE MONKS held a long meeting to consider my request to stay in the monastery until my "close friend" returned from Japan. Their votes fell in my favour, given that there was no hotel in Pagan (which had been reduced to the size of a small village since the earthquake); and two extra woven mats—one for my interpreter and one for myself—were laid down in Tumchooq's house on stilts, a little way away from the monks' dormitories. Before going to bed that night we went to wash beside a well. I untied the black silk belt securing my scarlet *tongyi*, a long piece of fabric which I wore around my waist like the Burmese women, and poured a bucket of water over my head. As the water ran over my hair and seeped into my *angyi* (a sort of blouse with a high neck and full sleeves), it billowed and filled and I thought I would finally experience the peace that Heaven had so far refused me. What if, I wondered, I end up like my interpreter, with silver bracelets all the way from my wrists to my elbows and a pretty ring, a "nose flower," in my nose?

As I climbed the stairs back to the house on stilts I fainted for the first time; scalding waves of heat washed over me, I

shivered with cold, chilled to the bone by the draught coming up through the woven bamboo floor. My old demon was
back again, but was no longer satisfied with drenching me in
a cold sweat and making my whole body feel like a thawing
pond; it had its eye on something else, although I didn't
know what. My repeated fainting fits worried me more than
the fever. I couldn't find these symptoms listed anywhere,
not even in the most exhaustive medical manuals, and I was
worried they were a warning that I was losing my memory.

The following morning my interpreter went to the dis-
pensary at the lacquer school but, apart from medicines for
everyday illnesses, she found nothing that would ease my
suffering. She was reduced to pushing my hair aside in sections so that she could massage my scalp, as well as my
temples and nostrils, with Tiger Balm. Towards the end of
the afternoon the monastery deputy arranged a healing session with my consent; it was held in Burmese and I don't
understand a single word of the language, but the ritual itself
was so explicit I grasped its significance perfectly. I felt as if I
were sliding into the abyss of time and becoming part of this
scene described by Marco Polo:

They have no doctors, but when they are ill they call for their
magicians. These men can charm the devil and it is they who
serve the idols. When the magicians arrive, the sick tell them
what ails them. And the magi immediately begin beating
their instruments, singing and dancing until one of the magicians falls over backwards on the ground, foaming at the
mouth, looking dead, and this is because the devil is in his
body. He remains in this state, as if dead. And when the
other magicians, because there are several of them, see that

one of their number has fallen as I have described, they start talking to him and asking what illness the sick man has . . .

As Marco Polo's words ran through my mind, providing a commentary for the action in which I was the passive—not to say paralysed—protagonist, I tried to remember whether Paul d'Ampère had written any notes about it. This attempt proved treacherous, for I was soon lost on a tide of words, French, Chinese and Tumchooq, clashing together, intermingling, forming and re-forming, glittering or going out like dead stars.

A fragment of text surfaced from my memory, a short text I myself had written, not one of those countless projects I never saw through to the end, but a school essay, and the incongruity of its sentences struck me as even more grotesque than the scene with the magicians. The monks' chanting lulled me until I sank into unconsciousness again. It was years since I'd slept as well as I did after that ceremony, and I spent two whole days immersed in cataleptic but peaceful sleep. When I finally woke my fever and listlessness had disappeared and I was quite overwhelmed with happiness at this resurrection. Feeling my way, I crept out of the house without waking my interpreter.

8

CLIMBING DOWN A WINDING PATH THROUGH
the woods beside the monastery, I came across everlasting seedlings (which I recognised from the bird-like shape of their red and yellow flowers) as well as mango, orange and avocado trees with cocoa pods peeping from beneath them. As I cut across the wood my footsteps were, admittedly, still tentative but my energy gradually came back to me until, passing in front of a Saman, a rain tree, I clung to its great supple vines, although I wasn't sure why, and swung through the air like a child.

The monks' dormitories were dotted about under these luxuriant trees, whitewashed wooden buildings, each comprising over a dozen rooms and, through their open doors, I could see the beds which consisted of planks of wood laid over vertical logs driven into the beaten earth of the floor. Outside the huts, the monks' robes and tunics hung on washing lines, still wet and pegged close together. Behind the buildings, which apparently had no wells, I saw the monks doing their morning ablutions round barrels positioned under drainpipes that channelled water from the roofs. By way of toothpaste, they snapped off a branch from a tree I didn't recognise, some sort of hibiscus, and crushed one end of it to polish their teeth. As soon as they saw me they seemed embarrassed and looked away.

The mill where the paper for sacred books was made stood outside the confines of the monastery, in a loop in a river, probably a minor tributary of the Irrawaddy. It was a timeless relic with massive wheels, which I didn't see straight away because the morning fog was still thick, but I could hear their jumbled purring and then all at once they loomed out of the mist like giants made of massive moss-covered rocks, dripping with water and seeming to come to meet me, with an ancient, ponderous slowness, before becoming weightless, swallowed up by another, still thicker blanket of mist.

The fog crawled over the ground, sprawling and occasionally hanging motionless, so that soon I couldn't work out whether I was dreaming or had been struck down by the tropical fever again, particularly when I stepped over the threshold and made my way inside that mysterious, ghostly architecture, its structure blackened by the passage of time. I felt lost in the clouds. A few rays of morning sunlight probed through small high windows, and I saw two monks working away in the half-light, keeping an eye on the millstone, speaking to each other sometimes loudly, sometimes in hushed tones. As the millstone circled around, they emptied baskets of raw materials into it, bark from some sort of local tree, white on the inside. With its repeated turning, the millstone ground the bark, compressing it until immaculately white raw sap spilled from it. This was then mixed with water to form "Pagan paper pulp," which, I was told, repelled insects.

I crouched down and, with the tip of my finger, touched the warm, viscous fluid whose smell reminded me of Chinese medicines. Just as that thought came to me, I shuddered, thinking I could see him in the white fog. It's him, I thought, it's Tumchooq, right here, on the other side of the mill, the same stature, the same way of leaning towards a basin of water as I saw him bend over baskets of aubergines so many times. I came very close to calling out his name, at the risk of giving everyone doubts about my mental health. The illusion dissipated as I drew closer, but I was still disturbed by the resemblance between Tumchooq and that monk who stood stripped to the waist plunging a big wooden sieve loaded with wet paper pulp into a basin and, when the water was up to his elbows, freezing in that position with such concentration that the gesture, which lasted only a fraction of a second, seemed to go on for an eternity. He shook the sieve in the water, so gently the movement was almost imperceptible, then lifted it straight back out again: the shapeless lump of pulp had transformed itself into a sheet of virgin paper, as if he had wrested it from the depths of the void. All that remained was to dry the sheet outside. But when he looked up and recognised me his smile gave way to embarrassment mingled with a hint of fear.

In the xylography workshop, on the other hand, complete silence reigned. From a distance I thought I saw little points of light gleaming like minute yellow halos over the heads of saints in religious frescoes, but as I came nearer I realised they were the shaven heads of twenty or so monks sitting side by side in a huge room, busy engraving wooden plates for printing sacred texts. Most of them had a magnifying glass clamped over their right eye, some over their left eye, and each of them worked under a lamp whose beam lit a specific area. I had to strain my ears to hear the wood creak under their engravers' styles, sometimes a slight crack followed by a sigh. Perhaps because of their watchmaker's glasses, I felt as if I were surrounded by the assorted ticking of clocks, alarm clocks, watches, every sort of timepiece of which xylography itself is a perfect example.

First a sheet of paper bearing the text in manuscript is placed facedown on a wooden plate about the size of a book and stuck onto it until the ink seeps into it, leaving a clear imprint of the writing; then the paper is removed and the wooden plate (preferably made of a hardwood) is pared away little by little, millimetre by millimetre, until only the letters are left in relief. The chiselling work, line-engraving the letters, was so subtle that my eyes eventually clouded over while I watched, as if staring at an ant eating a grain of rice. Engraving just one letter took ten or twenty minutes, I could barely make out the progress of a single upstroke. I later learned that engravers can work only two lines of text a day, that it often takes them a good ten days to finish a page— a wooden plate—in Pali text of the teachings preached by Buddha two thousand five hundred years earlier; and just one second's distraction, the slightest carelessness, can mean they have to start all over again.

The sound of chisels, the fragmented light, the watchmaker's glasses behind which their eyes were hidden, probably fixed, motionless, slightly protruding and perhaps very beautiful, a little cough, an engraver's right hand sculpting the wood, a panoply of chisels in different sizes clamped in his left hand, mouths blowing softly over the plates raising a fine wood dust changed into powdered gold by the lamplight—it all constituted a separate world.

Several monks were repairing old plates, some as much as a

hundred and fifty years old with areas that needed reworking with a jigsaw, because the letters were so worn, a clear sign of an abundant print run. Here time was immutable, immutable as dogma, and I started trying to gauge the three years Tumchooq had spent here engraving—in relief or intaglio—two lines a day, not to mention the years he spent in the kitchens and the paper mill. He might never have launched himself on the same trail for which his father had already suffered so much, the pursuit of the integral version of the torn manuscript, if he had had the least idea of the patience this titanic Long March would require. I found it difficult, almost impossible, to imagine the look on Tumchooq's face when he first engraved a whole plate, bringing it up to the light to check a few details, then taking off his watchmaker's glasses to appreciate his work as a whole, the solemn letters, the exquisite widening of lanceolate forms, the contrast between the width of a vowel and the narrowness of a consonant, between thick vertical strokes and fine horizontal ones, the clarity of a small ligature, the assurance of the strokes, the accuracy of the diacritical symbols. No one is left indifferent by the beauty of a printing plate. Then he would deliver it to the printing workshop, a layer of ink was applied to the surface, a sheet of blank paper laid over it and, by lightly brushing over the back of the paper, the page was printed. It was removed straight away. The letters in relief on the cut-away surface of plate appeared black, shining and still moist, on the white background of the paper. Only the chapter headings, whose letters are carved out of the wood, are printed in white on a black background.

The sun was only just up, the meticulously swept path with not a single fallen leaf on it glittered beneath my bare feet, and each of my footsteps, I was aware, was an act of

meditation. With its sand and its occasional stones positioned here and there, as if among the extinguished, collected, cooled ashes of our passions, without the least spark
of an ember to reignite them, that little path was like the life
of whoever walked along it. Perhaps its maker wanted it to
remind us that our footprints, like the happy days of our
lives, disappear with the first gust of wind, without leaving
any trace at all. I suspected this path of sand had been made
by Tumchooq himself, because it was so like the "sea of
stones" at the château at Saint-Paul-de-Fenouillet that I visited as a teenager, a "sea" devised by Paul d'Ampère, who
later described its soft lapping of waves to his son.

That sandy track took me right to the entrance of the
Cave of Treasure, where its keeper, an elderly monk, was
cleaning an antique printing plate with sandalwood pulp.
When I arrived he lit a cube of camphor on a copper dish
and, gesticulating furiously to make himself understood,
invited me to run the tips of my fingers through the flame
and bring them up to my forehead. Then, without a word, he
opened the door and let me in.

The cave was enormous, unfathomably deep, and filled
with shadow, if not complete darkness. Daylight barely
reached inside, filtered through a single gap carved through
the rock and half-covered with vegetation, but it went astray
somewhere along the way and was swallowed up before
reaching the floor. By this pale glow, which could be mistaken for moonlight, I made out the silhouette of a gigantic
multi-tiered stupa standing in the middle of the cave: at the
top of its prodigious height a gold roof twinkled.

All of a sudden, as if hallucinating, I heard the click of an
electric switch and the edifice, lit up from the inside by

countless lamps, appeared in all its splendour. Its pyramid-shaped base and each of its eight levels borne on pillars were made of finely sculpted white marble, but the walls were of glass, affording glimpses of shelving, which went right up to the ceiling on each level and was laden with engraved plates, all tightly packed together, like thousands and thousands of hefty volumes of an encyclopaedia, the largest in the world, an encyclopaedia in raw wood, overrunning the eight levels of that stupa and its shelving, which carried on as far as the eye could see, into infinity for all anyone could tell. Its prison of rock cut it off from the outside world, erased the present, the past, seasons, rain and heat, making it barely possible to distinguish between day and night. Voices, the sound of footsteps, the least little cough produced a subtle echo like the diffuse hubbub of a river or the rumble of an underground tremor. Swallows, which I at first mistook for bats, flew to and fro through the air around me, skimming my hair with the tips of their wings, some coming very close to crashing into the glass walls, lit up like a palace of memories in that amphitheatre of eternal printing plates.

It was only when I climbed the long, steep staircase at the centre of the stupa and reached the shelving up a bamboo ladder that I found the first personal touch from Tumchooq: numbers traced in curcuma formed a lustrous bronze embellishment to each sacred plate, probably an inventory system, numbers in a familiar hand, like those I saw long ago in the greengrocer's written in chalk on the price boards, or in pencil in the shop's accounts book. Seeing the particular care Tumchooq had taken over the top floor, I realised that this had been the focus of his attention, towards which all of his efforts—and even his suffering—had converged over the years. A filigreed wooden frame hung on the lintel over the doorway, and written in golden capitals on a blue background was the word "*Jataka*"—the sacred works relating Buddha's previous lives, which constitute one of the most significant bodies of sutras in the Pali language, and whose narrative style and content, according to Paul d'Ampère, come closest to the Tumchooq text on the torn scroll.

There were very many engraved plates there, with labels indicating their titles and giving summaries in Pali and Burmese, which—to my great regret—I couldn't decipher. Some of the labels were accompanied by a simple illustration (the archivist's whim or instructions to illiterate monks?), often drawings of the animals in whose form the future Buddha was incarnated: buffalo, lion, elephant, ass, horse, camel, stag, tiger and lots of birds—partridge, blue tit, sparrow, dove, stork, turtledove, etc. The creator of these pictures seemed to have a predilection for the grey parrot, and I then remembered that his father had told him these birds were the most eminent living linguists on the planet: the silky grey of their plumage, their black beaks, the red tuft crowning their heads, and most of all the incredibly human look in their eyes; I knew he'd been thinking of his father as he drew those birds.

As with the house, there was no furniture, except for a hammock in faded fabric hanging between the shelves, and its thick ropes had carved the furrows of passing time in the beam it was attached to. In places the worn rope held by only a few twisted, muddled, blackened fibres, while the woven rush matting over the floor had been flattened beneath the master's feet. How many times did he walk up and down in one night of insomnia? Thousands? Inspired by a desire to know, I counted the engraved plates, first on that floor, then, going from one level to another, in the whole stupa: the total figure, insofar as my estimate could be accurate, was in the region of two hundred thousand, without counting the damaged plates, icons, matrices and wood engravings piled up in great sacks in the basement. Considering the average sutra comprises thirty pages, and therefore thirty engraved plates—a hypothesis reached after some deliberation—I reckoned Tumchooq must have examined seven thousand texts of the Buddhist canon through his watchmaker's glasses. Day and night, summer and winter, year after year, his eyesight must have deteriorated, clouded, been ruined as he worked exhaustively through the monastery's incalculable collection, probably without ever achieving the goal he had set himself eleven years earlier beside his father's grave: to find the integral text of the torn scroll, in whatever language he could.

I felt intuitively that his trip to Japan was all part of this interminable quest, his unfinished project, like a step in a new direction, perhaps even the last. That sutra which was believed lost for ever could resurface out of nowhere at any moment and against all expectations—in the antique book markets of Kyoto, in the cellars of a Japanese military library or religious institution. I wondered whether, in his obsessive search for the sutra, this man who was used to living and managing on so little and who, like his father, was first and foremost an adventurer, I wondered whether he would resist the temptation to repeat his Burmese experience in Japan, to disappear only to roam far and wide with no identity or official papers, researching, learning the local language, researching further until he found another collection as priceless as the one at the Pagan monastery.

The door to the cave opened and two black silhouettes,

almost like shadows, appeared against the daylight, slipping silently inside: it was the monastery deputy and my interpreter coming to invite me to a major ceremony of exorcism and prayers to Buddha, asking him to bless and protect their superior, Tumchooq, who was threatened by the spectre of misfortune. I should have guessed there had been a dramatic development from the awkward way the monks behaved whenever I came near. The words uttered by those two shadows, still with the light behind them, reverberated around the cave and their echo lent them such an other-worldly quality that I had trouble understanding my translator, but I didn't need her explanations to guess as my legs shook, my knees gave way and the stupa seemed about to crumble beneath my feet.

The news had come two days earlier while I was laid low by fever. According to a telegram sent by the Kyoto Buddhists' International Conference, Tumchooq had been arrested by the border police at Tokyo airport, and a Japanese monk who had come to greet him had witnessed the scene. Tumchooq was accused of being in possession of a false Laotian passport. ("It was the first passport he ever had," the monastery deputy told me. "He bought it a few days before he left, through a man who specialises in that sort of transaction, in a slightly offhand, last-minute way. Unfortunately, instead of a Burmese passport, he was given a Laotian one. A false one.") Despite his religious robes and the intervention of his Japanese co-disciple, Tumchooq was immediately deported to Laos and handed over to the judiciary, and this in a country where the sentence for identity fraud was liable to be life imprisonment.

EPILOGUE

PEKING

OCTOBER 1990

SURREAL, COMPLETELY SURREAL, THAT was how the sequence of events felt to me, and I can only describe them now in broad outline, because Tumchooq's arrest and imprisonment so clouded my thoughts. The white mists engulfing my mind mingled with the bluer ones of the Irrawaddy, which lapped at the foot of the walls around the monastery. I remember nothing of our leaving, nor of the boat that took us to Mandalay, still less of how we first approached the Burmese government on the subject of Tumchooq's release, but the only thing I can be more or less sure of is that we very soon decided to wage the war on two fronts, Laotian and Chinese: the monastery deputy went straight to Laos to mobilise monks there and I took the first flight to Peking, where I was to find Tumchooq's mother and obtain documents from the Public Records Office to establish her son's identity.

It had been eleven years since my flight from Peking. The light, which had been so distinctive in late afternoon, was no longer the same, nor the smell; there was a hundred times more traffic than before, so that, when my taxi came off the motorway between the airport and the city centre, it found itself trapped in an endless queue of cars, groaning and edging almost imperceptibly forward, only to grind to a halt again. The physiognomy of the cars and passers-by seemed to have changed, too. Their clothes were brighter, their faces darker and more strained, but it was the look in their eyes that really struck me. They looked at me without a glimmer of curiosity. They no longer had that probing policeman's expression, but that of an experienced salesman who was absolutely meticulous in his accounting and gauged each customer as he came into the shop. A professional eye, looking after its own interests. Still, I recognised Peking by one detail: the taxi driver, irritated by the traffic jam, wound down his window, cleared his throat and spat forcefully into the road, proudly watching his spittle's parabola until it landed bang in the middle of the street, and not even contemplating any kind of apology.

I decided to stay at the Cui Min Zhuang Hotel, not for its proximity to Wang Fujing Street, which is a sort of Peking Champs-Élysées, but because it is close to the East Gate of the Forbidden City, a few hundred metres from the residence for museum employees where Tumchooq's mother had two rooms in a brick-built house at street level, with a traditional courtyard in the middle of which, if memory serves, there was an exuberant kaki tree with deeply scored black bark and, in summer, leafy branches reaching beyond the walls and bowing under such a weight of fruit you expected them to crush the tiled roof. Not forgetting the tap for running water that Tumchooq had mentioned so many times, I felt I had already seen it.

"One morning," he had told me, "after a stormy night, I

looked out of the window and saw my mother going out of the house. Her red boots marked out her footsteps in the glittering white blanket of snow, right to the middle of the courtyard, where she turned on the tap to wash some vegetables. She chopped white turnips into little cubes, put them in a basin and sprinkled them with a thin layer of salt as white as the snow. The basin was in white enamel and on the bottom it had a red peony with green leaves, and the enamel was chipped in places."

The sun had set some while ago, even though I hadn't wasted any time in my fifteenth-floor hotel room with its view over a tide of giant modern buildings with flashing luminous signs on them. A few metres from the hotel the indistinct silhouette of a slender bridge spanning a major traffic artery appeared above the tiny, fine and mostly broken roof tiles of a few very old houses, all curved lines and low-slung frames. A white cat, perhaps a Persian, ran along the roofs, jumped, climbed up a sad single wall among the demolished houses to the thrumming of bulldozers that I could hear but not see. When I left the hotel and turned into the first side street, the headlights of the machines toing and froing across the demolition site lumbered towards me incredibly slowly, blinding me. There were a few traditional old houses left, waiting their turn to be demolished, and the lights still lit in their doorways looked like the pitiful flames of candles burnt almost right down, exhaling their last glow, their last breath of warmth, while the bulldozer headlights peered at them like monsters examining victims paralysed with fear, before pouncing.

This part of the city had been my favourite place over a long period, not only because of the emotional connection with Tumchooq and its proximity to the Forbidden City, but because for two thousand years it had represented the real

Peking, and Tumchooq had had a map of it on the wall of the greengrocer's, so that, night after night, word by word, he could learn the Chinese characters most frequently used in daily life (and often the most beautiful): those that made up the names of the streets in the city. The map was a lithograph representing a bird's-eye-view panorama of the entire Imperial City (which surrounded the Forbidden City) with its four gates and Tiananmen in the middle. The tumultuous profusion of *hutong*, Peking's narrow streets, were picked out as white lines on the black background of the map, forming a spider's web so clear it was worthy of the very best engravings. The lines were often straight, cutting across each other, spreading east, west, north and south. Sometimes they changed into fluid ribbons snaking around lakes, white marks dotted here and there like whimsical drops of mother-of-pearl. In places the lines were cut by a bridge, a villa or an aristocrat's residence, while in others they melted into marshland. Along each white line representing a *hutong* there was a name, in the writing of the day, carved with noble skill. Tumchooq made me read them out loud with him, road by road, quarter by quarter. Some of the names, the way their ideograms were combined, sparkled with exquisitely nuanced elegance; others captivated me with the sound they made: subtle, sensual, occasionally exuberant, particularly when he said them, my Tumchooq with his attractive Peking accent. Even though the Tumchooq method was elementary from a pedagogic point of view, it was terribly effective: at the time I could find absolutely any street in the city centre, however small, and any footpath, however twisting and winding, as if Tumchooq had carved the map inside my head.

I decided to go to Tumchooq's mother's house on foot, but I should have guessed this decision would lead only to disappointment, if not a nightmare. The further I walked, the more struck I was by the complete absence of simple street pedlars when there used to be an endless stream of them from morning till night, their bicycles laden with heavy bags of food, which bulged over both sides of their luggage racks. Tumchooq could do a brilliant impression of the ones who sold grilled sweet potatoes, the yellow flesh with a hint of red, so much better than chestnuts; or those selling sweet or sour apricots, which made you drool in summer; or hot, crispy, deep-fried cakes; spicy, salted crabs; dried carrots covered in chilli; steamed dumplings; stinking soya cheese; or even those selling aphrodisiac plants reputed to make a man pee higher than an electricity pylon . . . I couldn't hear anything except the rumble of bulldozers reverberating like thunder in the stifling night air and the long, irritable, aggressive toot of car horns.

Fifty metres further on I stood for a moment under a spanking new streetlight casting its light over a metallic sign on which the name of the street was written, but where I expected it to say EAST GATE STREET, there was another, unfamiliar name, the name of some ghostly impostor calling itself JOY OF THE EAST STREET. Disconcerted by the change, which I initially put down to a slip of memory on my part, I asked a passer-by whether he knew East Gate Street, but he looked at me as if I were mad and walked off without answering. Despite all this, I set off down the street, but the little restaurants where I used to have a bowl of warm soya milk and a steamed dumpling for lunch had disappeared like the *hutong*, without a trace. The street had become smooth, impersonal and wide, edged with concrete buildings some ten or twenty storeys high, some of them still under construction. Next there was a no-man's-land of luxury shops—Gucci, Dior, Chanel, Lacoste, L'Oréal—with flags by the door and brightly lit windows where Western-style mannequins adopted poses, blond women with green or blue eyes, beautiful black athletes with well-honed muscles, shiny, life-size photographs of Zidane, Beckham, Ronaldo . . . and all at once I understood.

Gone, alas, was the world of the old map in the lithograph. Gone, alas, the spider's web of tiny streets, which had constituted the flesh and bones of Peking since the Yuan dynasty in Marco Polo's day. I wondered whether anyone had made a note of how many *hutong* had disappeared in this neighbourhood, which now belonged to a new era. A thousand? Two thousand? What a shame! Even if only for their names with their wealth of retroflex consonants, which only natives of Peking could pronounce, their diphthongs and other exquisite sounds. Not sure what I was doing, in despair, I started to run and was soon going frantically, foolishly fast. Like a lost child. As if trying to exorcise something. There were cars in front of me and others coming to meet me, ruby of rear lights, dazzle of headlights. I couldn't breathe properly. My legs weren't really under my control, disobeying my need to escape, in places refusing to take the turning I wanted. I let them carry me through that world of illuminated signs for boutiques, financial corporations, estate agents, cosmetic surgery clinics offering breast enhancements, remodelled noses and tautened eyelids, dubious hair salons with red lighting, Indian or Thai massage parlours, Finnish saunas, Turkish baths, Brazilian grills, advertisements for foot baths using forty Tibetan plants, shops selling aphrodisiacs, which all claimed to deal in "contraception and adult health," sex shops offering gadgets more realistic than the actual thing, acupuncturists promising to cure stammers, restaurants with aquariums illuminated by finely tuned lighting to show off crabs with long pincers, soft-shelled turtles known for their curative properties, strange lobsters . . .

When I reached the bridge at the North Gate of the Forbidden City I couldn't see the single-storey house with the square courtyard where Tumchooq's mother lived. Paralysis of memory or losing my mind? I scanned the place again, concentrating twice as hard. No. It wasn't there any more. It had gone. The house had gone, along with the whole block of houses which used to be behind it, forming a small street called the Hutong of Figs, which started at the exact point where the palace walls turned eastwards on the corner of a watchtower in carved wood. The *hutong* wound its way between the moat and the tall imperial wall, which it followed for a kilometre until it reached South Pond Street. That, too, had disappeared, struck off the map. So had "lover's paradise," a discreet strip of wooded land along the moat from the North Gate right the way down to the beginning of the Hutong of Figs, a place that had been the secret haven of love for more than three decades, from the 1950s to the 1980s. There had been no streetlights. Every evening when the last glimmers of dusk had disappeared from the dark surface of the moat, couples would arrive from all over Peking, men and women, boys and girls, unmarried people who lived in collective dormitories, walking deep into the thickets, sheltered under the exuberant foliage to exchange a first kiss in the shadows, a fleeting embrace, rapturous fondling, in fact, the whole panoply of sensual pleasures provided by a lover's touch. This earthly paradise had had no more luck escaping sudden death: it had been replaced by a sanitised park with dodgems.

Back at Cui Min Zhuang, my hotel, I managed as best I could to get some rest after an eventful shower in a tub protected by a torn plastic curtain, with taps that needed constant adjustments, because the temperature of the water was so capricious and unpredictable. One minute I was screaming as it scalded me, the next dying of cold under its icy flow, because another customer had turned on a furred-up tap above, below or on the same floor as me. That shower was such a test of my nerves that I emerged from it completely dazed. I fell asleep as soon as I lay down and didn't even have the strength to turn out the light.

Despite the establishment's promising appearance, despite the pretty emerald tint to the tiles covering roofs all the way to the outer wall and even though, in the distant past, the building had been the secondary residence of Mei Lanfang, the best singer of all time at the Peking Opera, the rooms had absolutely no soundproofing, but nothing could have drawn me back from that sleep as my body gave itself up for dead, not the noises from the room next door, nor those from the one above, where the water gurgled through the pipes and a man sang in his shower.

In the middle of the night, perhaps towards dawn, a toilet flush thundered directly above me like a waterfall storming down a cliff face, so loudly that it woke me. The old cracks on the ceiling shuddered, widened and turned into gaping wounds with debris flying out of them, crumbling whitewash, dust, spiders' webs, soot, etc. The noise really is appalling at

Cui Min Zhuang, I thought to myself, but, before I had even finished the sentence, my body drifted back to sleep. My mind, however, did not, since I could hear voices: at first I thought they were coming from the television, which I'd probably forgotten to switch off, because I thought I could hear the crackle of its speaker, like fine sand running down the walls. I was so overwhelmed by sleep it was impossible to get up and switch it off.

The voices were low to start with, but suddenly became very distinct, a change I put down to the television set, which was likely to be just as unpredictable as the hotel's plumbing. As if in a dream, I could hear two men talking. The first was telling the other what had happened at the museum in the Forbidden City while he was on a poorly paid but instructive and eventful placement as an expert in ancient painting; all this reported in a voice devoid of involvement or emphasis, bordering on curtness but very precise.

The incident had happened two years earlier in Mr. Xu's office; he was the last leading light in valuations and, although he was already seventy-two, the Forbidden City gave him a considerable salary every month to delay his retirement. For several years he had been passing on his knowledge to young colleagues from various museums in the four corners of China. A single sentence from the master about calligraphy or a painting was priceless. His practised eye, familiarity with the works and phenomenal memory earned him a supreme position in China and international renown, because—as anyone who has read essays on Chinese art will have gathered— Western scientific methods are incapable of dating a work accurately and even less of identifying its author.

The scene took place in the second half of August, towards

half past six in the evening, at the end of a long day's work; most of the offices were closed when one of the guards from the Great Gate brought a young Manchurian of about twenty into Mr. Xu's office. He introduced himself as a school leaver who had been accepted by a highly reputed university in Shanghai, but his lack of funds to pursue his studies was forcing him to sell a collection of antique paintings, which had been in his family for generations. The acquisitions department of the museum was closed and he was in a hurry to catch the train to Shanghai, because he didn't have enough money to pay for a night in a hotel, which was why the guard had brought him to the master's office.

The latter smiled and entrusted his apprentices with the task of valuing the works. There were about thirty of them, tied up with string, relatively recent calligraphies and paintings of no great value, except for one which attracted the expert's attention. It was one half of a torn roll of silk, the silk itself very old, probably from the Han dynasty, yellowing raw silk covered in the seals of several emperors' collections, notably that of Emperor Huizong of the Song dynasty, although the red colour had blackened with the passage of time.

At that point the voice stopped and the sound of a toilet flushing thundered somewhere in the hotel. I held my breath, not daring to open my eyes, as if moving one centimetre would shatter the dream, if that's what it was, and interrupt what this man was saying, when I didn't want to miss a single word. The writing on the fragment of scroll was not Chinese but rather the unfamiliar signs of an unknown language, two horizontal lines written from right to left.

Strange though this may seem, Mr. Xu skimmed his fingers briefly over all the pieces, not lingering for a second over the torn scroll, as if it had no more value than the others. He wore the same polite little smile he had his entire life, no more, and the young student was already preparing to leave again with his property. But that is not what happened. The master asked the young man to follow him to the accounts department, where he told them to give him a sum of money which still seems astronomical today: twenty thousand yuan for all the pieces, way beyond the boy's expectations.

"The moment he left the accounts department," the voice went on, "the master asked me to go to the station with the boy, on the pretence that it was on my way home, to try to find out his address in Shanghai and, most importantly, where the piece of torn silk came from. In the Number 113 bus, heading for the station, the young man told me that one day in the 1930s his grandfather, who was a Manchurian peasant and the only man in his village with a bit of education, was working in the red sorghum fields when a Japanese military aeroplane flew overhead. A piece of silk fell from the plane, gliding through the air in the dazzling rays of sunlight, and landed about a hundred metres from him. When I reported this back to the master he was overcome with joy and disbelief. 'That's what I wanted to hear, a piece of silk falling from the sky!' He said that three times with tears in his eyes and explained that he hadn't dared offer more money to the boy for fear of awakening any suspicions in him that might have threatened the sale. 'It's impossible to put a value on this half scroll,' he added. 'Tomorrow I'll arrange for the museum to pay him another hundred thousand yuan as a mark of my gratitude. I'll also ask for the guard to be given a reward of fifty thousand yuan, because without him the opportunity to acquire this treasure would have slipped past the door and disappeared for ever. This is the most precious acquisition in our museum for fifty years, because, if memory serves, we already own the other half, which was obtained at the time by less scrupulous means, because its owner—a Frenchman granted Chinese citizenship—was condemned to life imprisonment so he would never be in a position to claim back his property.' "

It was only towards the end of this story that I looked at the television, but the screen was a blur. Broadcasting must have finished some time ago, because the screen was striped with evenly spaced lines. There was absolute silence, not the tiniest rustle or sound of water seeping somewhere. I didn't immediately grasp the importance of what I had heard, because I was so convinced I had dreamt the conversation, given that it hadn't been on television. "Only in sleep do certain things have a way of appearing unannounced." That Chinese proverb is what first came to mind as, going back over each sentence I had overheard, I gradually regained a foothold in reality.

A door slammed suddenly. The one to the room next door. Its occupiers came out and stayed on the landing for a moment, looking for something. One of their voices left me in no doubt: he had been the one relating the events earlier. I obviously hadn't been dreaming, because he now went on with incontrovertible clarity:

"Extraordinary though this may seem, I knew the Frenchman's wife from the Department of Imperial Archives. A beautiful woman, elegant and aristocratic-looking, who withdrew into a sort of perpetual widowhood out of guilt for her husband, whom the authorities had forced her to accuse. According to Mr. Xu, she was given the choice between charging him with a crime he'd never committed or losing the child she was carrying."

The following morning I was one of the first visitors into the Forbidden City; dawn was just skimming over the petrified golden waves of alternate peaks and troughs in that ocean stretching as far as the eye could see. The light of the sun was picked up by the myriad roof tiles on the buildings like so many mirrors in matt gold. And when the huge red disc was partly obscured by heavy clouds, its replicas on the roofs distorted into aubergine shapes, their lower halves soon twisting into as many monstrous snakes, before turning into long needles of light. Eventually, the sun spread glistening fluid over the roofs, a golden colourwash, a layer of twinkling icing. Flocks of crows, in their thousands, wheeled with fantastical elegance, their wings shimmering with the pink of reflected sunlight as they glided languidly above the walls, palaces, pavilions, white marble esplanades and paved courtyards stretching into infinity. According to elderly inhabitants of Peking, generation after generation of crows had enjoyed the privilege of breeding and growing up here, fed and housed by the imperial family to whom they devoted unfailing loyalty. After the last dynasty collapsed and the last emperor, Puyi, fled, the crows—refusing to see usurpers in their former masters' place—took to leaving the palace early in the morning only to return at nightfall, with such regularity and precision that their cawing in the evenings was the welcome signal for the end of the working day for all the museum staff.

Having skirted round the major edifices, I cut across

countless courtyards in the quarters once kept for widowed empresses and which now act as the museum's offices, closed to the public but teeming with two thousand employees. I walked past the Imperial Archives building, where Tumchooq's mother had worked for three and a half decades as a specialist in transcribing and often abridging ancient musical compositions from the notation of their day into notes and neumes.

At this early hour I couldn't find anyone; perhaps she had already retired. I thought I would come back later and ask for her new address. Outside the building stood the Bodhi tree Tumchooq had told me about, the one his mother used to bring him to as a child, often on Sunday mornings, to pick fruit when he was actually far more interested in the crows' nests perched up high and deserted at that time in the morning. If Tumchooq himself was to be believed, his mother radiated a volcanic youthfulness, a dormant volcano, which occasionally billowed out lava, belying her neat, married woman's chignon and the strictly dictated clothing of the time: a roomy, black corduroy jacket, wide beige trousers, flat canvas shoes . . . In that sacred tree she shouted at the top of her lungs with her son. Shrieking like a schoolgirl in the playground, she would mysteriously disappear, only to pop up again above him, in among the overlapping leaves, clinging to one branch, with her feet on another. Rosy-cheeked and with her chignon falling apart, she bombarded him with rock-hard fruit, burst out laughing, leapt back, climbed even higher, ran on all fours like a monkey, sat astride the end of a branch, which swayed beneath her weight, and there, looking indescribably sensual, she challenged her son to try to reach her, punctuating an entire Sunday morning with her laughter.

Thirty-odd years had passed since the days when they came to glean fruit from the Bodhi tree, and the windfall I picked up was such a charming thing, with fine gold stripes on its skin, that I put it in my bag and decided to take it all the way to the prison in Laos where Tumchooq was being held.

In the area for "Heritage Exhibitions," next to the great hall dedicated to Emperor Huizong of the Song dynasty, I found the "Tumchooq" room, a more modest space exhibiting "Renat's maps," which were forgotten in an archive for two centuries and discovered by Strindberg, who, before becoming a playwright, worked at the Royal Library in Stockholm, where he studied Chinese in order to make an inventory of a collection of books in that language.

Sergeant Johan Gustav Renat of the Swedish artillery was made a prisoner of war by the Russians after their defeat of Sweden at Poltava in 1709. He spent seven years in Siberia, near the Chinese border, before being captured by a group of Kalmouks, the Djoungars, whose sovereign, Tse-wang Raddan (1665–1727)—known for his violence and his ambition to create a vast Mongol empire between Russia and China—was delighted with this gift from heaven: an artilleryman who knew the secret of building cannons. Over the course of ten years a turbulent relationship developed between the tyrant and the Western captive, a combination of death threats, mutual mistrust and peculiar friendship. Renat returned to Sweden after the death of Tse-wang Raddan, who had given him two geographical maps, one drawn by his own hand on thick, yellowing paper with an uneven grain. Its easy flowing images depicted mountains in green, lakes in blue, his own residence with its scarlet columns and his spotless tents with their red doors, inscriptions in Kalmouk, and the vast territories of Ili and western Mongolia, not forgetting the Gobi Desert, coloured in light brown. In the middle of the desert a blue-green oasis by the name of Tumchooq was indicated beneath a Tibetan-style temple with a flat roof on which three silver tridents were positioned to ward off evil spirits. It was the only temple on the map. According to Strindberg's biographers, the young librarian and future great playwright pored over this map for hours on end, fascinated by the Tumchooq temple: Why had Tse-wang Raddan drawn it? Some raised the possibility of a pilgrimage, made by Renat, in an attempt to obtain spiritual protection for his son, the fruit of his love for one of the sovereign's daughters, for the child was an albino, a sign of bad luck in the natives' eyes, and therefore at risk of assassination at any time.

After this geographical display the exhibition was devoted to the origins of the Tumchooq kingdom, notably with a presentation of an entire page from a Tibetan manuscript discovered in cave 1656 at Dunhuang, preserved at the Peking Library, and in which Kanghan Zanbu, a twelfth-century pilgrim, explains the origins of this kingdom, which, in his time, was already buried under the sand: one day, in the middle of the Gobi Desert, the chief of a nomadic tribe met a goddess who had come down from heaven, and he married her. Shortly after their wedding he went off to war, and while he was away his wife had an affair with a foreign traveller; she became pregnant, but managed to conceal her condition and hid the child she bore under a tree, as agreed with her lover. When he came to collect the child, on a starless night, his burning torch was assailed by every moth in the woods, dancing, flitting, jostling each other and forming a thick cloud around him. Some, nudged forwards by the others, burnt their wings and perished. This strange procession went on all night. The baby woke the following morning with a beautiful butterfly stuck to his forehead, a variety called Thum-suk, because of the colourful markings, in the shape of a bird's beak, on its wings. And so the father called his son Thum-suk Blung (*blung* meaning "fog" in Mongol).

A few decades later Thum-suk Blung became the first sovereign of that part of the world and baptised his kingdom with his own name, omitting the word "fog" to keep only the attractive "beak of a bird," which was gradually palatalised and transformed into Tumchooq. His reign, which encouraged and developed silkworm breeding, produced wondrous silk and satin fabrics so beautiful they rivalled bird plumage and the fine scales on butterfly wings. The story of this first sovereign also gave rise to an entrenched custom, respected by every inhabitant, that a mother should baptise her child by the name of the first thing she saw after she was delivered.

Beyond a room filled with artefacts found during archaeological excavations, I ended up in the last part of the exhibition, a very small conference room with three rows of pink plastic chairs. A silent ghost—a middle-aged man, wearing the dark grey overall of a museum employee—turned off the light and closed the curtains, plunging the room into darkness. The torn scroll, known as the "Tumchooq Sutra," was so precious and in such bad condition that visitors could only view slides of it, and these slides soon made their timid appearance in a beam of light, quivering slightly on the screen stretched over a wooden frame, while the projector, handled by the employee in the grey overall, started to purr like a cat on someone's lap. The scroll, at once familiar and unknown, first appeared in its entirety, already restored, with no visible trace of the tear, at least not on the photograph. The writing was too minute for me to read. I had to wait for the successive appearance of several closer shots to see the scroll as it had been for eight decades, mutilated, amputated, before the other part, believed missing in 1932, resurfaced; some of the letters were almost erased and could only just be made out. One of the pictures was reminiscent of a photograph of the Turin Shroud, taken a century earlier, on which the barely legible imprint of a body appeared.

While these professional, detailed, impeccably focused images were projected onto the screen, I pictured the wavering image Tumchooq showed me of it in the greengrocer's shop when he initiated me into the sacred text, and I couldn't help myself speaking aloud his father's deciphering of the text, word for word as he had done:

ONCE ON A MOONLESS NIGHT A LONE MAN IS TRAVEL-LING IN THE DARK WHEN HE COMES ACROSS A LONG PATH THAT MERGES INTO THE MOUNTAIN AND THE MOUNTAIN INTO THE SKY, BUT HALFWAY ALONG, AT A TURN IN THE PATH, HE STUMBLES. AS HE FALLS, HE CLUTCHES AT A TUFT OF GRASS, WHICH BRIEFLY DELAYS A FATAL OUTCOME, BUT SOON HIS HANDS CAN HOLD HIM NO LONGER AND, LIKE A CONDEMNED MAN IN HIS FINAL HOUR, HE CASTS ONE LAST GLANCE BELOW, WHERE HE CAN SEE ONLY THE DARKNESS OF THOSE UNFATHOMABLE DEPTHS . . .

After a pause of a few seconds, which felt like an eternity to me, the projector lit up again, shimmering motes of dust hovered in the beam of light, and the missing part of the scroll which I was there to see appeared in close-up. I shook like a leaf, because I had such a strong sense of the dead being brought back to life. Without realising what I was doing, I stood up and walked towards the screen, where my own shadow swayed, about to fall, moved closer and came to a standstill. With tears in my eyes, I touched the letters one after the other, stroking the grain of the screen, which reminded me of Tumchooq's monk's robe and the rags hanging from the side-pieces of Paul d'Ampère's glasses, while the purring of the projector awakened an auditory memory which was as indistinct as it was distant, the song of the sand dunes that Tumchooq had described to me.

"At first it's a dull, hazy, distant murmur like the buzzing of an army of invisible mosquitoes trapped somewhere and looking for a way out. The murmur of a river beneath the sand, the soft whispering of a mythical source. The private rumble of a river carving its bed through the dunes. Then the buzzing draws nearer, a buzzing of bees, or rather a furious, swirling swarm of savage wasps and bluebottles. And then it stops. Scarcely an echo to be heard. A few seconds' pause, after which the buzzing starts again, intensifies, becomes a menacing vibration, as if ancestral spirits were beating drums beneath our feet and singing mantras; and the vibration swells until it sounds like the thrumming of a plane in the air, the roar of thunder low on the ground.

" 'That's the song of the dunes that you once heard in Manchuria,' Mum told me. 'Not all Manchurian dunes sing, only a few, outside the West Gate of the small town where your grandfather, Seventy-one, was exiled. Every year on New Year's Day, everyone went there, men, women, children, the elderly, rich or poor, all dressed in their best clothes. The only time I took you to my birthplace you were four years old. It was your first big ceremony. You'd been excited since the day before. You were frightened of being forgotten, or late. We got up at five o'clock in the morning, without having breakfast, but we took food with us. I dressed you up like a real Prince. Do you remember your robes with the peonies? No? In quilted, aubergine-coloured satin, lined with silk and embroidered with peonies, the New Year flower, with big petals in red, white and blue, green leaves and Tumchooq butterflies fluttering over the flowers in twos or small groups, so delicately embroidered that each of them had different-coloured eyes. The robe fastened on the right, true to the old imperial style, with a long opening at the side, edged with pearl-grey brocade, running straight up as far as the waist and cutting diagonally across to the round collar decorated with three blue silk ribbons, embroidered with little signs meaning *happiness*. It had wide sleeves, very wide, in black satin, as short as T-shirt sleeves, and coming out from underneath them were the yellow sleeves of your quilted jacket. It was really beautiful and you were so proud of it. We all were. And your silk boots, do you remember them? You looked so gorgeous, walking through the sand! The soles were white silk, the uppers dark blue silk and the legs yellow silk, a bright luminous yellow with pretty damask designs of clouds, in keeping with our rank as a family, the same ones your great-grandfather wore. The top of the boots was curved and the edge was decorated with braid in blue brocade, embroidered with golden dragons dancing in multicoloured waves. You refused to be carried by servants. You skipped about and climbed to the top of a steep dune with the others. The day was only just dawning, the sun was hiding behind the clouds, but there were already masses of people. We sat on the sand and ate sesame fritters. People were sliding down the sides of the dunes, with lots of shouting and laughter; some ran at the sand and ended up knee-deep in it. Others rolled down the slopes. Yes, you have to move and push and shove, or the dunes stay silent. And then the sun shone with a thousand needles of gold, and the dune moved with the shifting of the sand. It gave way. In the first avalanche, blocks of sand broke away, tumbling down the side of the dune where people had been playing. Slabs of sand, at first fairly compact ones, broke away, gathered speed, crumbled, and sprawled in every direction, raising clouds of dust, and from them came strange buzzing sounds, and everyone held their breath and listened. The same phenomenon was happening on neighbouring dunes. The sound produced by the avalanches of sand grew louder and louder and eventually an explosion rang out like a clap of thunder. You were so frightened you cried *Mummy! Mummy!* and blocked your ears with your fingers.' "

That song of the sands is what I thought I heard, too, as I deciphered the text of the missing part of the scroll, the end of the sutra:

"LET GO," RINGS A VOICE IN HIS EARS. "THE GROUND IS THERE, BENEATH YOUR FEET." THE TRAVELLER, TRUSTINGLY, DOES SO AND LANDS SAFE AND SOUND ON A PATH RUNNING JUST A SHORT DROP BELOW HIM.

ALSO BY DAI SIJIE

BALZAC AND THE LITTLE CHINESE SEAMSTRESS

Balzac and the Little Chinese Seamstress is an enchanting tale that captures the magic of reading and the wonder of romantic awakening. An immediate international bestseller, it tells the story of two hapless city boys exiled to a remote mountain village for re-education during China's infamous Cultural Revolution. There the two friends meet the daughter of the local tailor and discover a hidden stash of Western classics in Chinese translation. As they flirt with the seamstress and secretly devour these banned works, the two friends find transit from their grim surroundings to worlds they never imagined.

Fiction/978-0-385-72220-9

MR. MUO'S TRAVELLING COUCH

Fresh from eleven years in Paris studying Freud, bookish Mr. Muo returns to China to spread the gospel of psychoanalysis. His secret purpose is to free his college sweetheart from prison. To do so he has to get on the good side of the bloodthirsty Judge Di, and to accomplish that he must provide the judge with a virgin maiden. This may prove difficult in a China that has embraced western sexual mores along with capitalism—especially since Muo, while indisputably a romantic, is no ladies' man. Tender, laugh-out-loud funny, and unexpectedly wise, *Mr. Muo's Travelling Couch* introduces a hero as endearingly inept as Inspector Clouseau and as valiant as Don Quixote.

Fiction/978-1-4000-7714-4

**Meet with Interesting People
Enjoy Stimulating Conversation
Discover Wonderful Books**